Praise
Adira: Journey to Freedom

Simply put, Lynne's vision for *Adira* is otherworldly. I love everything about it: the creativity, the storytelling, the new spin on an old story— and one of my favorites at that. Highly recommend.

—*Dr. Kary Oberbrunner*
Wall Street Journal and USA Today bestselling author,
CEO Igniting Souls

In *Adira: Journey to Freedom*, Lynne Modranski provides a time machine that transports us to the days of Nehemiah. It is a primer for the "biblical imagination."

—*Michael Card*
singer, songwriter, theologian,
and author of The Biblical Imagination *series*

Lynne Modranski's first novel, *Adira,* is a thoroughly engaging read. Beautifully written, the narrative gave me a picture of life in the Biblical days of the prophet Nehemiah. The dialogue is so true to the times I felt I was present. Her character Adira trusts God to guide her life while she struggles with the meaning of true freedom. "Now, I would wait for Yawheh's next big move," she says at the end of a chapter. So, I too, as the reader, had to wait and reached a satisfying ending.

—*Rita Gerlach*
author of the Daughters of the Potomac *Series,* Wait Until Morning,
and Barbour Books Novella Contributor

Very heartwarming story. I loved being able to go behind the scenes in what may have happened in the Bible. Once I really picked it up, I couldn't put it down.

—*Nikki Kovach, Goodreads member*

This historical fiction book is such a good read. It takes you into Bible times and makes you really think about what people may have had to endure. It is filled with suspense and romance. It will take you on a journey with Adira while she learns to grow up the hard way and finds God along the way.

—*Julia Jenkins, Goodreads member*

Enjoyed the whole storyline and following Adira's family on their journey. Loved all the history that was put into the writing. I felt like I was there.

—*Linda Mader, Goodreads member*

Adira
Journey to Freedom

Other Books by this Author

Devotions

Devotions Inspired by Life

Devotions for Church Leaders and Small Groups

A Reflection of the Beauty of God

First Steps for New Christians

Bible Studies

Dive In to a Life of Freedom

Be A Barnabas

Advent Readings

Advent Through the Eyes of Mary

In Search of a Silent Night

A Christmas of Heavenly Peace

Children's Curricula

Jesus, Teach Me How to Pray

Heroes, Heroines, Champs & Chumps

The Fruit of the Spirit is . . .

Journey to Greatness: Lessons from the Life of Joseph

Children of the King: Developing Kids with Noble Character

Adira
Journey to Freedom

LYNNE MODRANSKI

Mansion Hill Press

Adira: Journey to Freedom

© 2022 by Lynne Modranski

Published by Mansion Hill Press

Steubenville, Ohio

LynneModranski.com

LCCN: 2022910492

ISBN: 978-1-953374-08-0

E-Book: 978-1-953374-09-7

Kindle: 978-1-953374-10-3

Thank you to my friend and artist

Rita Warrick

for Adira's cover art

*Dedicated to
all who've journeyed
into places unknown
and are looking
for a way home*

Table of Contents

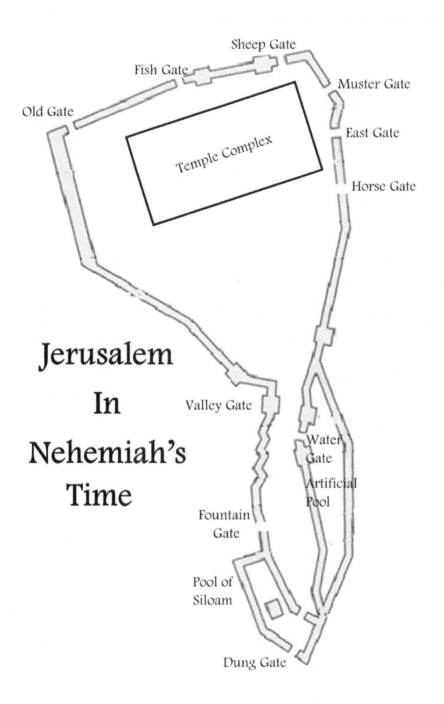

Sheep Gate

Fish Gate

Old Gate

Muster Gate

East Gate

Temple Complex

Horse Gate

Jerusalem

In

Nehemiah's

Time

Valley Gate

Water Gate

Artificial Pool

Fountain Gate

Pool of Siloam

Dung Gate

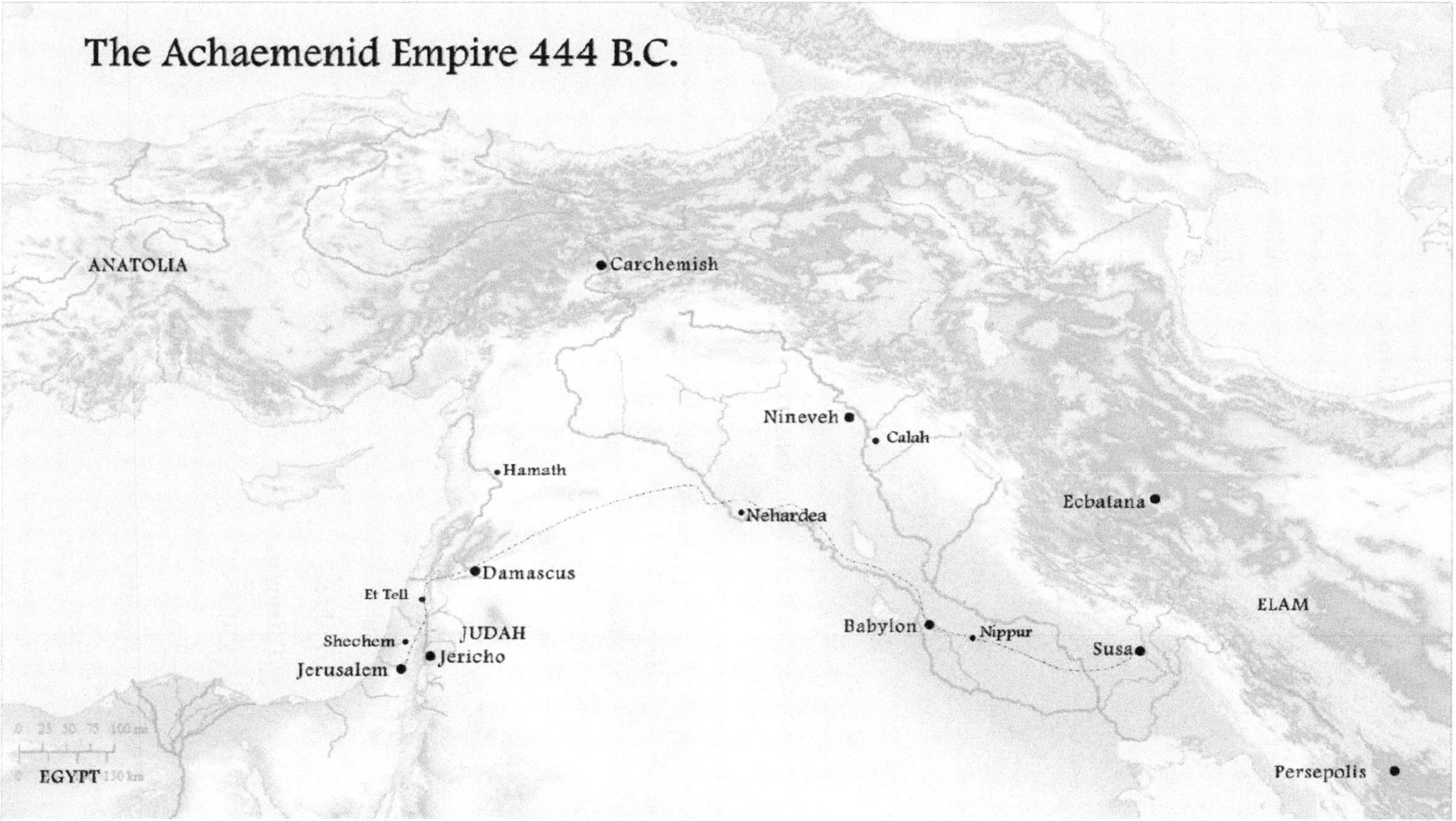

The Achaemenid Empire 444 B.C.

ANATOLIA

Carchemish

Hamath

Damascus

Et Tell

Shechem

Jerusalem

Jericho

JUDAH

Nineveh

Calah

Nehardea

Babylon

Nippur

Susa

Ecbatana

ELAM

Persepolis

EGYPT

0 25 50 75 100 km

Definitions

This list is a few of the Hebrew words I use
to help put you in Persia with Adira

Ab/Abba	Father/Daddy
Em/Emi	Mother/Mama
Dohd/Dohda	Uncle/Aunt
Sabba/Savta	Grandfather/Grandmother
Mitpachat	Women's Headcovering
Hammam	Bathhouse
G'veret	Mistress
Reebon	Master
Serai	Home or Sleeping quarter
Guest serai/Caravanserai	Like a Hotel

Hebrew Months of the Year

Nisan	March-April
Iyyar	April-May
Sivan	May-June
Tammuz	June-July
Av	July-August
Elul	August-September
Tishrei	September-October
Cheshvan	October-November
Kislev	November-December
Tevet	December-January
Shevat	January-February
Adar	February-March

Adira
Journey to Freedom

Part One
Adira

I had not been sad in his presence before, so the king asked me,
"Why does your face look so sad when you are not ill?
This can be nothing but sadness of heart."
I was very much afraid, but I said to the king,
"May the king live forever!

. . .

Then I prayed to the God of heaven, and I answered the king,
"If it pleases the king
and if your servant has found favor in his sight,
let him send me to the city in Judah where my ancestors are buried
so that I can rebuild it."
Nehemiah 2:1-5 (NIV)

I didn't know I was a slave
until I found out I couldn't do the things I wanted.
Frederick Douglas

One

"Adira." I heard Em's whisper, but my foggy brain refused to respond.

"Adira, I have news." The teasing lilt in my mother's voice made me roll toward her. "News of Ab."

"Abba?" I sat up. "You've heard from Abba!" My father had been gone for more than a year. And while caravans traveled through Susa every day, few brought news from Jerusalem.

In the soft light of the oil lamp, my mother's face beamed. "He's home!"

"Home?!"

Em raised her finger to her lips. "You don't want to wake the twins."

I lowered my voice again, "But, when?"

"He arrived long after we'd gone to sleep." Instinctively I turned toward my parents' mats. "He's up and gone. You'll see him soon."

Where would Abba go before dawn?

Em read my mind. "He went to talk to your uncle. Nehemiah's day begins as early as mine." Lifting her mitpachat to cover her head, she bent to kiss the top of mine.

My mother serves the royals each day, trusting me with the three small rooms we call home. The twins don't wake until sunrise. So, each morning after I share a barley loaf with my older brother, I roll the sleeping mats and sweep the room I share with my parents.

Today, Ab's early morning visit to see his brother stirred my disdain for Jerusalem. My parents call it home, but they've never lived anyplace except Susa. Well, here and the other royal cities.

King Artaxerxes and his nobles like the change in scenery, and Em oversees the harem's meals. So, while they never travel to Babylon, the queens follow the court to Ecbatana to escape the heat. Several extremely cold winters even took us south to Persepolis.

The gods have blessed my family. Ab and Em both serve the king's household, so we have everything we need. But their homeland often robs me of Abba.

You should hear their stories of my grandparents' trials under the rule of the old Chaldean Kings. Sometimes I wish Abba would keep those tales to himself. Over and over, he shares Israel's history, including Nebuchadnezzar's invasion of Judah and his great-grandparents being taken to Babylon as slaves more than one hundred fifty years ago. Still, when my parents talk about Jerusalem, you'd think the exile happened in their lifetime. I don't understand the fascination. Yet, despite my dislike for the place, Ab's stories draw me in.

Stories—Abba will have many to tell tonight. I'll save my sewing. If I stay quiet in the corner, they'll allow me to listen late into the night. Twice before he'd gone to Jerusalem and returned. Ab always made his travels sound like a great adventure.

The twins stirring interrupted my thoughts. Time to stop daydreaming. I'll never get my morning chores done if I don't get busy. Plus, I'm sure we'll have company after the evening meal.

Our small home sat on a far corner outside the palace complex near the stables. Just beyond the first row of servants' quarters, a grand courtyard created a beautiful boundary leading to the world of the nobility. Only those with official business passed through the massive archway that opened to the government buildings. Em and my older sister, Natalia, crossed daily as they served the queens and the harem, and Ab reported to the king's staff as one of Persia's chief builders.

I seldom walked this way, but I'd grown impatient. As my brothers and I neared the open area, I saw Abba talking with some men.

Picking up the pace, I motioned Jok and Jon to keep up.

As soon as he turned from his conversation, I called out, "Abba, Abba!"

His face brightened, and when he squatted and opened his arms, I broke into a full run. Abba's strong arms holding me tight erased moons of worry. Though she certainly doesn't need it, I try to help take care of Em when Ab goes to Jerusalem.

My joy was short-lived as my father widened his embrace to include the twins. I wish Abba still pulled me onto his lap and told me stories of the god he called Yahweh. I'd always loved those tales, but during the last four years, he'd spent more time in Jerusalem than Susa, and after I passed my tenth year, Em said I was too old to curl up on Abba's knee.

"What would you like for your welcome home meal, Abba?" I asked as our embrace unfolded.

"Ah yes, my youngest daughter has taken over the household duties since her sister serves Queen Esther. Surprise me, sweet Adira. After the limited food we had the last two days in the wilderness, whatever you prepare will be wonderful. Perhaps you could find some extra fruit and lentils for after the evening meal. My brothers will be visiting. We'll probably talk late into the night, and the snack will be welcome."

"Do you have exciting news for my dohds?"

"Nothing to concern yourself with, wee one."

"Ab, I'm not really a wee one anymore."

"Precious Adira," Ab pulled me close one more time, "you will always be my wee one. Now hurry and corral your brothers before they get into mischief."

I turned to where Ab pointed. The boys were climbing over the half wall that separated this small open area from the main courtyard. Each brother had straddled one of the columns that supported the arched gate. Ab's proud smile was all I needed to gather the young gymnasts and herd them toward our little living space.

"King Artaxerxes treats us well, but entering the courtyard is a privilege," I scolded. "Had guards caught you climbing, we'd have been detained. And some of the guards may have enjoyed it a bit too much."

A snack of apricots and bread kept the boys busy while I prepared the afternoon meal. The family would be gathering soon. Em slipped home for a few hours each day between the queens' midday and evening meals. So, we'd always eaten late in the afternoon.

Avraham should be waltzing in any moment. My seventeen-year-old brother served in the king's stables, a coveted job among our people. Most boys his age worked in the fields. Avraham hoped to be noticed by one of the soldiers so he could be trained to drive a battle-ready chariot. Having an uncle who is cupbearer to the king does have advantages.

Two

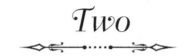

By the time Em returned, our afternoon meal covered the low table. While we waited for Ab, she sent Avraham for an extra jar of water and dabbed on one of her precious perfumes. I forget my strong, independent Em misses her husband terribly when he travels.

Rounds of hugs gave the stew a chance to cool when Ab made his appearance, but finally, everyone found a cushion. As we ate, Ab talked about the weather in Jerusalem and his sandals wearing out in the desert. Avraham caught him up on news from the soldiers, and we discussed Sabba Hacaliah's failing health. I started to ask about his adventures, but Em's wink reminded me those stories would come tonight after his brothers arrived.

Em rushed out to finish the queen's evening meal, and Avraham took Jok and Jon to help clean stalls. My trip to the market would be easier without the rambunctious boys. I might even have time to slip over to the hammam—late afternoons were usually quiet in the bathhouse.

The mid-winter sun set long before Em returned from serving the harem's evening meal. She brought Natalia with her. My fifteen-year-old sister usually stayed in a room off Queen Esther's chamber, but when the generous queen heard Ab had returned, she'd given Natalia leave to visit with us until early tomorrow morning.

It had been so long since our entire family had gathered for a meal. I felt thankful as the room grew silent so Abba could pronounce the evening blessing.

My father's deep calming voice filled the room and calmed my soul. Even though I couldn't understand my parent's attraction to this singular God who'd sent my great-great-grandparents into exile, Abba's strong and steady timbre brought a tremendous sense of comfort and peace. Avraham did His best to reproduce our father's blessings when Ab traveled, but his recitation of the memorized prayer lacked the warmth of Abba's.

As we cleared the remnants of our meal, Ab's brothers began to arrive—each oil lamp adding to the warm glow in our small space. Natalia and I sat out snacks and filled several wooden goblets with wine before retreating to a corner to mend our brothers' robes and listen in on Ab's adventures.

Dohd Nehemiah arrived last. His duties as cupbearer kept him confined to the king's quarters most of the time. Even here, the king's chief steward would know where to find him. As he lowered himself onto a worn, red cushion, he redirected the conversation, "So, Hanani, give us the details. What's going on in the homeland?"

Ab took a deep breath and shook his head, "It's distressing, brother. No one would know Cyrus let the first of our people return a hundred years ago. Rubble still marks her boundaries, and massive piles of burned wood lie where the twelve gates should stand. Jerusalem is in trouble, and though the king allows a few to return with every caravan, those who traveled with me the last time just added to the burden. The city sits in disgrace."

As Abba continued to describe the city and his trip, my mind wandered. My family's obsession with Jerusalem once again confounded me. I loved my life. Other Jews in our station wished they had it so good.

As my attention returned to the conversation, Dohd Nehemiah's countenance troubled me. His anguished face made it look like he heard nothing his brothers were saying. After a few moments, silent tears began to fall. Ab had everyone's attention, so no one else seemed to notice until Em interrupted, "Nehemiah, what is it?"

The focus turned to Ab's youngest brother. I doubt anyone had ever seen him so distressed.

The room stayed quiet waiting for Dohd to speak. Finally, my uncle rose from his reclining position and fell to his knees. He reached his hands toward the heavens and began to pray. No one could understand his tear-filled mumbling, but we all bowed our heads with him until he emptied his heart before Yahweh.

Three

My mother's hushed voice invaded my slumber. "Hanani, you just got back."

"I know, Chava, but Nehemiah has a plan, a grand plan. We won't leave right away. Nehemiah needs the king's permission, and there's no predicting storms this time of year."

Dohd Nehemiah's duties required him to stay close to the king. Like Natalia, he had a small chamber in the quarters of his charge. Though his schedule seldom let him visit, he and Ab had talked late into the night every evening since his return, even after Em went to bed.

"That won't be an easy conversation."

"Nehemiah's already started praying."

My heart sank. I loved having Abba home. Everything felt right. I pulled the blanket tight as quiet tears soaked my mat. I could only grant my grief a few minutes. Em would leave for the harem soon, and I'd need to get something ready for Avraham and the boys to break their fast.

Avraham rose with me each morning. And though normally the task of the women, my brother filled the water jars while I prepared the morning meal. Today I'd need a little of the cold liquid to freshen my swollen eyes.

Before I could check the water bucket, Ab spotted me. He held a steaming cup in his hand. Em had prepared him something before she left. "My sweet Adira looks as if she's been crying." Even though only one candle lit the room, Ab could tell.

"Did you overhear me talking to Em?"

My eyes burned as I nodded. Abba stood and pulled me close. His strong arms temporarily chased the fear away. What would I do without him for another year?

"Come, sit with me."

I poured a glass of goat's milk and joined him.

"Adira, you know I have to go, right?"

Words couldn't get past the catch in my throat.

"Wee one, it's time for our people to go home, but until the city is secure, it won't be safe. During this visit, I plan to build a real home for our family. One where my beautiful daughters each have their own room. We'll finally be free."

No amount of blinking and steady breathing would hold back the tears now.

"But Abba, I don't understand why we can't just stay in Susa. My friends live here. We have a good life. We live near the palace and travel with the king and queens. Many of those free Persians in the market aren't dressed as well as you and me."

My father grew quiet as his own tears threatened.

"Adira, no matter how good you think we have it, here in Susa, we are slaves. Yahweh created us to be free. Our great ancestor, Father Avraham freely followed Yahweh. He started not far from here, but

God led him to the Promised Land. Yahweh chose Yaacov over his brother Esau and gave the younger twin the name Israel. We are Yahweh's chosen people, wee one.'

"Yahweh has rescued our people many times. You've heard the stories. He raised Joseph from slave to second-in-command to save the patriarchs from famine. And He rescued Moses so he could lead our people through the Red Sea and deliver them from Egypt.'

"My sweet daughter, have I not told you of the grand victories of Joshua and the grace Yahweh showed when our people rebelled during the time of the judges? Don't you remember the history of King David? He had great success because his heart chased after Yahweh. For hundreds of years, Adonai blessed Judah and Jerusalem. But our ancestors failed Him. Evil kings came to power, and our people chased after them and their false gods instead of our Creator.'

"That's why we're here, Adira. More than one hundred fifty years ago, after many warnings, God allowed all of Jerusalem, including my great-grandfather, to be drug into slavery. This is why the sons of Aaron remind us of the law. If we turn our hearts to Yahweh, He will deliver our people once more. Since the time of Cyrus, these Achaemenian kings have helped with our deliverance."

Abba's face radiated as he spoke. I nodded, but my lips refused to smile. I knew the history, but Abba talked of traveling far away to a place broken down and burned, all to follow a single God. Hadn't he noticed the wealth Ahura Mazda gave to these Persians? I wanted to share his dream, but he saw something beyond my imagination.

"Adira." Ab's voice broke into my thoughts.

"Adira, what are you thinking?"

Not even the songbirds broke the dark silence. I finally spoke the only words I believed wouldn't cause him pain, "I just don't want you to go away again, Abba."

His loving smile drew me to him even before his strong arms. He held my chin as he released me, "It's time for me to get to work. I'm expected at the new construction site on the other side of the palace, but don't let this worry you, wee one."

My wrinkled brow and half-smile conveyed my thoughts.

"I know, I know, you aren't my wee one, anymore." His hearty laugh lifted my spirits. "But there's no need to worry. I'll be here a few more moons."

Abba opened the door just in time for Avraham to enter with two more pots of water. Jok and Jon would be rising soon, and my busy day would be underway. I knew it would be full of silent tears and confused thoughts.

Four

Kislev 13, 445 B.C.

Life had a predictable routine. We rose early, mother tended to the harem, father built the king's grand structures, and I took care of my six-year-old brothers and looked after our cozy space.

I often overheard Avraham and his friends talk about getting out of this peasant slave life and returning to Judah, but I never understood. Why did they say, 'returning' when they'd never lived there? And why go to a city with no walls—a place that has rubble for houses? Even worse, Abba said wild animals are just one of Jerusalem's many enemies.

I missed Natalia. She and I once shared every secret, but since her move into Queen Esther's quarters, I seldom had time alone with her. She slipped away for a meal with us once or twice each week, but Queen Esther and the harem lived on the other side of the palace complex. Em walked the round trip twice a day, but no one needed her after they finished their meals. Natalia and the other maids were at Queen Esther's beck and call day and night.

Today, she slipped away for an early midday meal. Avraham took the twins to the stables, so I walked her back as far as the courtyard.

"I feel so blessed to live in Queen Esther's quarters."

I frowned. "Not living at home makes you feel blessed?"

"Let's face it, I stayed home with you and the boys a lot longer than most girls my age. Sometimes I wonder if Em hid me away knowing the queen's former maid was aging."

My sister was right, she could have ended up scrubbing palace floors.

"Queen Esther is so kind, and I love to hear her stories. She's told us all about Xerxes and his battles, but Queen Esther's own story is the best. Did you know she is a Jew?"

"I think Ab mentioned that."

"Oh, probably, but his stories always bore me."

Perhaps our differences kept us close. I loved Ab's stories.

Natalia continued, "When Queen Esther was my age, King Xerxes started looking for a new queen. His first wife had done something to make him angry—I can't remember what exactly. Anyway, Queen Esther—she wasn't queen then—came to live at the palace. Actually, she wasn't even called Esther then. Her cousin, Mordecai . . ."

"Wait. Esther isn't the queen's real name?"

"Nope."

I waited a moment for Natalia to reveal her name, but she just kept going.

"Hold up. What was her name?"

"Oh yeah," Natalia chuckled, "Hadassah. Isn't that pretty?"

"It sounds weird, Queen Hadassah." I laughed. "So, you mean when she was your age, she chose to leave her family?"

"Her parents had died, so she lived with her cousin. But she didn't get to talk with him much after she moved into the palace. She came to the palace with dozens of other girls. Each one spent a year preparing to meet the king."

"A year? You're kidding."

"Truly. Then after a full year of beauty treatments, she had exactly one night to impress the king."

Abba had never told us this part of Queen Esther's story. Did he even know?

"Queen Esther laughs about it. She says for her the year of preparation wasn't for one night; it was for a lifetime because the king married her."

"What a perfect story."

"Oh, there's more, but I have to get back. I'll tell you the rest the next time."

"Come on, Natalia. You can't leave me hanging!"

"No, I asked for a short break while the maids served lunch and the queen took her nap. She'll be ready for her afternoon walk when she wakes. Two of us go with her each day. But I can't wait until you hear how Yahweh answered her prayer."

And with that, Natalia headed back toward the queens' quarters.

So, Queen Esther worshipped the God of Israel. I assumed after forty years in an Achaemenid palace she'd embraced Ahura Mazda.

I had so many questions for Natalia. I wanted to talk to her about Abba leaving.

Natalia was right, I needed to get home, too. The evening meal wouldn't prepare itself. As I turned my back on the courtyard, I wished I could be more like my sister. She seemed so content. She could probably find a blessing in Ab's return to Jerusalem.

Five

Dohd Lemuel and Dohd Reuben arrived just after sunset. Sabba Hacaliah hobbled in with them. My grandfather had grown so thin in the last few moons. Ab had just helped him settle his frail bones when an exhausted-looking Dohd Nehemiah came in.

"Thank you for fasting with me, brothers." Dohd took a cushion next to his father.

"You said it was important, Nehemiah," Dohd Lemuel spoke for the brothers.

How had I missed Abba not eating? I guess refereeing Jok and Jon distracted me more than I realized.

"I believe we can build that wall."

What was Dohd talking about?

"If I were twenty years younger. . ."

Abba interrupted Sabba, "Nehemiah, I think you underestimate the damage. Not one inch of the wall remains. Besides that, Sanballat and Tobiah will do everything they can to stop it. Jerusalem's neighbors have created obstacles for every rebuild in the Holy City since Cyrus sent the first exiles back. It took forty years and a second edict from King Darius to get work on the temple moving, and it's still not finished."

"We can do this, Hanani. I have fasted and prayed since your return."

I could feel anger rise from deep within. Dohd had orchestrated this need to go back to Jerusalem. *How could he take Abba from me so soon? How could Abba agree to go?* Sitting in the corner, I concentrated on my mending to keep from screaming. Obviously, I had missed some important conversations after that first evening.

As the four men discussed the pros and cons of the trip, I moved my needle quietly until my little lamp went out. Then the winter darkness allowed me to sit unnoticed. The longer they talked the more grief I saw on Dohd's face. Or perhaps the flicker of the lamps tricked my weary eyes. No, Dohd Nehemiah's grief had led to tears.

"Hanani, the burden on my heart for Jerusalem is great, more than I can bear. I believe Yahweh wants me . . ." Uncle took a deep breath. "No, He demands I go."

Then, as he'd done on the night of Abba's return, Dohd moved from his seated position to his knees, this time with his face to the ground.

"Yahweh, God of heaven." Uncle's voice broke as he prayed. "You who are great and awesome, who has promised to love those who show You love and keep Your commands, please hear the words of your servant and see my distress."

Dohd's tears had turned to sobs, and everything else grew silent. Even sounds from outside the window ceased. One by one, each adult joined Dohd in his humble position. I watched the full moon rise high in our small window as we waited for him to rein in his weeping enough to continue.

"Yahweh, Mighty God, I confess the sins of Your people, the sins of my people, the sins of the sons of Hacaliah. Our nation acted wickedly before You. We neglected Your commands and ignored the words of Moses."

The essence of Dohd's prayer filled the room. Abba joined the weeping, and Em cried out, "Forgive us." Tears fell from my uncles and grandfather, and one by one they added their voices to the prayer.

From my corner, I watched in fear. I'd never seen such a display of emotion from my family. I considered waking Avraham—perhaps he could protect me or help me understand.

Dohd Nehemiah finally gained some composure, and the room grew quiet again. Though no one moved from their semi-prostrate position, I thought the spectacle must finally be over until Dohd took up his prayer again.

"Yahweh, we plead with you to remember the promise you made to Moses. You told him that when your people sin, You would scatter us among the nations, but when we returned to You and obeyed your commands, You would bring us out of exile and return Your people to the land you gave to our fathers, to Avraham, Itzhak, and Yaacov, the land you chose for the dwelling of Your Name."

Sobbing raised and subsided once more until only sniffles broke the silence. I wished I had my blanket as the flames on the lamps began to dance in the cool Kislev breeze. Still, my family remained quiet before their God.

Dohd's prayer weighed heavy on everyone in the room. I almost slipped out to the safety of my sleeping mat, but even if I could've found a path through my uncles, the Presence in the room paralyzed me with a weight I couldn't comprehend.

Just when I felt like I could breathe again, Uncle continued, "Yahweh, we are your servants."

Ab, Em, and the others raised their voices in affirmation. Then Dohd Nehemiah finished, "Yes, Yahweh, we are your servants, the people you redeemed by your great strength and mighty hand. Adonai, hear the prayer of your servant. Attend to the cries of your servants who delight in bringing reverence to your Holy Name. Grant your servant success and favor when he stands before the king."

Dohd Nehemiah remained in his kneeling position. Dohd Rueben rose first and helped Sabba up, then each family member exited quietly. I retreated to my mat in my parent's room leaving Dohd and Ab to their prayers.

Dohd's occasional mumblings continued through much of the night. And while I'd like to blame them for keeping me awake, processing the evening's events was the real culprit. If only Natalia still shared my sleeping space. She would help me understand my feelings or at least listen while I tried to sort it out. The heaviness I'd felt as Dohd prayed had been uncomfortable, but ever since it lifted, I longed for it. There had been something soothing in that Presence that far outweighed the fear it brought.

My family revered Yahweh, but I felt torn. Thanks to my Elamite friends, I'd been enlightened years ago to the folly of limiting my worship to one God. I might be young, but I'm old enough to see the power of Ahura Mazda and his array of lesser deities, each possessing one or more of a variety of powers. How could I limit myself to a single God who had deserted the nation of Israel for 175 years?

Our people had more integrity than any others I'd encountered.

So, if Yahweh was truly so powerful, and Jerusalem His city, why did He let the Babylonians drag the grandparents of these good people into slavery? Why didn't He protect His precious Jerusalem? Putting all my eggs in Yahweh's basket made no sense.

A barrage of emotions stirred within. Dohd said Yahweh compelled him. How can that be? I'd never heard anyone talk that way about the god of Elam, not Ahura Mazda or any of his underlings. And, if this was true, if Yahweh pressed Uncle to this decision . . .

I will never understand this God my father embraces.

If Yahweh forced Dohd, will He force me to do something?

Abba said Yahweh was different, but if He makes His people do things against their will . . .? Well, I certainly don't see any good difference.

Confusion turned to fear and then anger, each emotion on repeat as they took turns feeding the silent sobs that rose from deep within until I finally fell into a restless, fit-filled sleep.

Six

Morning came too early the next day. Emotionally spent, the dark of winter didn't help me give up my blankets. Unfortunately, the boys would wake soon, and I'd already heard Avraham with the water.

I rolled my mat and walked through the daily routine, but my emotions kept bubbling, rushing through me like the Karkeh River after the spring rains. Jok and Jon must have sensed my pensive mood because they did their chores without complaining and played quietly all day.

One week after my family's turbulent prayer session, my friend, Yasmine, joined me in the market while the twins went with Avraham to help at the stable following midday meal. Yasmine's mother served the harem, too. We'd been friends for as long as I could remember.

At the market, we liked to pretend we were regular citizens of Susa instead of servants and slaves. We hung the soft silk scarves over our arms and admired the embroidered gowns. The merchants knew we didn't have money to make such extravagant purchases, but most let us indulge our imagination as long as we stayed out of the way of paying customers.

"I'm glad my ab doesn't leave us for moons," Yasmine said after I shared my angst about Abba heading back to Jerusalem. I knew she would understand.

"Dohd said Yahweh compels him to go rebuild the wall. I don't know why Ab wants to go back already."

The conversation paused when we reached the food booths. Em and I mended for the merchants in exchange for fresh fruit and extra grain. Yasmine's family bartered eggs.

After we made our trades, Yasmine continued, "How does your Yahweh compel a person?"

"I'm not sure, exactly. But when Dohd and Ab pray, I feel a strange Presence in the room, and both say they hear their God in the silence."

"What does Yahweh's statue do when He speaks?"

"Yahweh has no icon. He forbids them."

"That doesn't sound right. What kind of god has no icon? Does he have a consort?"

"No, Yahweh says he is One. Like Ahura Mazda, except with no lesser gods. Ab says Yahweh is the true Creator."

"But with no statue, what do you look at when you worship?"

"Ab and Dohd close their eyes. They lift their hands and sometimes kneel with their faces to the ground."

"You should borrow one of our household gods. Maybe they can help convince your Ab to stay home." Yasmine offered.

"I couldn't. Ab and Em would be so hurt and disappointed if they found a foreign god in our house."

Since neither of us could explain the oddity of Yahweh, we changed the subject to handsome boys and our most recent sewing projects and headed back.

Seven

When winters turned especially cold, the harem often traveled to Persepolis. The builders of Susa's palace complex had reproduced the southern royal headquarters with only minor differences, so even here, we occupied a small three-room apartment on the southern corner near the stables.

Dohd Nehemiah remained in Susa with Artaxerxes, and Avraham stayed with the horses; however, Natalia traveled with Queen Esther to the warmer location.

The past three times we'd come, Ab had either been in Jerusalem or forced to stay in Susa to oversee a rebuilding project, but this time the king sent him to take care of maintenance on his southernmost palace.

Natalia joined us most Shabbats in Persepolis. Ab led us in prayer and taught a Psalm. I couldn't help but wonder how many he had memorized. He ended each Shabbat evening with a story from Israel's history and more prayer.

As we sat in the glow of lamps listening to Ab this Shabbat, he surprised us, "Chava, I just got word from Nehemiah, several in Susa and a few of us here have decided to celebrate a fast on the thirteenth of Adar in honor of Queen Esther."

"Why would we fast in her honor, Ab?" I asked.

Natalia spoke up, "Because the people of Israel fasted with her for three days after Haman cast the purim to choose a date to execute our people."

Ab smiled, "Has my oldest daughter begun to enjoy the history of Israel?"

"I'm afraid Adira will always be the history lover, Ab; however, I do enjoy hearing the queen share her own story."

"Then maybe you should tell your siblings the rest of the story," Abba laughed.

Natalia beamed, "I'd love to. Queen Esther said Haman hated our people. He especially despised the queen's cousin, Mordecai. Unfortunately for Haman, he didn't realize Mordecai had once saved the king's life. He also had no idea the queen was a Jew.'

"Haman convinced King Xerxes to proclaim a day when every Jew in the empire would be killed. When Mordecai found out, he reported it to Queen Esther. Mordecai told her she had to make a plea to the king. But going to the king without an invitation could mean death, even for a queen. In answer to her fear, Mordecai told her, 'perhaps God put you in this prominent position for such a time as this.' So, she agreed and asked Mordecai to have every Jew in Susa fast and pray with her."

"That's why Abba wants to hold a day of fasting!" Jok chimed in.

"Correct, son. After twenty-five years, the memory of Queen Esther's bravery has begun to fade. We don't want to let that happen."

"Wait a minute. Natalia, what stopped Haman from assassinating our people?" Jon asked.

"Queen Esther told me that after the three days, she revealed her heritage to the king and told him Haman planned to kill her and her people.'

"The enraged king stepped into the garden to consider what to do next. Meanwhile, Haman tripped and fell on Queen Esther."

A series of gasps filled the room, but Natalia kept going.

"The king returned before Haman could get up. You can imagine Xerxes' anger. He immediately had Haman dragged out and killed. Then he allowed Mordecai to create a new edict that gave our people permission to protect themselves from the people who wanted them dead.'

"So, on the fifteenth of Adar, the people of God fought back against the army of Persia. Many of Xerxes' men didn't even fight. They'd heard about Yahweh's power, and it frightened them. Our people not only won, but many Persian citizens also became Jews that day. Esther and Mordecai helped demonstrate the power of Yahweh to protect His people."

"I couldn't have told it better myself, Natalia." The fading lamps made it difficult to tell for sure, but I think Ab had tears in his eyes.

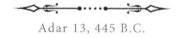

Adar 13, 445 B.C.

Over the next week, word spread quickly among the Jews in Persepolis. Even Queen Esther decided to fast when she heard. When the day arrived, Jok and Jon passed on the cheese and bread I set out for them to break their fast. My little brothers made me proud. Many called it the Fast of Esther.

Those fasting gathered for prayer early in the day then moved to the courtyard outside the harem's quarters. Queen Esther came out on her balcony to greet the people. She praised Yahweh for raising her up to help save the people of Judah.

I went to bed hungry that night, but for the first time in my life, I found myself proud of my heritage.

As Spring emerged, the harem returned to Susa, and anxiety returned to my soul. Dohd and Ab would leave for Jerusalem soon. I could feel it.

Eight

Nisan 2, 444 B.C.

I hadn't fallen asleep yet when Ab came in. " . . . Two weeks . . .," From my sleeping mat I could only catch a word now and then. "Natalia . . . stay . . . "

"Oh, Hanani . . ." Em's broken voice had a sound of tears. "And Avraham?"

I missed everything in Ab's muffled reply.

" . . . be ready," Em's words left me confused. My mind raced as I tried to make sense of the clipped conversation. I assumed they discussed Ab's upcoming trip, but . . .

"Nehemiah's worries for Jerusalem are beginning to show on his face." Perhaps I was wrong, maybe Em hadn't been crying.

"I know. I worry for him." The whispers grew to an audible level.

"The king won't tolerate him looking so downcast."

"I'm fasting for him. We can sense the time draws near."

"I will pray too. Yahweh will answer."

The next morning, I found both my parents on their knees. They were finishing their morning prayers as I rose, and with just a cup of water, they were on their way. Em only had time to tell me she expected Natalia for the evening meal. I couldn't wait!

Natalia arrived early. Queen Esther's other six maids would cover her duties for the entire afternoon and evening. We could talk late into the night.

My sister and I laughed and shared stories as we chopped vegetables for the stew. It felt like old times. Jok and Jon even grabbed knives. I wanted to talk to her about my worries, but I couldn't bring myself to spoil the fun.

When Dohd Nehemiah arrived with Ab, my heart grew heavy. Fortunately, no one seemed to notice my mood change.

After everyone enjoyed the stew and sweetbread, Natalia and I cleared the table. Ab made the story of David come alive. I laughed to think no one invited the young shepherd to the meal where Samuel anointed him king.

Eventually, Em turned the conversation to Passover preparation. Though our celebrations paled in comparison to those of King David and King Josiah, we always removed the yeast from the house and had a great dinner of lamb as the Nisan moon grew full. Jok and Jon now shared the traditional questions that allowed Ab to remind us why we eat the bitter herbs with our shoes on.

"Will the queen allow you to join us for the Passover meal?" Em asked Natalia.

Before she could answer, Ab interrupted. "Chava, before you get too carried away with Passover preparations, we need to talk. Natalia, I'm so glad you're here this evening." Then he turned to Dohd, "Nehemiah, tell the family what you told me this morning."

After weeks of seeing Uncle so distraught, I loved seeing his lightened countenance. He, Ab, and Em had eaten heartily this evening. The mood of the meal had lifted all my worry, but as Dohd began, the feeling of dread returned.

"Yahweh looked on me with favor today. My heart had become so burdened for Jerusalem, I couldn't hide it, and today the king asked about my downcast face.'

"After seeing how the king treats those who ruin the mood of his meals, his question caused some fear. But I told him, 'May you live forever great King. How can I not be sad when the city of my ancestors lies in ruins with her gates burned and walls lying in heaps?'"

Dohd continued, "I expected the worst, but King Artaxerxes simply asked, 'What do you want?'"

"I quickly raised a prayer to Yahweh, and told the king, 'Please allow me to go to Judah to rebuild.'"

Dohd's face beamed when he asked us, "Can you guess what the king answered?"

Em laughed, "By the look on your face, I assume you've already packed for Jerusalem."

"You are correct, Chava. He only asked when I would leave and how long I'd be gone. So, right there, on the spot, I told him I would leave on the sixteenth day of Nisan. I know it's soon, but isn't it fitting we leave this bondage of slavery on the anniversary of our ancestors' escape from Egypt? Passover will have a double meaning this year."

"This is why I'm glad our sweet Natalia is with us tonight." Abba's eyes glistened, "Our journey comes with a price that makes my heart heavy. The king has released your mother from service to the queens; however, Natalia and Avraham, after talking with Queen Esther and Shemu'el, King Artaxerxes has requested you stay. You won't be able to come with us."

Come with us? Panic rose within me. *What does that mean?*

I could barely breathe as I processed the conversation and Em's free-flowing tears. *Does this mean the rest of us are going to Jerusalem?* Natalia and Avraham looked so calm. Both smiled with wet cheeks. *Am I the only one who understands the gravity of Ab's words?*

Avraham spoke first, "We'll be fine, Em. You've raised us well. That's why they can't let us go. Natalia and I work harder and carry more responsibility than others our age. It's a testimony to your love and hard work. Shemu'el has been asking me to move into a room off the stables for some time. He wants to promote me. I'm sure he was pleased when Ab spoke with him."

"And Queen Esther is the most pleasant person to serve," Natalia continued. The tears in her eyes confirmed she'd miss us, but her voice sounded steady and confident, "Avraham and I will stay close. We'll be fine, Emi."

Fine?! Fine?! Nothing would be fine! How could they accept this so readily?

As my family continued to talk about preparations, I heard nothing. Anger boiled up inside me—anger toward Ab for springing this on us and anger toward Em for agreeing so readily, but I couldn't even look at Dohd. How could my uncle do this to me? I could never forgive him for this.

Nine

Nisan 14, 444 B.C.

The next two weeks passed without me. My body went through the day-to-day motions while my mind ran the gamut from numb to angry to inconsolable. Every task I performed reminded me of my future—my last walk to the market with Yasmine, the final laundry day in Susa. And as I rid the house of leaven, I began to question our annual ritual. Why do we still celebrate Passover? The deliverance from Egypt was twelve hundred years ago.

The longer I worked, the more I realized this plan to ruin my life wasn't Dohd's fault; the blame lay with the God my family worshipped. A real and mighty God wouldn't leave His people in Susa. And Shabbat—couldn't a Creator God force this day of rest He supposedly commanded? Only the nobility take days of rest in Elam and Media, the servants and slaves don't get any days off.

The day before our scheduled departure, Natalia and I managed to have some sister time. Queen Esther had excused her from her duties for three days. So, while Jok and Jon went to the stables to inspect Avraham's new room, we grabbed our small baskets of soaps and perfumes and took advantage of the quiet to go to the hammam. Natalia looked so content.

"Your face doesn't hide your pain well, little sister."

I'm not sure she expected an answer.

"I thought you'd be excited to return to Jerusalem. Even Queen Esther looks forward to hearing about Ab and Dohd's success."

A million replies raced through my mind. Servant training served me well in this moment.

"Adira," Natalia continued, "Elam and Media are not our home. Abba tells us this almost every night. Little sister, you are going home. Yahweh is delivering you from this life of slavery."

I couldn't contain my terse remarks any longer. "How can a place we've never seen be home? I was born in our little house, right here in Susa. Except for summers in Ecbatana and a winter or three in Persepolis, I've never lived anyplace else. My friends are here. You are here."

Once I began my tirade, I couldn't make it stop. "And 'delivered from slavery?' I've heard about the trip to Jerusalem; it will take almost four moons. Then I'll wake up in a place with no walls for protection. The lions and bears roam free. Will I even have a roof, or will we have to live in tents? Are there any hammams in Jerusalem, or is this my last proper bath? How can that be better than serving royalty here?"

"You will be free, Adira."

"Free to do what? Forage for food, cook in the open, bathe in rivers and ponds?"

"Perhaps you've had it too easy. You don't see Abba using his master-building skills constructing palaces for kings while we live in a hovel. You don't get to see Em prepare lavish meals for queens while we eat stew, cheese, and barley bread every day. And in Jerusalem, you'll be free to worship Yahweh the way He intends to be worshipped without having reminders of Ahura Mazda in every corner."

My mind had already formed the words of my sarcastic response, but Natalia's look of sincere reverence stopped me. Her countenance softened my heart, "But, Natalia, how can you be so certain Yahweh is the greater God?"

"Not the greater god, Adira, the only God. Don't you remember all of Abba's evening stories? Moses led our people through the sea on dry ground. The Creator fed them manna for forty years. Don't you remember how He raised up David and the immense growth of Judah and all Israel while the people followed Yahweh?"

Natalia's passion showed. "Even here in Elam, kings have dreamed dreams only Yahweh could interpret. And in Babylon, the Almighty rescued Daniel from the lions. God brought several Jews to power even under those ruthless kings. It reminds me of Joseph."

"How do you know these aren't just ancient folklore?"

"Besides the fact Queen Esther knows people who served Daniel—it's our history, Adira, important facts passed down from father to daughter and mother to son. Don't you listen when Abba shares?"

"We rarely hear Abba tell us about Israel anymore. He's been in Jerusalem more than Susa since the twins were born."

I could tell from the look on her face she was beginning to understand, "I'd never thought about it. Jok and Jon have missed hearing the stories of Israel, haven't they?"

"Avraham tries to take over for Abba, but he's much better with the horses than retelling history."

We continued in silence. The hammam for the servants was much smaller than the royals' bathhouses, but our small home would have fit in this hammam more than five times. Two arched porticos provided entrance to the large stone structure. Inside, a pool large enough for twenty women took up most of the space, and fire pits full of rocks to provide steam sat in strategic spots around it.

We used the large tools to place some rocks in the pool to warm it a bit, removing the cooled ones and placing them on the firepit. The refreshing water washed away my anxious spirit with the dirt. We bathed quickly, and by the time we finished, the conversation had turned to friends and young men as well as the queen's newest robes. Only for a moment did we remember our previous conversation, when, just before we put away our perfumes, I held my sister tight. No words exchanged but her tears told me she understood.

Part Two
Journey to Jerusalem

And because the gracious hand of my God was on me,
the king granted my requests.
So, I went to the governors of Trans-Euphrates
and gave them the king's letters.
The king had also sent army officers and cavalry with me.
Nehemiah 2:8-9

They who would give up an essential liberty
for temporary security,
deserve neither liberty or security.
Benjamin Franklin

Ten

Our bittersweet Passover celebration included Sabba Hacaliah and many cousins. Ab answered Jok and Jon's scripted questions with more passion than ever. His face held a mixture of sadness and anticipation. Though we'd leave Avraham and Natalia behind, our next Passover lamb would be sacrificed at the temple in Jerusalem.

Nisan 16, 444 B.C.

We rose before the sun, but the Passover moon provided plenty of light to load our meager belongings onto the wagon. Three other families would travel with us, but only ours and the small band of cavalry the king sent for our protection would continue all the way to Jerusalem.

Everything within me rebelled, though only silent tears betrayed my heart. Natalia and Avraham held me tight as our parents put the two sleeping six-year-olds in the back of the wagon. Would I ever see my older siblings again?

The captain and three cavalry guards led the way on horseback. Dohd rode too. Em and I would walk with Ab as he guided the camel that pulled our wagon. The king had been gracious to Dohd, giving him everything we needed to make the journey. The other three families followed, and two more guards brought up the rear driving the supply wagon.

By the time the sun began to warm the spring air, our small caravan had been traveling for some time. We stopped only long enough to eat a cold midday meal. Jok, Jon, Em, and I took turns riding in the two spots Ab had left in the back of the wagon. We tried to convince him to take a break and ride, but he said he was used to the long walk.

Unlike Ab, my market trips and jaunts to the hammam didn't prepare me for all-day hiking. Blisters caused my feet to throb. I could barely keep my eyes open as I helped Em heat the stew when we stopped for the night.

Five wagons created a fortress around the fire. And as we enjoyed a magnificent sunset, Ab speculated, "I wonder if this is how Moses and Aaron felt the first night after they left Egypt?"

Dohd laughed, "They may have had a bit more anxiety considering they were constantly looking over their shoulder for Pharaoh's army."

"You're probably right, brother. We are blessed."

Blessed. I didn't feel blessed. I gathered Jok and Jon and headed for the wagon.

The spring air turned cool quickly as the stars appeared. I hoped the fire would keep us warm all night. Pulling my blanket tight, I slid under the wagon with my brothers and listened to Ab and Uncle talk about Moses bringing the Israelites out of Egypt.

Bijan, head of the only Elamite family traveling with us, asked, "What are these stories you share, Hanani?"

Abba's voice grew strong. He loved retelling the stories of Israel. I fought to stay awake so I could enjoy his rich timbre.

"These are the histories of Israel from the Torah. But in order for you to truly understand, I need to take you back to at least Avraham."

"Father Avraham. I know about the father of Ishmael and Midian."

"Yes, but Avraham's first legitimate son, Itzhak received Yahweh's covenant. Avraham's wife, Sarah, longed for a baby, but she grew old. When our ancestor was seventy-five, Yahweh promised him a son to make his name great. But Sarah grew impatient and gave her servant Hagar to her husband. That's where Ishmael came in."

Dohd chimed in, "Sarah's child of promise was born to her in her ninetieth year just as Avraham reached one hundred."

"And Midian was born long after that," Bijan added.

I wanted to hear more, but my heavy eyes won. As I drifted off, I heard Ab. "Correct, Bijan. After Sarah died, Avraham took a second wife who gave him twelve more sons. But that was after he almost sacrificed our ancestor Itzhak . . ."

Eleven

Every limb of my body ached. How could walking make my fingers hurt? Fruit and matzah greeted my hungry belly. Though I never cared for unleavened bread, one week each year, I forced it down.

"We have to get moving early today if we want to make it to the caravanserai by sunset," the captain of the guard bellowed.

The night hadn't provided much relief for my blistered feet. Thankfully, Ab said we'd stay at the caravanserai for Shabbat. My whole body would appreciate the day off.

Just before sunset, the caravanserai came into view. Everyone quickened their step a bit. I wondered if I'd even bother to eat when we got there. I just wanted to sleep. But as we drew closer, the structure caused me to forget my hunger and need for sleep.

When Ab had said we'd be staying in caravanserais along the way I'd expected a large house like the guest serais in Susa. The fortress that appeared in the middle of the wilderness looked more like a small city. The ornate entrance with large wooden gates rose even higher than the two-story walls. If each window corresponded to a sleeping room, there might be fifteen rooms on each level, thirty rooms on this side I could see. The setting sun made other details difficult to make out, but curiosity had wakened me.

"You made it just in time." An oversized Persian greeted us as the gates closed behind our small entourage. "We close the gates at dusk to keep out bandits, but we saw you carrying the king's standard while you were still far off."

Quick introductions and bartering the cost of rooms took a few more minutes, but I heard little as I took in the sight. Torches outlined the massive courtyard and large troughs for the animals sat on either end. Arches opened into sleeping rooms and stalls. Dried grass on the floors would make for a much comfier bed than the cold desert ground offered last night.

The commander secured three upper rooms for him and his men. These rooms had doors to provide privacy. The rest of our party rented four open sleeping rooms and two stalls for the horses and camels.

Jok and Jon fell asleep before Dohd and Ab returned from caring for the animals. We'd traveled hard; there would be no stories tonight. Everyone needed a good night's sleep.

Nisan 18, 444 B.C.

The bright sun peeking over the walls of the caravanserai woke me. How could I have slept so long? Em would need me to get the boys' breakfast. My aching muscles soon settled the panic. Does freedom include sleeping past sunrise? Maybe I could learn to enjoy this.

With little to do but feed and water the animals, even the soldiers joined our celebration. I'd never known a proper Shabbat before. In Susa, we set aside the day to focus on Yahweh, but Em still had to serve the queens, and King Artaxerxes expected Ab to work on the current construction project. Today, we sang several Psalms after each meal, and Ab shared parts of the Torah from memory before he led us in lengthy prayers.

Spring had turned a bit cold for mid-Nisan, and rain clouds threatened in the western sky. So, everyone gathered around a fire in the late afternoon. Bijan interrupted the small talk and laughter, "Hanani, your history lesson left me wondering what happened next."

Abba laughed, "You enjoyed the Torah's tales of Father Avraham and Ishmael's brother, Itzhak? Let me tell you more about his son. Our ancestor, Yaacov, lived up to his name. He tricked his brother Esau twice to secure his birthright and his blessing before running to Aram to escape his brother's rage. There he spent seven years working for his uncle to win the hand of his love, Rachel. But the day after his wedding, he discovered his father-in-law had tricked him. Instead of finding Rachel in his wedding bed, he found her older sister, Leah. Now, while you might think that's a scandal, we are personally grateful, because our ancestor, Yehudah, was Leah's fourth son." Abba laughed lightly.

Dohd Nehemiah finished, "But Yaacov did get his love after a week."

"Yes, Yaacov worked another seven years in exchange for Rachel. Leah and Yaacov's concubines gave him ten sons and a daughter, and Rachel gave him one more son." Abba continued, "He acquired great wealth in Aram. After twenty years, he returned to

Canaan. He lost Rachel to childbirth and gained his twelfth son on the way back home, but fortunately, his brother had forgiven him."

Dohd interjected, "Yaacov caused some friction among his own sons though."

"That part of the story always surprised me, brother. You'd have thought after all the problems he had with his twin he would have wanted his sons to get along."

Bijan asked, "What did Yaacov do to antagonize his sons?"

"Honestly, most of them had no problems," Dohd explained. "But they were all against Joseph. You tell it better, Hanani."

"Well, as I said, Rachel was Yaacov's true love. So, after she died, our patriarch favored her oldest son. The ultimate insult to Leah's sons was a richly embroidered and ornamented robe he gave to Joseph."

"Yes, I can see how that could cause some sibling rivalry," Bijan laughed.

As Abba shared the story of Joseph's dreams and his brothers' deception, I just enjoyed the sound of his voice. His deep melodic cadence gave me a feeling of peace. But as I let my thoughts turn inward, my peace turned to anger. Six years of hearing Abba's deep soothing tones had been stolen from me. I didn't know these ancient stories as well as Natalia and Avraham because my father had given himself to Jerusalem. I grieved silently. Not just for myself, but for Jok and Jon who hadn't heard any more than snippets of the tales since their birth. Jerusalem was a thief, and here we were—traveling to rescue it.

I meant to leave the circle quietly, but the rage inside caused me to knock over my cup.

"Adira, are you alright?"

"Fine, Abba." I may have spoken a bit too quickly to be believable, but if I didn't get out of there, tears would betray me.

From the sleeping room, I heard Em apologize for me. I sat against the wall and pulled my knees close while tears flowed.

Only a few rays of sunlight lingered on the horizon when Em's soft voice woke me. The water she used to wipe the dry tears from my face felt nice. I knew she'd warmed it just for me.

After a long hug, she broke the silence, "Are you hungry? We're going over to the great hall to eat." The meals that came with the room weren't nearly as good as Em's, but they filled my belly.

Nisan 19, 444 B.C.

The next morning, we headed out. My feet hadn't healed, but the caravanserai's hammam had allowed me to get rid of the grit and grime.

Two more nights sleeping under the wagon and then another caravanserai. Dohd said Kings Cyrus and Darius had ordered these luxury overnight houses to be built for the merchants who traveled much faster than our small party.

With each fire, Ab's stories continued. Though I heard Moses and Aaron's tale every Passover, each retelling left me amazed at the details I didn't remember.

This time I realized just how cruel the Egyptian slave masters had been. I only knew about slave life in Elam and Persia, where slavery was merely a social class, like the peasants or nobility. Slaves fell just a little lower than the servants on the social ladder. Each class had its place, but Cyrus had insisted all be treated with respect. We never experienced the cruelty our ancestors bore in Egypt.

And for some reason, I counted the plagues this time. I knew there'd been a few, but ten? And how had I missed Israel plundering the Egyptians before they headed out? I guess Moses stretching his arms out over the Red Sea causing it to split had overshadowed the other specifics.

Ab always went into great detail about the crossing. He made it sound so exciting, but this time the pillar of fire that stood between Egypt and Israel caught my attention.

"The Egyptian army chased the people of Israel. The Israelites could see the chariots thundering toward them, but the sea blocked their escape. Trapped, the people started crying out. Panic moved through the ranks, but then the pillar of cloud that had led them to this moment moved behind them. Moses stretched his hand over the water, and right before their eyes, the sea parted. A wall of water as high as this caravanserai stood to the left and the right, and Moses told them to walk through. Those who led the way hesitated for just a moment, but when they started across, amazement set in. The seabed, though it should have been silt and mud, was completely dry.'

"It took a full night to get the people across the Red Sea. Hundreds of thousands of men, women, and children hurried across as the pillar of cloud turned into a pillar of fire. It sent the Egyptian army into a state of confusion as they tried to break through with no success.'

"When the last Israelite crossed the sea, the pillar returned to the front of the nation of Israel, releasing the Egyptians to follow. Can you imagine how much fear must have filled those people watching the army come after them?"

Bijan sat with his mouth hanging open, "What? After all that, your God allowed the Egyptians to catch your people?"

Dohd laughed, "Oh, just wait until you hear what happened!"

Abba continued, "After the last member of the Egyptian army entered the seabed, God released the walls of water, and every chariot and soldier drowned in the rushing water."

I loved hearing Abba tell the stories. But they brought as many questions as answers. If Yahweh did all that, why didn't He still protect? Why did we have to leave Susa to rebuild Jerusalem? If a pillar of cloud and fire could hold back an Egyptian army, couldn't Yahweh raise those walls Himself? Ahura Mazda never let such devastation fall on Persia. Was this God my family trusted really as mighty as Abba believed?

Each night, Bijan and the others asked Ab to tell more stories. His passion and excitement drew everyone in. Even the soldiers had begun to listen. But every story left me wondering—if Yahweh could provide water and manna, why didn't he protect Jerusalem from Babylon one hundred seventy-five years ago?

Twelve

After a week, my blisters became callouses making the walking a bit easier. Ab and Dohd kept us on a schedule that allowed us to reach the caravanserais before sunset on the sixth day so we could spend Shabbat under cover. I couldn't tell whether our days of rest frustrated the cavalrymen or made them glad for a break.

Iyyar 3, 444 B.C.

Two Shabbats had passed, and I'd spent the morning moping, missing Natalia and Yasmine. But when we topped a ridge shortly after midday meal, my pity-party mood quickly changed. There in the distance spread a mighty city. The Great River flowed right through the center. Though Ab had told me Babylon wasn't much bigger than Susa, the huge ziggurat that occupied as much space as the palace and the heavy gated fortress made Babylon appear massive.

The cavalry commander held back to talk to Ab and Dohd, "We need to pick up our pace a bit if we want to reach the city before the sun goes down."

As the former capital grew larger before us, a second waterway surrounding the city appeared. The wall's fifty watchtowers loomed high over the city while soldiers kept watch atop the remarkable wall.

We made it to the city with daylight to spare, but by the time we settled into the guest serai, Shabbat had begun. I would have to wait until first day to explore.

Ab's Shabbat story included Israel's journey through the desert. He told us Joshua and Caleb tried their best to convince the people to enter the Promised Land, but fear stopped them. When Ab described the size of the Nephilim who lived there, I decided I may have voted against Joshua and Caleb, too.

Iyyar 5, 444 B.C.

After a restful Shabbat, Em squashed my plan to explore the grand city.

"Emi, I go to market alone in Susa all the time. I'll be fine."

"Babylon is not Susa." And with that, the discussion was over.

Fortunately, Ab invited me to go with him when he went out to look for work for the few days we'd be staying in Babylon. As we passed through the second gate into the inner city, I'm sure everyone could tell I'd never been here before.

Glazed brick murals, bigger than anything in Susa, decorated the massive gates, and the ziggurat could be seen from every corner. It dwarfed Artaxerxes' palace. Glistening off the yellow and blue tiling, the sun gave the temple the illusion of a gold coating. The closer we got to the focal point of the city, the more temples, idols, and altars, all dedicated to the pantheon of lesser gods, dotted the street corners.

So many people and so much to see; I had no idea how many turns we'd made. I quickly understood Em not allowing me to explore alone. Getting back to the guest serai without Ab would be impossible.

I assumed Ab knew where to look for work, he'd been here at least twelve times in the last five years. But it appeared as though we were about to walk out the other side of the city. As we approached the small bronze-covered gate, I heard a low gurgling. Rather than leaving the city, we'd reached the halfway point. This gate gave passage to the Great River where bronze gates lined the banks offering access up and down the huge waterway.

"The river runs high and fast today, Adira. This spring must have been unusually wet further north. Babylon rarely receives much rain. Praise Yahweh, He's kept our path dry."

On the way back to the guest serai, Ab stopped to talk to a few merchants, men he seemed to know well. He arranged to repair a few wagons and shops, and I focused on staying close to Abba as the crowds pressed in.

We spent three days in Babylon. Ab and Dohd worked, and the cavalry commander replenished our supplies. Em, the boys, and I made trips to the hammam and the river. We washed our travel-weary robes and took care of the animals. Dohd also sent a message back to Artaxerxes. With the speed of those couriers, the king would have word of our progress before we left Babylon.

Thirteen

We loaded the wagon before sunrise. Only Bijan and his family continued with us, but two more wagons heading north were more than willing to join a caravan that included the king's guard. The Euphrates, often wider than the walls in Babylon, led us on our journey. The Great River ran wild and high, and its cool refreshment became a welcome distraction as the days grew warmer.

Natalia would soon be packing Queen Esther for the annual summer move to Ecbatana. The heat in Susa during Tammuz and Av had been unbearable the last few years, so the entire court moved into the northern palace for three or four moons.

Iyyar 18, 444 B.C.

For ten days, we walked the western bank of the Euphrates, stopping twice for Shabbat. The well-worn road passed through many small towns and caravanserais, giving us shelter at night. Each day several merchant trains passed going both ways. When the traders stopped to chat, I stayed close to the wagon. I'd heard how young girls end up as slaves or commodities at one of the few remaining bridal markets.

Every evening when we stopped, the men unloaded one or two of the wagons and added a coat of pitch. Ab said we'd appreciate the protection when the wagons floated across the Euphrates.

By the time we reached Nehardea, the sun hung low in the western sky. Though close to town, we camped by the river. The stars in the clear night sky seemed brighter than usual. Their beauty called to me, so I laid my blankets outside the protection of the wagon. I would fall asleep stargazing.

The stars brought so much peace—until the voices in my head began battling. My friends in Susa told me Ahura Mazda created these stars, while Abba insisted Yahweh hung them there. The god of Persia offered so much more freedom than his Jewish equal. Ahura Mazda, while chief god, allowed the lesser deities to share in his glory. Yahweh, on the other hand, would not share His position or His honor.

And then came the tears. Again. Robbed of the wonder of the night by my own struggle, one I hated but couldn't seem to stop, I rolled over and attempted to get some sleep.

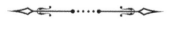

Iyyar 19, 444 B.C.

When the caravan started to stir before first light the next morning, my body cried for more time, but that wasn't going to happen. The horizon revealed a glimmer of light when the army commander started shouting orders.

"Rains upriver have made the Euphrates much higher than

normal for this time of year. I'll lead the way; my officers will stay on either side of your wagons."

Abba lifted Jok and me onto the camel's back while Em held Jon on top of the wagon. Abba would lead the camel while Uncle rode his horse. It was time to ford the Great River.

Before we started across, Dohd prayed but it didn't quench my fear. We'd forded other small tributaries since we started, but none came close to the size and speed of the Euphrates. Even the Tigris didn't compare. The commander's horse stepped into the rushing water on the lower side of a wagon. As we watched the first camel fight the current, my fear rose. The wagon and camel were pushed off course by the rapid flow, but they made progress.

One by one, the wagons entered the river. The men leading them walked as far as possible because once their feet left the riverbed, fighting the current became a daunting task.

Abba led my mount down the bank with Dohd riding next to us. When my feet hit the water, it sent a chill through my entire body, and I pulled my legs higher on the camel. I felt bad for Abba. Already chest-deep in the cold water, staying in line behind the wagon in front of us became difficult. As Abba began to swim, Dohd tried to stay close enough so he could reach the horse's halter. Dohd's horse kept him safe. A cupbearer doesn't have the strength of a carpenter and stonemason.

Behind us, the wagon the men had sealed two moons ago stayed afloat as planned, but pushed by the current, its weight put a huge strain on the camel.

Without warning, the current shifted the wagon in front of us. Abba stretched, attempting to grab the back before it tipped over, but much of its contents already floated back toward Babylon. Two women clung to the side of the wagon. Would they have the strength to fight the current if they let go?

Abba handed our camel's rope to Dohd and swam hard to reach the wagon, but on its side, the current powered it south even faster. Fear consumed me as I watched Ab and one of the other men try to save the loose wagon. How long could they fight the frigid water?

Even with the officers' help, they couldn't get the wagon upright. The water pushed Ab further and further downstream. I heard Dohd cry out in prayer as he pressed forward trying to stay focused on getting our wagon to the other side.

Helpless and afraid, I held Jok tighter as I clung to the camel's straps. I glanced back at Em. Tears streamed down her face.

When I turned back, Abba was gone. The wagon had been pushed close enough to the eastern shore that the camel could walk again, but I couldn't see Ab. Hiram, the owner of the wagon, now held it tight until someone could help him turn it upright. But Ab should have been there, too.

Focused intently on the tragedy unfolding before my eyes, when my camel stepped on the bank, the slight incline caught me off guard. As I righted myself and Jok, one of the cavalrymen grabbed the camel's rope. Dohd dismounted and made sure our wagon made it to dry ground before he and the two soldiers ran to help the distressed wagon.

I still couldn't see Abba. Had he been pulled downstream?

Dohd reached the overturned wagon at the same time as one of the soldiers. The three men easily righted it, and the camel pulled the crippled vessel onto the bank. Two hundred cubits further downstream a movement caught my eye. There, Abba rose from the raging water carrying one of the women. As soon as he reached the riverbank, Ab collapsed. Both the woman and her savior lay lifeless, and there was no sign of the second woman.

"Stand right here," Emi told Jon as she ran to kneel beside her husband. Ab attempted to get up but quickly fell. Stuck high on the camel's back, I held Jok tight as the final wagon emerged from the river.

The sun seemed to stand still as we waited to see Ab and the woman he'd carried show some sign of life. Every adult in the caravan had gathered around them, so I couldn't see a thing.

Finally, Dohd stood and reached down. The crowd parted just in time for me to see him pull Ab to a sitting position and hand him a blanket.

I breathed a sigh of relief as my brother broke the silence, "Is Abba okay, Adira?"

"I think so, Jok."

"Hallelujah"

I pulled my little brother closer.

Fourteen

Abba and the woman finally stood. It was Hiram's wife. My chest wrenched thinking about her sister. As the group headed back up the riverbank, several men stopped to assess Hiram's wagon, but my gaze was fixed on my parents. I didn't even notice Dohd leave their side until he lowered Jok from the camel.

We made camp and built fires so everyone could dry out. Ab rested while the other men made repairs. Dohd said only Yahweh could have kept Hiram's wagon from being completely destroyed in that current.

The loss of Hiram's sister-in-law weighed heavy on the entire party. The grieving couple sat with Ab while the rest busied themselves with repairs and preparations. As the day ended, Em fed the children, and the fasting adults gathered round the heartbroken couple. After making certain my brothers were sleeping, I slipped into the space between Em and Ab. Em gently squeezed my hand and Dohd offered a smile from across the fire. My family understood I'd chosen to cross into adulthood.

We sat in silence. No one would say a word until Hiram or his wife spoke. As the half-moon moved high in the sky, the others gradually left the warmth of the fire. Only our family and Bijan and his wife remained when Hiram finally spoke, "We can't stay here for the time of mourning."

Dohd let the darkness mourn with us for a bit before he replied, "I think we should travel to the next caravanserai for safety and remain there until after Shabbat so your family can mourn, even if it's not a proper Shiva. I'll talk to the commander about it tomorrow."

Abba and Bijan nodded in agreement.

Fifteen

Iyyar 20-25, 444 B.C.

The somber mood of the next day kept even Jok and Jon quiet, but the three days of mourning and Shabbat gave us some desperately needed rest. By the time we left the caravanserai, the moon had nearly disappeared. Natalia would be leaving for Ecbatana any day. I hoped Avraham would be sent with the king's horses so my siblings wouldn't be alone.

The days passed uneventfully as we continued along the road that followed the Great River. Ab shared more stories, and my feet grew more callused every day. Ab said we'd stay on this route until the next full moon; then we'd head south.

Each caravanserai hosted merchants heading to Babylon and Anatolia with wagons full of precious gems, purple cloth, and vast amounts of silver wares. The oversized sinister-looking men traveling with the merchant caravans obviously served a purpose.

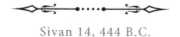

Sivan 14, 444 B.C.

The caravanserai at the Karbhak river marked our arrival at the King's Highway. Bijan's family continued on the Royal Road with the others. They headed toward Anatolia while our family headed south with only the soldiers as companions.

The moon shrunk into a sliver as we moved closer to our destination. Every night, Abba shared stories of Judah's history. Gideon's story amazed me. The youngest son from a small family and a tiny tribe led a meager army of three hundred to defeat the nation of Midian. How could that happen without the help of a god? Could Israel's Yahweh be greater than I'd once thought?

The King's Highway offered few caravanserais, but the nights under the stars grew more comfortable as the Tammuz sun moved to the northern sky. Someone watched over us. The rains only soaked us a few times in three moons.

When the route offered no caravanserai, we celebrated the Shabbats in the shadiest campsites we could find. Even after two moons, I couldn't get used to being still from sunset to sunset. Dohd found a tree just outside of each camp and spent most of the day on his knees. The closer we got to Jerusalem, the more time he spent in prayer.

Tammuz 4, 444 B. C.

We arrived in Damascus on the first day of the week. While an impressive city, it paled in comparison to Babylon. Artaxerxes had a palace here, but the court never visited.

We stayed in Damascus for several days, but much like Babylon, Em didn't allow me to explore. The night before our scheduled departure, Dohd and Ab came in looking frustrated.

"That didn't go well," Dohd told Em.

"Did you expect it to?" Ab replied. "Sanballat enjoys his large satrapy; though I doubt he's ever ventured to the southern part of his jurisdiction."

"I hoped the letters from the King would keep us safe. But Sanballat didn't seem pleased to see us either despite his kind words."

I could hear the hint of laughter in Ab's reply, "Yes, he couldn't have been more obvious with his questions. But honestly, Nehemiah, what did you expect? You were cupbearer, the most trusted non-noble in the kingdom. Sanballat knows you'll be the next governor of Jerusalem."

"That's ridiculous. Jerusalem is part of the Damascus satrapy."

"Brother, if you want to succeed in this building project, you're going to have to understand you are a threat to Tobiah and Sanballat. They know once those walls go up in Jerusalem, Artaxerxes might well decide the area needs its own ruler. That's all Sanballat sees. I know you serve Yahweh, but these guys only serve their own interests. You need to think like they do."

Dohd grew quiet. Only one word stuck in my mind—governor—Dohd Nehemiah could become governor.

Sixteen

Tammuz 7, 444 B.C.

Because we traveled with the king's guard, several wagons in Damascus were anxious to join our caravan. This time the list included a girl my age named Miriam. Her parents had died, and her grandparents were headed to Jerusalem to stay with her dohd.

Miriam and I quickly became good friends. Her presence made the journey so much better. Originally from Nineveh, her family had started toward Jerusalem just after her parents died. The four-moon job her Sabba Zabbai had taken in Damascus to give them more travel money had turned into four years.

I wanted to ask how her parents died but couldn't find a way to bring it up. Her cheerfulness hid the truth of her past, and I never heard her complain. I wondered if I could be so pleasant if I lost Ab and Em. My mood shifts each time I start missing Avraham and Natalia.

When not spending time with Miriam, I began to imagine what it might be like to be the governor's niece. Dohd had no children. Would he invite us to live in his home? The governor probably had a small palace. Jerusalem might not be so bad after all.

Each day, I grew more excited to see where the person

appointed by the king might live in my parent's homeland. The royal complex in Damascus had been small compared to the grandeur of Babylon and Susa, but the homes surrounding the palace had given me hope. This free life my parents talked about might be worth it.

The rough terrain of the Damascus road left riders bruised and walkers tired. Without a caravanserai to offer rest, we traveled fewer hours each day. The slow pace left time in the evening for storytelling around the fire, but now four men shared the tales they'd memorized from their youth. They told of battles where Israel's enemy defeated themselves before God's chosen arrived. One time the men of Israel heard Yahweh's army marching in the treetops.

Ab beamed with pride when the four began to recount the story of Esther. "My daughter, Natalia, is in the service of Queen Esther, and Chava cooked for the queens and concubines."

Miriam's grandfather had been a young man when Haman's edict to kill all Jews had reached his family. "Everyone began to panic," he said. "We knew unarmed servants and slaves were no match for the armored soldiers. When the second edict came through, no one understood how it happened, but everyone praised Yahweh."

Ab gladly filled in the details of the story Natalia had gotten directly from the queen.

"Did you know Haman's dislike of our people started when the Queen's cousin refused to bow to him? For years Haman stewed over Mordecai, but the man had convictions. He would only bow to Yahweh."

Ab and Em delighted telling the story Em and Natalia had heard directly from Queen Esther.

Ab finished the story, "Last year we celebrated a fast for Queen

Esther to commemorate the day the lot was cast in Israel's favor."

"I remember when the second order came to Nineveh," Zabbai shared. "Everyone was so relieved. Not much blood was shed in the north. The Persians didn't take the chance."

"What is Queen Esther like?" Miriam's savta asked.

Em chimed in again, "She is the kindest of any nobility I've ever met. No more humble a person can be found in the entire harem." Em paused. "But now these children need to go to bed."

We didn't miss the fire as we crawled onto our mats under the wagon. The warmer nights were a welcome gift.

Each evening after dinner, Ab and Dohd shared stories of Susa and Babylon for our new Jewish friends. Both loved telling everyone their great-grandfather had been a friend of Shadrach, Meshach, and Abednego as well as Daniel. Stories of those early exiles had traveled east over the years, but everyone enjoyed Dohd's third-hand account of the three men surviving the fiery furnace and Yahweh shutting the mouths of lions.

Seventeen

Summer nights in Galilee were so much more comfortable than those in Elam. Though we usually went with the court to Ecbatana, I remember spending a few summers fighting the unrelenting heat in Susa.

As we journeyed, we learned more about the families traveling with us. Joiada and his wife had three children. They'd been living in Damascus for a long time, but like Dohd, they felt a stir to return to Jerusalem.

Zabbai and his wife, Leah, had planned to come to Jerusalem for years. His son, Baruch, had gone before Miriam was born. Miriam's parents had finally raised the funds to make the trip, but before they could leave, Nineveh had been hit by raiders, killing the couple, and destroying their home. Leah had found six-year-old Miriam hiding in a grain barrel.

Hakkoz and his wife, Renana, were the oldest. Their grandson, Meremoth lived in Jerusalem. He seemed more pleased than any of the rest to be returning. His grandfather had been a young boy in Jerusalem and had told him magnificent stories of Jerusalem's previous glory. Hakkoz had heard first-hand stories of the exiles being carried off to Babylon. Ab and Dohd listened intently when the old man shared the tales his grandfather had told him of Jerusalem's greatness before the Babylonian invasion.

Though they'd been with us the entire trip, the soldiers never shared our fire. We'd been with them for almost four moons, and I knew none of their names. Thank the gods, their presence kept the thieves at bay. At least once a week, the soldiers told Ab they'd noticed the faint silhouette of a suspicious traveler. They seemed to move on once they spotted the trained sentries. Ab said Yahweh blessed us by sending the cavalry with us.

Eighteen

"We're almost home, Adira," Ab looked pleased as we stopped to give the horses and camels a break after a long climb. "Just beyond these hills lies the country of Judah."

Gentle mounds rising from the wilderness took the road in almost as many turns as the Euphrates. The camels slowed as the road wound up the hill.

Two Shabbats had passed since we'd seen any sign of a city. But as the third approached, the soldiers announced we'd be in Et Tell before sunset. If not for the Summer sun, we'd never have made it to the city gates before they closed. The small village had no guest serais, but a kind fisherman offered grass beds for the four women, the young children, Miriam, and me. Ab, Dohd, and the rest of the men slept in the courtyard under the wagons.

Tammuz 17, 444 B.C.

"Adira." Ab's soft voice forced one eye open. Why do my parents insist on waking before the sun?

"Adira." A second whisper. I'd really grown accustomed to sleeping past sunrise on Shabbat, but Ab seemed insistent.

"Take a walk with me, wee one."

"But Abba, we traveled so long yesterday."

"I'm sure your brother and sister in Susa wish they had it so rough." His gentle reminder guilted me out of my grassy bed.

As my father and I walked toward the southern gate, the smell of the city hit me. I must have been too tired to notice last night. Or perhaps the wind had been blowing the other way. When the breeze picked up, it carried a much more pleasant smell. On the other side of the gate, the wind blew strong, accenting the fish smell as well as this other scent I couldn't quite make out.

Only Ab's clay lamp lit our way in the early moonless hours. The sun hadn't even attempted to light the eastern sky.

"Let's sit here for a bit." Ab moved his light to reveal a grassy spot on the sloping terrain. We sat quietly as the earth began to wake. How did the toads and birds know the sun was about to make its daily debut? These creatures had awakened me every morning in Susa. Nature's early risers told humans to prepare for daybreak.

But one sound in the darkness left me curious. I couldn't identify the soft, soothing noise. Repetitive and rhythmic, yet different every time, this early morning sound left me clueless. Just as I considered breaking the silence to ask Ab about it, the almost-full moon of Tammuz broke over the hills, its haunting light revealing the source of my mystery.

There before me, a small harbor opened into the greatest body of water I'd ever seen. Wider than any point on the Great River, the shimmering sea seemed to go on forever. For just a moment, the birds and toads hushed their harmonies, as if they too were in awe of the beauty. Only the sounds of the lapping sea remained. Soon the hills gave way to the fullness of the sun, and my winged friends broke the silence.

"Ab, this is beautiful," I whispered so as not to spoil the majesty.

"I thought you might appreciate a quiet Shabbat morning. Tomorrow this lake will be covered with those boats that line the shore, but we've finally reached a town that will observe our sacred day."

Ab let the silence settle in once more before he continued. "We're almost home, Adira. In this town, you'll find that even those who are not Jews celebrate our day of rest, a habit they developed just after the exile when the Assyrian kings tried to find ways to appease Yahweh." Joy filled Ab's voice. "Today you will celebrate your first true Shabbat."

We sat in silence enjoying the grandeur. Soon Dohd, Em, and the boys joined us. No one said a word. The enormous lake cradled in the rolling hills mesmerized even my rowdy brothers.

As I sensed our morning worship drawing to a close, Dohd Nehemiah began to pray. "Yahweh, Creator of the sun and the moon, You who laid before us this magnificent scene, we praise You. We thank You for giving us the king's favor and providing safe passage. You are the great and mighty Creator, and we stand in awe of your handiwork. Hallelujah and Amen."

The artistry drew us in until Jok and Jon began to get restless. We rose and slowly made the short walk back into the town. Only the twins' laughter and running interrupted creation's song. Ab's face held a peace I'd never seen before. Is this why he kept returning to Jerusalem?

Back in the village, our hosts invited us to share their meal.

Afterward, Em and I gathered our hammam basket and walked toward the sun. We found a spot on the river that offered privacy and washed away weeks of dirt. The cool water felt so refreshing, and a clean robe would be welcome. Before we scrubbed ourselves, we washed out the family's soiled clothes.

"This will be the last Shabbat we'll do laundry, Adira. In Jerusalem, we'll be able to go to the temple and truly make it a holy day."

We finished the washing and laid the clothing on rocks to dry, then Em and I laid in the warm Tammuz sun.

"Em, did you want to come to Jerusalem?"

"Adira, we go where your father tells us to go."

"I know, Em, but did you want to? I mean, you were born in Susa. Sabba and Savta are buried there. You had good friends in the queen's quarters." I paused for just a minute. I didn't want to hurt her. "Em, we had a good life in Susa."

"Yahweh certainly blessed us, didn't He?" Her short response didn't answer my question. But just as I considered asking again, she continued, "Yes, even with all these blessings, I wanted to come. When I was your age, your sabba and savta talked often about someday returning to Jerusalem. Unfortunately, they never had the means to travel so far. This is a costly trip.'

"Yahweh gave the land of Judah, and even this land we lie on now, to His people. Then He chose Jerusalem as the place for His name to dwell. He chose our ancestor Yaacov over Esau. We don't know the reason; except He is the mighty God and can do as He pleases. Our people failed Yahweh, Adira. Even though He blessed them time and time again, they failed Him. That's how we ended up in

Susa.'

"But now God has provided a way for us to return. When your father realized the king would pay all the expenses for his and Dohd's travel, he asked permission to bring us along. We are definitely blessed. If not for Nehemiah petitioning the king for this trip, we may have been in Susa forever."

As I soaked in the sun, I allowed Em's words to soak in, too. I'd never considered the cost of travel keeping my grandparents in Elam. I thought they stayed because that was their home.

As the sun slowly rose to its highest point in the sky, Em began gathering the clothes. We'd finish our day of rest listening to Abba share the ancient stories, and tomorrow we'd leave early. Ab said we'd be in Jerusalem before next Shabbat.

Nineteen

Traveling around the sea was beautiful. The Tammuz heat had withered the greenery along our path until now; however, here everything grew lush and full. Ab made this a short day so we could stay in Magdala. He said the small serai would be one of the last we'd see. Since it offered only enough room for the four families, the cavalry attachment camped outside of town.

The smell of the sea and the green vegetation slowly faded as we continued south. For two nights we slept under the wagons, but on the third day, we entered Shechem, the largest city we'd encountered since Damascus. As soon as the town came into view, Abba began telling stories.

"Adira, did you know our people buried Joseph's bones here?"

"I thought Joseph died many years before Moses brought our people out of Egypt?"

"You've been paying attention, wee one."

I must have twisted my face at him without even knowing it, because he gave me an ornery smile and winked at Em, "Oh yes, you passed your thirteenth year just before we reached the sea, didn't you?"

I had! Each Tammuz I mark another year passing, but in the

traveling, I'd forgotten.

As we reached the city gate, Father continued, "When the people of Israel left Egypt, they brought Joseph's bones with them and buried them right here." His voice grew somber. "Our fathers, Yaacov and Avraham walked on this ground, Adira. Yaacov and his sons dug a well that lies not far from here."

All Abba's stories began to come alive. In Susa, they'd seemed like fables, but now we stood on the ground where our ancestors had walked. They had touched these same stones I touched as they built wells and walls. I could almost see the people of old walking through the plaza to buy and sell and visit friends.

The evening meal gave Abba an opportunity to share even more of Shechem's rich history. He, Dohd, and the man who owned the serai kept everyone at the table spellbound as they took turns with their favorite parts of Israel's story. Some I'd heard since I was young, like the story of Israel's sons avenging Dinah and grazing their sheep nearby. But Joshua's covenant and the trouble the city had seen with the Canaanite kings were new. Ab captured Jok and Jon's attention with the stories. I smiled to think how bored Natalia would be.

A short travel day put us in Lebonah. Dohd immediately went to his knees. When Em and I served the evening meal, he passed. "Even if I wasn't fasting, I don't think I could eat tonight, Chava. I can't believe I'll get to see the Holy City tomorrow."

We rose early on preparation day. According to Ab, today would be long but we should reach our destination before Shabbat began. Dohd offered a blessing before we started our journey. His voice gave way to the excitement we knew he felt having Jerusalem within his grasp.

This final trek required pushing hard. You could see everyone's exhaustion when we stopped for a midday meal at Bethel. But even in our haste, Abba took a moment to point out that Father Avraham had pitched his tent here when he came to the land Yahweh had led him to.

"Yaakov slept here, Jok." The boys were mesmerized by the tales. "No serai to provide shelter. Only the stars to keep him company. He named this place Bethel because here he saw a vision of angels going up and down stairs to heaven. He said it must be the House of God."

"Why did Yaacov travel alone, Abba?"

"Well, Jon, our great ancestor was not always the most noble of men. He had just deceived his father and stolen Esau's blessing, plus he'd tricked him out of his birthright years before. So, to keep Esau from killing him, his mother, Rebekah, sent him to Aram to live with her brother and find a wife."

"Did he find one, Abba?"

"I really have to catch you boys up on Israel's history, don't I? He ended up with two wives, Jon."

The boys' eyes widened. "Two?"

"Was he a king?"

Abba laughed, "Not exactly, Jok." And he recounted the story of

Yaacov, Rachel, and Leah. "Yaacov had an interesting story, boys, but his journey to becoming a great nation began right here in Bethel."

Dohd interrupted, "Brother, if we want to get to Jerusalem before the sun sets, we need to get moving."

"Dohd Nehemiah is right, boys. It's time to head for home."

Part Three
Building the Wall

They were all trying to frighten us, thinking,
"Their hands will get too weak for the work, and it will not be completed."
But I prayed, "Now strengthen my hands."
Nehemiah 6:9

For everything that is really great and inspiring
is created by the individual
who can labour in freedom.
Albert Einstein

Twenty

Tammuz 23, 444 B.C.

The sun hung low in the western sky by the time Jerusalem came into view.

"The city will be on full alert soon, sir," the commander addressed Dohd. "Two of us will ride ahead to ensure safe passage."

"Ab, you said we had to get here before they closed the gates, but I don't see . . ."

"I know, Adira." Ab looked toward Jerusalem with joy. "Our Holy City has no proper gates or walls right now. Regardless, men stand guard to protect her. We don't want to surprise them after dark."

The sight in the distance left me speechless. Piles of rubble lay in a haphazard outline where walls must have once stood. The visible structures could easily be counted. Only one building, what I assumed to be the temple, stood tall on the horizon.

Dohd would be governor of this? I doubted we would find any kind of ruler's mansion behind the cubits of debris. Suddenly, the ramifications of what I saw hit me, "Ab, where will we live?"

"Adira, I thought I told you only a few houses remain standing."

He had. I remembered now. The thought of Dohd becoming governor had stirred images of grandeur, and I'd fixated on them since

Damascus. Tears stung. We'd left the palace complex of Susa to come here? Why would Em agree to this? At least Natalia still lived in the luxury of the queens. A bit of envy settled in as a little voice from within reminded me, *but Natalia is a slave.* Perhaps a slave, but luxury just the same.

By the time we reached the scorched break in the rubble, only our torches provided any light. Despite the late hour, several men from the city greeted us.

Dohd Nehemiah dismounted, "Good evening, gentlemen. I didn't expect such a grand welcome."

"The courier from Damascus delivered your message more than a week ago. It said King Artaxerxes sent you. We wanted to make sure the King's liaison had a proper welcome."

The city officials continued, "We appreciate you letting us know you were coming. We've been working since the courier arrived to prepare something suitable, but so few houses still stand."

"Any shelter will do. We left Shechem before sunrise, so we'll be thankful for any place to rest these weary feet."

Dohd was right. I would not be complaining about the accommodations tonight. We'd only traveled this hard one or two days during the last four moons. My feet ached, and my eyes did not want to stay open.

They led us to a place with walls and a roof we'd share with Miriam and her grandparents. It could hardly be called a house. A similar structure attached to the back would provide shelter for the other two families. The soldiers joined the small detachment permanently assigned to the city. But could you honestly call it a city? A place with no walls or gates and a few dozen run-down houses?

Twenty-One

Everyone welcomed the mandatory day of rest. Even Ab napped after our time of worship.

The following day, Ab and Dohd left early. After we helped Em and Leah unload the wagon and put away our few belongings, Miriam and I took Jok and Jon exploring. I admit, the city appeared less dismal in the light of day. There were more houses than I'd originally seen, and the temple looked even more impressive with the sun gleaming off the polished stone. Ab told us he'd spent the bulk of the last six years working on it.

The Jerusalem market left me unimpressed. Just a few permanent vendors selling nothing but necessities. Only one traveling merchant had trinkets, jewelry, and idols. Not that I had anything to barter with, but Miriam and I enjoyed browsing.

We were most entertained on our adventure with Jok and Jon's new friends. The young boys used cracked pots they'd rescued from the dung gate for target practice. Miriam and I watched from a distance. I enjoyed seeing the twins with boys their own age.

"Do you think Em will let us bring our slingshots here tomorrow, Addy?" one of the boys asked on the way back.

"I don't know, Jon. Em may want to resume your lessons now that we've settled again."

Both of my parents had been taught to read and write, a luxury for a slave. And they'd made sure each of their five children had the skills, too. We often heard how our ancestors had been taught in secret before Cyrus took the throne. Sabba Hacaliah's parents had been true slaves in the household of Babylon's kings. The stories of their trials made me appreciate my life.

"Do you think your mother would teach me, too?" Miriam asked.

"I'm certain she will, and I'd love to help." I'd never considered Miriam might not be able to read or write, another reminder of how blessed I am.

"Adira. Miriam. You're just in time. We'll need more water for the afternoon meal. Did you find the pools in your exploration?"

Ab finished for Em without bothering to hear an answer, "Just keep walking south, girls. You can't miss them."

After cooking for the entire harem and all their maids and slaves in Susa, Em didn't need much help preparing meals for the eight living in our shelter. I wouldn't be surprised to find the other two families sharing our pot when we returned.

Twenty-Two

By our third day in this new city, we had a routine. After the morning meal, Em spent hours writing in the dirt as Jok, Jon, and Miriam learned to read. Miriam's grandmother beamed as my friend pronounced the words the characters formed. Outside, Ab and Dohd reinforced the shelter trying to make it more of a home.

"Can you get us more water for the mortar, wee one?" Ab's wink told me he knew my eye roll was more for show than protest. How could he see so deep into my heart?

The cool jar felt good on my shoulder as I walked back to the work site. "Who do we trust enough to inspect the wall with us, Hanani?" I'm sure Dohd didn't mean for me to hear. "Word will get back to Sanballat soon enough, I don't need to invite spies."

"I believe we can trust Zabbai's son, Baruch, and Hakkoz's grandson, Meremoth. They'll be here soon. They volunteered to exchange labor. Both will help us here, and when we're finished, we'll help them add rooms for Hakkoz and Renana, and Zabbai, Leah, and Miriam."

"Miriam's moving out?" I'd just begun to enjoy having a sister again.

"Hello, Adira!" Dohd sounded surprised. "I didn't hear you return."

"Wee one, you knew she'd go live with her uncle after we all got settled in. Don't worry, Baruch may live in the southern part of the city, but it's inside the eastern wall."

Dohd winked and whispered, "Or where the wall will be."

"Here, add that water to this sand. Just a little. Stir as you go, we need a nice thick mixture. The work will keep you from worry." Abba believed hard work and prayer solved every problem.

But he was right. Concentrating on getting the mortar to a good consistency put Miriam's impending move in perspective. Of course, she'd go live with family, and I'd still see her every day. I hated being so selfish. Yet, what I knew in my head didn't change what I felt in my heart, and with every stir of the mortar, my emotions stirred within me. I was losing my best friend. The thought felt like one more burden on top of a mountain of hurt. I'd lived the past six years without Ab, and then just after we were reunited, my friends and siblings were stolen from me. My family had constantly talked about freedom, but this didn't feel like freedom. I missed my friends. I missed Natalia. I missed my comfortable life.

"Tonight then." Dohd's voice called me out of my own thoughts. "You, me, Joiada, Meremoth, Zabbai, and Baruch." What were Dohd and Ab getting into now?

Twenty-Three

The dark Tammuz sky made it difficult to see as Dohd mounted his horse. Only Em, Leah, and Meremoth's grandparents stood watch, or so they thought. Miriam and I hid in the shadows as Ab led the way on foot. The group headed quietly toward the southern part of the city.

"Where are they going at this time of night?" Miriam whispered the question that rattled in my head. With my finger to my lips, I pointed toward the grownups. I'm not sure why we felt the need to sneak, but we kept vigil there, out of sight, worrying about my ab, Miriam's sabba and our dohds.

Our vigil ended up less than vigilant because when the voices woke me, I found myself on my mat with no idea how I got there. Miriam and the boys remained lifeless. Only the glow of the dying fire offered any light.

"It's worse than I imagined, Hanani."

"I tried to tell you, brother."

"Are there any sections worth saving?" Hakkoz's voice shook.

"None. You saw for yourself the northern walls when we arrived. And the Valley Gate—though gate is a generous description."

"It's more like a pile of rubble." I loved Abba's laugh.

"I've never seen such intentional and needless destruction."

Hakkoz provided the answer. "From what my sabba said, those Babylonians were terrified of Yahweh. They hoped leveling the dwelling place of His Name would stop Him forever. They underestimated the power of the God of Israel."

With no real reason to rise before the sun, I rolled over, thinking about Hakkoz's statement as I drifted off. When have I seen the power of the God of Israel?

Twenty-Four

The sun had barely reached the second-hour mark when Dohd set out to invite every family head and important official to meet with him in the center of the city. Ab, Meremoth, and Baruch finished the wall that would create a sleeping room for Ab and Em. The room they'd created first for Zabbai and Leah would be for me and the boys after they built the extra space on Baruch's home. Ab said work at Meremoth's should be finished within the week.

Meremoth had come to Jerusalem with Ezra thirteen years ago. All six of his children had been born in Jerusalem. Hakkoz had told us his story one night as we'd sat around the fire.

Hakkoz's grandson had studied for the priesthood since his thirteenth year. Dedicated to becoming a true servant of God, Meremoth immediately answered the call when Ezra asked priests and Levites to join him in rebuilding the temple in Jerusalem. He married Abigail just before they left.

"I would have loved to have traveled with Ezra back then," Hakkoz had shared. "But I was one of only a few priests training the next generation. So, when Meremoth asked Uriah's blessing to join Ezra in the Holy City, none of us questioned it for a second." Tears had formed in the old priest's eyes, "We never imagined Uriah would be gone just ten years later."

Em, Leah, Miriam, and I stood in the back of the crowd as Dohd and Ab addressed them.

"Men of Jerusalem!" When Dohd raised his voice, the crowd grew quiet. "My brother reported to me the state of things here in our Holy City upon his return to Susa last fall. I immediately felt God speaking to my heart. So, my brother and I fasted and prayed. God's gracious hand was upon me, and I have a letter from King Artaxerxes blessing our work. Gentlemen, last night, my brother and I, along with several others, inspected the southern part of the wall. I believe God wants us to work together to rebuild."

The crowd began to hum with excitement. Only three men standing in the back with us looked less than excited. They left before plans could be made. Meremoth shouted first, "Let's rebuild." Soon scattered voices rose from the crowd.

"I agree."

"My family will help."

"When do we start?"

"It's time!"

Voices began to get lost in the commotion, and Ab gave Dohd a huge embrace. When the crowd quieted, Dohd continued, "Many of you worked on the temple with my brother, Hanani. You already know the opposition we'll face, so I think we should start immediately before our adversaries get word. Hanani will be on horseback going from site to site to answer building questions. Each family will take the spot closest to their home.'

"We'll need some who will gather stones and others who can mix mortar. Those with the most experience will lay the stones. Work will begin tomorrow at sunup."

Twenty-Five

On the first day of construction, Abba let me ride with him while Jok, Jon, and Miriam had their lessons. Jerusalem looked different sitting high with Ab's arms wrapped around me.

We began near the temple. Abba introduced me to Eliashib, the high priest. He oversaw the priests as they worked on the section of the wall closest to the sheep gate. "Do you see this pool, Adira? Each lamb that enters through this gate will be washed here before the sacrifice."

Ab seemed surprised to see the group working on the next section, "Old friends, what brings you all the way from Jericho?"

"Zakkur left Jerusalem to tell us the news as soon as your brother finished speaking yesterday."

"I knew they would want to help," Zakkur shouted as he carried stones to their section.

"We left Jericho before sunup. Couldn't miss this chance to help our friends."

We found Meremoth hard at work just past the next split in the rubble. I recognized this path. "This road leads to Damascus, right, Ab?"

"Yes. Old maps call it The Fish Gate. The merchants selling fish from Tyre and Galilee once entered through here."

Ab answered Meremoth's questions, and we continued along the pile of rubble. I could just begin to see where the next gate would stand when Ab dismounted and handed me the reigns.

"Problems, friends?"

"No, I think we have everything under control?"

"How many men do you have carrying stones? Looks like you got a late start."

"This is all of us. We've been discussing who will do what. Came in from Tekoa early this morning thanks to Zadok. Our good friend rode out to see us yesterday afternoon. We couldn't wait to help."

"Alright, then. If you need anything, ask for Hanani. I've been building since my youth, ready to assist anyone who needs it." Abba walked toward me, grabbed the horse's halter, and turned to go back the way we'd come. But he paused before he mounted.

"Zadok, good to see you."

"Hanani!" The man greeted Ab with a bear hug. "I was surprised to hear you returned so soon. Didn't you say you were going to stay with your family for a while?"

"I brought them back with me!" Ab turned to me, "Zadok bar Baana, meet my daughter, Adira."

"Pleased to meet you, young lady."

"And you, sir."

"Zadok, what do you know about these guys from Tekoa?"

"Not much. When I rode down there yesterday to recruit some help, I talked to the men who had worked on the temple. But this morning, these guys came looking for me. They haven't even picked up a stone."

"And they don't take hints either."

"I'll try pressing them again, but I don't know how much good I can do. I'll probably end up doing this section too."

"Well, whatever you can do to get the job done, we appreciate it."

Zadok headed over to the stalled work crew as Ab mounted and we rode away.

I saw our new friend, Joiada, working on what Ab said was the Old Gate, and once again he dismounted.

"Melatiah!" Ab found someone else he knew. "How did you hear of our plans?"

"I just happened to be in Jerusalem finishing a project when your brother spoke. I knew I had to be a part of the rebuild."

"Well, it's good to see you, my friend."

The scene repeated itself many times as we rode south out of the shadow of the temple.

"Abba, how do you know so many?"

"All these men helped on the temple. I worked with them every time I visited Jerusalem. I've been here many times since you were born, wee one."

Everyone worked. I'd never seen anything like it. Ab introduced me to two of the city's district rulers as they labored over their sections. Near The Valley Gate, one of those rulers had enlisted his daughters to help.

As we continued our journey south, the space between the walls narrowed. In between the rows of scattered houses, we could see the men working on the eastern wall. Ab stopped once or twice to answer questions.

"This gate leads to the dung piles," Ab explained when we reached the southernmost part of the construction project. "And that gate on the eastern wall just ahead will take you to the Pool of Siloam. At one time the kings had lush gardens here. And it still boasts the coolest water in Jerusalem flowing up from the Gihon Spring."

When we reached the Fountain Gate, Abba introduced me to two more of the district rulers. Men of their station would never be doing this kind of work in Susa.

"This is where our great King David is buried, Adira. He originally built this Holy City. And right about here is where the quarters of his mighty men once stood."

"Mighty men?"

"Yes, David's army included thirty soldiers that he called his mighty men, the best soldiers in all Israel." Ab paused his story. "Baruch! Zabbai! How are you doing?"

"Everything's going smooth here," Baruch replied. "I don't think my father has seen this much work in a long time. He got soft living in Damascus."

"I can still keep up just fine, son." Zabbai laughed.

Just ahead I saw another familiar face. Ab looked puzzled. "Meremoth, didn't we see you up near The Fish Gate?"

"Yes," Meremoth laughed, "but none of the folks working here had experience, so I'm going back and forth to keep both sections going. Did you see Sabba this morning before you rode out, Hanani? How are he and Savtha?"

"They were well at morning meal. I'm sure Chava is taking good care of them."

The sun rose high as we rode toward the next space in the

rubble that represented a gate. "This is where you sent Miriam and me to get water."

"The Water Gate. Not a very original name, but it opens to the headwaters of the Gihon Spring." Ab filled our skins before we finished our journey.

The Temple came into view again as we passed a few of the finished homes. Even the guards and merchants wielded chisels and mortar tools.

"This gate once led to the King's stables, Adira, and the Temple Solomon built sat right here on the high part of the city."

We finished the circuit just in time to see all the women begin to bring midday meal out to their husbands and sons. Ab decided we better get to the house before Em came looking for us.

Twenty-Six

Work on the wall paused for Shabbat. Ab bought a prize lamb from one of the local herders, and we all walked north to the Temple. Em and I stayed in the courtyard while Ab, Dohd, and the boys took the lamb to the priest. It felt so strange. Not that I'd never seen a sacrifice before. I'd witnessed plenty to Ahura Mazda in Susa, but never before had I seen Abba bring a sacrifice.

Em knelt, so I followed her lead. Only the lambs' bleating and a faint murmur of a dozen women's prayers broke the eerie silence. I wished I could pray. Ab's deep voice speaking the blessings gave me so much comfort, and no one prayed like Dohd. Somehow his cries to Yahweh sounded like they rose straight from his soul. His anguish often brought tears to my eyes, and when he turned to thanksgiving, I could feel my heart fill with praise.

But those were not my prayers.

I hadn't thought much about Susa's god since we arrived in Jerusalem; however, Yahweh, who seemed so real to my parents didn't seem much different than the statues of Persia to me. Yet each time I flirted with giving my loyalty to Ahura Mazda, I struggled with the fact all those gods looked like carved dolls.

Back at our shelter, a courier from Damascus waited. The young man seemed sympathetic to Dohd's mission. "Two of my comrades, Sanballat's personal couriers, arrived in Damascus early yesterday. They told Sanballat you made a lengthy speech about rebuilding and the men of the city rallied." The young courier continued, "As soon as he heard the news, Sanballat's face turned red, and he started yelling." *Was that a smirk on the young man's face?* "I believe he called you 'feeble Jews.' Tobiah stood with him, and they incited the entire army against you. When I heard him talk of sending a message, I immediately volunteered to deliver it."

"Thank you, son. But what makes you so sympathetic to our cause?" Dohd asked the question I was thinking.

"Sir, as with most born in Damascus, my father is an Ammonite, which works to my advantage because Sanballat trusts me. However, few in the city know my mother was born here in Jerusalem. Her great-grandparents were among the extremely poor left here when the Babylonians destroyed the city. She loved to tell me about Jerusalem and Yahweh. I feel blessed to find a way to honor her memory."

Dohd embraced the young man, "Yahweh found another way to encourage us." He wiped the tears from his eyes, "Well, let's see what old Sanballat has to say.

"From: Sanballat, governor of the Trans-Euphrates," Dohd began to read. "To: Nehemiah. What do you think you are doing?" Dohd looked up and smiled at Ab. "Looks like we got his attention, brother.'

"When you presented your letters from the king requesting safe passage, I had no idea you would be so rebellious as to try to rebuild the walls of Jerusalem." Dohd continued, "You've taken on a project only the king's professional builders can accomplish. Even Tobiah knows a fox climbing on a wall built by your people will make it crumble. Stop your foolishness."

As soon as Dohd finished, he began to pray, "Hear us, O God. Hear the words of the people who despise us. Oh Yahweh, turn every insult back on them. Send them into captivity, punish them for their insults."

The courier finally broke the reverent silence, "Do you have a message you'd like me to take back to the governor?"

Dohd pulled out a piece of parchment and spoke out loud as he penned his reply, "From: Nehemiah, cupbearer to King Artaxerxes and servant of Yahweh. To: Sanballat.'

"Yahweh in heaven will give us success. We will rebuild the wall. As for you, you have no share or right to this holy city, Jerusalem."

I didn't know much about how to deal with government officials, but I had a feeling Dohd's note wouldn't go over well.

Twenty-Seven

Av 27, 444 B.C.

Work continued for almost a moon. It started looking like a real wall. Everyone in the city did something. Jok and Jon helped gather supplies every day after their lessons, and Miriam and I carried water from the spring to the workers all around the wall. Our backs and legs got used to the demanding work, but that first week was brutal.

Miriam and I had just delivered water to Dohd when the young courier stopped in again. Dohd listened to the young man then called together some of the city officials. "Tell them everything you told me."

"Couriers and traders passing through here have brought word to the governor that you've continued work on the wall. To be honest, it looks even more impressive than we've heard." I liked this guy's smile.

Malkijah ben Rekab spoke up, "Sanballat has always been a thorn in our side. We can handle him."

"Yes, but he's stirred up Tobiah, the Arabs, the Ammonites, and even the city of Ashdod. I overheard them plotting an attack on Jerusalem. Fortunately, a message needed to be delivered to Bethlehem, so I volunteered."

Dohd explained, "The boy offered to stay and help with the wall when he delivered Sanballat's last message, but Hanani and I encouraged him to return to Damascus. We can use some eyes and ears in Sanballat's inner room."

"I really must go. If I'm not back before the gates close, they'll be suspicious."

Dohd detained the young man. "Stay while we lift this to Yahweh. I'd like to pray for your safe travel, too. Eliashib, will you begin our prayer?"

"Brothers and sisters, let us kneel before our creator." All the district rulers, guards, and priests bowed as the high priest began his prayer. Miriam and I knelt at the back of the crowd. Sometimes the invisibility of girls worked to our advantage.

"Yahweh, Adonai, we praise you for the courage of this young man to be your messenger, and we ask your protective hand be upon him as he rides with the wind."

Shallum ben Hallohesh picked up the prayer, "Creator, Rock of Israel, we praise you for the strength you've given us to complete this work on your Holy City."

"Yahweh Nissi," Ab would be disappointed if he saw me looking around, but I couldn't identify the voice, and curiosity got the best of me. It was Hashabiah who prayed, "You are our protector and our strength."

Around the circle each man took up the prayer, "You are our hope."

"El Shaddai, Mighty Warrior, fight our battle."

"Yahweh Sabaoth, Lord of Hosts, bring your heavenly army against our enemies."

"Hear our prayer, El Roi."

When every priest, official, and guard had poured out their heart to Yahweh, the circle grew silent for a moment before Dohd finished, "El Elyon, I praise you for these leaders and add my petition to theirs. I believe you put this on my heart moons ago in Susa, so I trust You to carry it to completion so Your Name may be glorified in all the world, Amen."

A great "Amen" came from all around the circle as everyone rose. Ab gave the courier a hearty slap on the back and sent him on his way.

"Shemiah," Dohd spoke to the guard from the East Gate as Miriam and I passed skins of water. "How many guards can we post at each gate?"

"I have enough armed men to put three sentries at each of the northern and western gates and one more at each of the four southern gates. I'll talk to the smith about taking a couple days off the wall to forge more weapons."

"Excellent. Ok men, let's get back to work."

At evening meal Ab spoke to me and Miriam, "Girls, I don't want you outside the gates, even to get water, unless one of the guards goes with you. Do you understand?"

"Is it that serious, Hanani?"

"The threat is real, Chava. The number of our enemies has grown. This wall strikes fear. Jerusalem has always been a formidable city. That's why the Babylonians destroyed the wall a hundred and fifty years ago. And that same fear now drives Sanballat and Tobiah."

Twenty-Eight

The next day, Miriam and I heard the murmurs as we carried water to the workers. The additional guards caused some to worry, and those working on top of the wall near the Fish Gate had seen dust rising on the horizon.

Near the Old Gate, we heard Dohd talking to the men of Gibeon. I felt pretty impressed with myself that I remembered who these men were.

"Nehemiah, my crew is growing weary, and the rubble gets in the way. We need some of the young men to start carrying the mess out to the dung pile. They can use my wagon."

One of the other Gibeonites continued, "Besides that, we've had men from Damascus making threats in Gibeon. We left our strongest behind this morning to protect our city. Sanballat is stirring up trouble. He sent scouts to find our weak spots and spread rumors they plan to kill anyone who helps with the wall."

"I've heard similar stories from the men of Tekoa." Dohd sounded tired. "Everywhere we turn they plan to attack. Let me go check on those extra weapons."

Miriam and I walked with Dohd to the smith. "How are those

extra knives and arrowheads coming?"

"Yahweh has been with us. My sons and I worked all night after Shemiah called us away from working on the wall. We should have a healthy supply for you by tomorrow."

Elul 1, 444 B.C.

Ab and Dohd missed evening meal. The stars hung bright by the time they arrived. "I'm sorry, Chava," Ab said as Em put bowls of stew in front of them. "We wanted to make certain every family had plenty of swords, knives, and arrows."

"Fortunately, the smith said he'd have more tomorrow." Dohd sounded so distraught.

"We're doing all we can, Nehemiah."

"I know, Hanani, but I feel responsible. I brought this trouble on the city."

"I thought you said Yahweh put this job on your heart."

"He did, brother." Dohd smiled at Ab. "Thanks for the reminder."

Before I could bring him a second glass of milk, Ab rose and put his sword and his knife in their sheaths.

"Where are you going at this hour, Hanani."

He leaned down and kissed Em. "I'm standing guard for second watch. Nehemiah will take third watch."

"From now on, half the men will stand guard while the other half works on the wall," Dohd said.

"And even those doing the building will keep their swords and knives ready," Ab finished.

Hakkoz spoke up from the end of the table, "I know I haven't been much use building the wall. These old bones just can't keep up anymore. But I still have an old ram's horn I used when I fought for Xerxes. I'm willing to sit as a sentry with it one watch each night to give someone a break."

Renana protested, "Are you sure you should be out there, old man?"

"I'll be fine, old woman," Hakkoz teased.

"And we truly can use every man."

"It's settled then. Let me dig out that horn, and I'll go with you, Hanani."

Twenty-Nine

For more than a week, Ab never removed his sandals or outer tunic. He worked on the wall half the day then switched places with someone on guard for the second half. He returned home with the stars then left again to keep second and third watch. He and Dohd each slept only one watch a night.

Miriam and I could feel the fear in the air as we delivered water and food each day. The wall around the spring was nearly finished, still, Ab didn't want us past the gate. Guards brought in large vats of water, and we filled as many skins as we could carry. Now and then we'd hear the men arguing.

"We need to abandon this project. Everyone's life is in danger."

"We'll never be safe if we don't finish it."

"He's right, we'll have enemies even without the wall. It will keep out the bear and the lion just as effectively as Sanballat's men."

Only a few skirmishes ensued, and the guards handled them. I heard someone wounded Shemiah, but it only put him out of commission for a few days. Perhaps Abba's God did watch over the city.

Dohd met with the city officials each morning to check on the work and encourage the people. I heard him remind them often, "God will fight for us."

Elul 15, 444 B.C.

It had been nearly two weeks since we'd had trouble from the enemy. Dohd heard they'd given up after they discovered Jerusalem never slept. Even though the threat seemed to have passed, the workers kept their swords, and the watchmen stood guard day and night.

When the king's courier entered the gates late one evening, news reached our shelter long before the horseman. The sentries had seen him coming, his crest and colors giving him away. Everyone in the city was anxious to hear what Artaxerxes had to say, so Dohd read the letter during the next morning's regular gathering.

"From: Artaxerxes, Emperor of the realm of Persia, Judea, Egypt, and the entire world. To: Nehemiah, son of Hacaliah, cupbearer to the King." The crowd grew quiet. Even the slight murmurs we heard most mornings were absent. "I have heard progress on the wall is moving quickly. I write today to officially appoint you governor of Jerusalem and the vicinity. Each satrapy around yours will receive a copy of this announcement. Continue with your work on the wall."

When Dohd finished reading the letter, the crowd erupted. They may have heard the rejoicing in Bethlehem. Everyone loved and respected Dohd.

Elul 18, 444 B.C.

Unfortunately for Dohd, the rejoicing lasted only a few days. One by one, residents of Jerusalem visited our shelter. Each shared the same concern. Though the spring rains had been plentiful, Sivan, Tammuz, and Av had been dryer than usual. Crops should be ready by now, but there was nothing to harvest. Everyone wanted the new governor to help feed their families. We heard Dohd and Ab talking about different plans each evening.

One day as I cleared the table from the evening meal, three men stopped. "Governor, this famine is destroying us."

"I'm going to meet with the district rulers tomorrow to make plans to bring in more grain," Dohd replied.

"Come on. Let's go. I told you it wouldn't do any good to talk to him," one of the other men said to the first. "They're all in this together.

Dohd stopped them. "Wait a minute. All in what together?"

"Those district rulers already own mortgages on our land."

"What?" I couldn't tell if Dohd was more surprised or outraged.

"All we have left are our children and our own lives." The second man chimed in. "Plus, we still have to pay the king's tax on all those fields."

The third man spoke through tears, "Each of us has been forced to sell our oldest daughter to pay the tax."

The color left Dohd's face, "Who bought these daughters?"

"Those same officials who mortgaged our land. Men who we believed shared our heritage."

As the men turned to leave, Dohd stood, "I appreciate you letting me know what's been going on. I assure you I had no idea. I've been so focused on the wall."

Ab had kept silent during the entire exchange, but his clenched fists and white knuckles betrayed his thoughts. After the men were gone, Dohd sat down across from him, and Ab's tears began to flow.

"Nehemiah, I brought Adira here so I'd never have to see her in service to another. Losing Avraham and Natalia to the king was enough. This is not supposed to happen in Israel." I had no idea my strong Abba worried so. I thought my siblings fortunate for holding such prestigious jobs in the kingdom. It never crossed my mind they were lost to the king.

"Hanani, how could I have missed this? I talk to those nobles every day. We need to be in much prayer so I have the right words tomorrow. I can't afford to lose their support on the wall, but this enslavement of the children of Israel cannot go on!"

Ab began, "Yahweh, great God in Heaven, Creator of all things and Redeemer of Israel, hear our prayer."

Em bowed over her sewing, and I knelt on a cushion in the corner as Dohd continued.

"Forgive us, Adonai, for not seeing this travesty. Lord, forgive our people. Give us wisdom tomorrow as we speak to these officials. Let us convince them they do not honor you when they take your children into slavery; and let us lose no time on the wall because of this great sin."

We sat in silence for a few minutes, but I could feel the prayers of my elders. Ab's strong voice had moved me before, but this time their prayer hung thick in the room, and I could sense its weight. Like a blanket, the hush turned into soft groans that brought comfort and warmth. Finally, it became quiet again, and Dohd signaled the end with a reverent, "Amen."

Ab sighed and rose. "My turn to stand watch."

"Stay safe, Hanani," Em whispered as he bent to kiss her cheek.

Thirty

Elul 19, 444 B.C.

Dohd and Ab rose and left before dawn the next day. Miriam and I brought water to those working around our area of the wall then dropped in on Meremoth's wife to help with her house full of children. It wasn't until evening, after Jok and Jon had gone to bed, that Ab and Dohd Nehemiah had time to tell Em what transpired with the officials.

"Nehemiah handled it tremendously, Chava. They could tell he was angry. Even before he began to speak, the crowd grew quiet. Then he let them have it!" Ab's smile and sparkling eyes gave away the end of his story.

"Nehemiah started with, 'You're charging interest to your own people?!' Not one man said a word. Then he continued, 'We've spent years getting Jews out of slavery. So much money has been spent buying our people back from the Gentiles, only for you to enslave them again?!'" I almost laughed as Ab tried to imitate Dohd. "You should have seen it, Chava. Even the birds hushed their song while the governor spoke!"

Dohd smiled, "My brother exaggerates. I simply told them that they didn't honor Yahweh. I explained the need to walk in the fear of our God."

"He did more than that. He demanded they stop charging interest and return every vineyard, olive grove, and house as well as one percent of the commodities they'd taken as interest."

"And to my surprise, the whole assembly said, 'Amen'."

"Then Nehemiah took off his robe and shook it. He said, 'May Yahweh shake out of their houses and possessions any who don't keep this promise.'"

"I made them swear an oath they would return the lands and people and stop charging interest."

"They readily agreed and praised God with us."

"God must have graciously prepared their hearts, Hanani."

"You're right. I truly expected some resistance."

"But God was with us, brother."

"He was indeed."

Dohd looked at the ground. "There's one more thing I have to do. And I'll need your help."

"Anything, Nehemiah."

"Not yours, brother. Chava's."

I wonder if they heard my gasp as Dohd looked over at my mother. I glanced toward Miriam. *What could he want Em to do?*

"Me, Nehemiah? I'm not sure how I can help the governor."

"Those nobles feast from the king's tax. As governor, I'd like to cut that tax on the people and have you prepare food for the nobles to save money. These people have been paying forty shekels a month, plus donating food and wine. That's too much. I'll still have to collect enough to send to King Artaxerxes, but I think we could feed them for much less."

"All that experience I got cooking for the queens won't go to waste, I guess. I'll recruit a few women to help. Give me three days to get it organized."

Thirty-One

Dohd's plan meant more than just cooking meals for the elite. It also required a move. Abba said many in town had been suggesting Dohd transition into the governor's quarters ever since the king's announcement, but Dohd liked to keep things simple.

My mouth dropped when I walked through the gate. I'd passed by here almost daily to get water for the workers, but I always imagined this walled courtyard belonged to one of the city officials. Em said it had been the governor's quarters ever since the first exiles had returned.

The shelter we lived in now would fit into the courtyard twice. Even though the dry season kept the weeds at bay, the neglected garden gave evidence no one had lived here for some time. The porch had several doors that opened into a great dining hall to make a large space for entertaining. Behind that room, Abba showed us a spacious kitchen and several sleeping rooms. "You'll have your own space, Adira. Em and I will have the room closest to the kitchen and Nehemiah would like the room on the end, but you and your brothers can have your pick of the final three."

My own room. I took my sleeping mat and peeked in each door.

The room closest to Ab and Em would be perfect for Jok and Jon, so I took the next. At first, it seemed like a dream come true, but it didn't take long for me to realize I enjoyed being in close contact with my family.

I found them sitting on cushions in the kitchen around a small table that probably once gave refreshment to the governor's servants.

"Jok and Jon can do that. And here comes Adira now. She can take care of the cushions."

"I can?" I questioned, not sure what my mother had volunteered me and my brothers for.

"In the dining hall. There are plenty of cushions for the guests, but they haven't been used since the last governor. So, they'll all need to be cleaned."

"You're right, I can take care of that." I poured myself a cup of goat's milk and headed toward the dirty cushions as they continued their conversation.

A short bench lined the back wall of the room, and on it lay more pillows than I could count. This would take most of the three days! Thankful to have something to do, I looked around for something to start the job. A door off the hall led to a small closet where I found a rod that would work nicely.

After sweeping a spot to place the cleaned cushions, I took handfuls to the other end of the room and began the process of beating out the dust. The job gave me plenty of time to think. It occurred to me that I hadn't thought about my friends in Susa since I'd met Miriam. And without them, the idea of a pantheon of gods had become a lot less attractive.

Ten cushions later I stopped for some milk to let the dust cloud settle. Abba had come to Jerusalem for freedom, but it seemed he worked twice as hard here as he had in Susa. And Em left cooking for queens to cook for nobles here. I couldn't see the difference. But I kept hearing Abba's voice, 'I lost Avraham and Natalia to the king.' *Had I really been rescued from something I didn't know I needed saved from?*

As I gathered another handful of pillows, I heard something in the courtyard. Jok and Jon's laughter always made me smile. Em must have put the boys out there to pull weeds and tidy up outside.

We didn't finish before the evening meal, but we still had two days before the first guests would arrive.

Elul 22, 444 B.C.

True to her word, on the third day, Em rose early to prepare an evening feast for the officials and their wives. Every day except Shabbat she prepared a banquet for the nobles. Not once did she seem flustered. Watching her organize it all made me think the queens allowing her to leave may have been a miracle.

Miriam and I added kitchen duty to our daily water deliveries, and Jok and Jon became wood carriers for the great fires required to cook the daily banquets. Everything ran smoothly under Em's direction. Despite the drought, all the necessary supplies arrived each day. Em said it was nothing short of a gift from Yahweh.

Thirty-Two

"We did it, Chava, we did it!" Em still had the knife in her hand as Abba lifted her off the ground. "The last gate has been set in the wall. I've never seen anything go so smoothly," he said as he deposited her back in front of the high table built especially for preparing meals.

Em laughed, "Smoothly, huh? I'm not sure your brother would agree with your description considering you've been holding swords as you work."

"Alright, smoothly might not be the right word, but fifty-two days. We rebuilt the entire outer wall in just fifty-two days. That has to be some kind of record. The temple took years. In fact, we're still working on it as time permits."

"Well, I guess tonight will be a special celebration then."

As we prepared the evening meal, the room buzzed with excitement. Everyone talked about how Yahweh had accomplished such a grand project.

Nobles kept pouring into the dining hall. Even the heat of the late summer didn't deter them. In Susa, only the most important were invited to parties like this.

Suddenly it occurred to me—I might be noble. Dohd was

governor, and even though Em oversaw the kitchen, she had a staff of five cooks and ten table servants, and each evening she removed her kitchen garment and replaced it with her best robe as she sat and ate with the officials. But if we were nobility, why did I still feel like a servant?

The celebrating went on late into the night, but when Abba left to take over the watch, I went to my room.

My room—I ended up sharing it with Miriam. Not because I had to but because I chose to. She moved in with us to give her dohd more space, but she could have had the extra room. I finally had everything I dreamed about on the road from Damascus, yet I felt hollow. I had danced at the celebration, but my heart only wanted to cry. Did I miss Natalia and Avraham? It was hard to believe I hadn't seen them for six moons. But no, my sorrow went deeper than that. Something was missing. I didn't know what I needed, but the hole brought silent tears again.

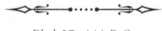

Elul 27, 444 B.C.

With the outer wall finished, Ab and Dohd were around a bit more often. They still took their turns at watch, and efforts to make the fortress impenetrable continued. Gatekeepers now had something to keep, and the Levites returned to their duties at the temple. Ab told me that when they finished the inner wall, dirt, stone, and debris from the old wall would fill the wide gap between the two, and guards would walk on top from tower to tower.

We'd just settled into a nice routine when Dohd made the announcement.

"Ladies and gentlemen." Every official stopped eating and gave him their attention. "I want to thank everyone for your hard work completing the wall. Since the king has appointed me governor of the region, I'll need to visit other parts of Judah. In my absence, my brother Hanani will be taking charge of the city. Hananiah will be commander of the fortress. No one fears God more than these two men. They will make certain the city gates remain closed until the sun is high each day and will keep guards stationed for your protection. They will speak on my behalf when I'm out of the city."

Everyone applauded and congratulated Ab and Hananiah. But as I went around the room refilling cups, I noticed one table seemed a little less excited.

Elul 28, 444 B.C.

The next morning as I walked into the kitchen, I discovered Ab and Dohd had noticed as well.

"Don't worry about them, Hanani."

"I'm not worried, brother, but do you know why they seemed less than pleased with your announcement?"

"Unfortunately, those nobles regularly exchange letters with Tobiah. A whole group here in Judah has sworn an oath to the scoundrel. Our own priest, Sheconiah, allowed his daughter to marry the ruler. And despite Meshullam's dedication to finishing the wall, he gave his daughter to Tobiah's son. Both men commend Tobiah to me almost every day. They think he's wonderful. I've shown them the man's threatening letters, but even that won't dissuade them.'

"Fortunately," Dohd continued, "he and our other enemies have been intimidated by the speed with which we completed the wall. Even they believe Yahweh had a hand in it. They might not be afraid of us, but they still fear God."

"Good. Perhaps while they're holding back a bit, we can get some of the houses restored." Ab was always thinking about helping others. He talked about building some homes into the fortress as they built the inner wall.

Dohd continued as I refilled his cup. "God laid it on my heart to do a genealogical registry. A month ago, I found the list of those who first returned to the land, and the High Priest helped me make sure everyone serving in the temple are true Levites. But I found that very few of the 42,000 who returned to Judah have settled in Jerusalem. We need more people here to defend the city. Those who are standing watch now are growing weary. I've already sent messengers to gather people from throughout the country."

Elul 29, 444 B.C.

The next day, Abba began overseeing the reconstruction of homes. Each night after we'd finished the evening meal, he'd tell us about how different men and women had stepped up to help with the project. "It's not easy work, wee one, especially since we don't have the help of the Levites or the men from Tekoa, Gibeon, and Mizpah anymore, but with Yahweh's help, Jerusalem will be rebuilt in no time."

Thirty-Three

People had been trickling into Jerusalem ever since the work crews finished the wall. I don't know what Dohd put in those messages he sent, but by the time the new moon came round again, the city was bursting. I hadn't seen this many people in one place since our trip through Damascus.

On the Shabbat after Ab announced the city gates' completion, droves of people began passing by our house, all headed in the same direction.

"Em, where is everyone going?"

"The same place we're going as soon as you and Miriam gather the boys," Em teased.

Jok and Jon shared my curiosity as we followed the masses to the large square that opened in front of the water gate. Everyone sat on the ground facing a huge platform that had been built in front of the gate as Ezra the priest climbed the stairs.

A tall table stood front and center on the platform and thirteen priests waited patiently for Ezra to get to it. He laid the scroll on the table, and as he unrolled it, people around me began to stand, and though still clueless, I stood too. But instead of reading from the scroll, the priest began to pray.

"Almighty God, Maker of Heaven and Earth, You are the One and Only, great Yahweh." People began raising their hands, and the murmur of amens could be heard throughout the crowd. Then Ezra continued, "We praise you for bringing us back to this land you gave our ancestors. We praise you because you blessed the work of our hands to complete this wall despite the threats from our enemies."

And as he finished, the people as one said, "Amen."

Something felt very different in the air. Ezra's prayer reminded me of Ab's. As the old priest began to share from the scroll, the words called me. I'd heard others read the law, but their droning quickly put me to sleep. Even with his pauses so the priests scattered throughout the crowd could repeat his words in Elamite, Akkadian, Aramaic, and Greek, Ezra spoke with so much passion and authority, the crowd remained silent. Men and women raised their hands and looked toward the heavens, while others fell to the ground and bowed before Yahweh.

As the sun reached its zenith, a soft noise rose from the crowd. Tear-filled eyes surrounded me, but some could no longer hold back the sound of their grief; while others had faces filled with joy. A handful of us remained unchanged, mere observers, but I wanted more. Ezra's excitement had captivated me. I knew he believed every word he read, each a repetition of something Abba had told us on more than one occasion over the past decade.

Ezra stopped reading as Dohd stepped forward, "My fellow Israelites, people of God, the sun is high, go and eat. Celebrate. Bring out the richest food and sweetest wine. Share with your neighbors. Treat today as holy. Wipe your faces, for today is a day of joy not weeping. Remember, the joy of the Lord is your strength."

As we walked back towards our home, I heard many praise God for Ezra and Dohd. Over and over, men and women said they finally understood God's Holy Word. Today's celebration overshadowed any I'd seen in Susa.

At the governor's residence, everyone laughed and praised Yahweh. Ezra joined us after the feasting was well underway. The moment he entered the room, applause erupted. I watched as all the officials stood to welcome him. The priest graciously accepted every extended hand and warm embrace. Dohd finally rescued him and led him to our family's table.

"Ezra, you brought Yahweh's Word beautifully today," Dohd began.

"I apologize for my tardiness, but I felt a need to pray alone."

"No need to apologize. You look exhausted my friend." I'd been thinking the same as Ab.

"Kind of you to notice, Hanani. I exert every bit of energy when I share the Holy message. It always takes a lot out of me.

Em filled the priest's cup. "Well then, eat up and rest. Enjoy the party."

The celebration continued into the evening. People wandered in and out, and nearly everyone stopped to greet the priest.

As the sun lowered on the horizon, Miriam and I went outside to get some air. We could feel the rainy season begin to settle in. I pictured Natalia back in Susa by now where the nights would still be warm. Susa didn't get this chilly until at least Adar. My friend and I pulled our wraps tight as we walked around the district.

"These people really know how to celebrate," Miriam said.

"What did you think of Ezra's reading today?" The priest's passion still monopolized my brain.

"I didn't understand most of it. Even with the Levites translating and explaining each phrase, it went over my head."

"But what did you think of it?"

We walked in silence for a few minutes. So many thoughts swirled in my head.

"I don't know how to describe it, Adira." Miriam brought me back into the noise of the celebration. "But everything I felt, I saw in my grandfather's face. Tears of joy covered his cheeks. He looked like he was greeting a loved one who'd been in a foreign country for years."

"I don't understand it, Miriam."

"Sounds like a conversation to have with your Ab. You know he'd love to talk about it. My grandfather has missed his stories while he's been busy with the wall."

"I can't talk to him. My doubts would break his heart."

"I think he'd understand. I've never known someone like your ab."

"You're probably right. But even in his understanding, he would have disappointment on his face. I can't bear to do that to him."

We walked the path back to our home in silence. Night was falling quickly, and we hadn't brought a lamp. Em had hired some young neighbor girls to clear the tables tonight, so Miriam and I headed straight for our room. Another big day awaited us tomorrow.

Thirty-Four

Tishrei 2, 444 B.C.

As much as I enjoyed listening to Ezra yesterday, I was grateful the men decided to go without us today. With all the celebrating last night, Em needed a lot of help to get everything ready for the evening meal.

The sun had just reached its high point when Ab stepped in the front door. "I'll gather the branches while you send the couriers, Nehemiah. I'll get enough for your family, too, Hakkoz."

Em wiped her hands on her outer wrap as the men grabbed bread and cheese, "Hanani, what in the world is going on?" Em's question echoed my own.

"Oh, Chava! Ezra read a part of the law today that I'd never heard."

There was part of the Torah my father hadn't heard? I stopped washing dishes to give Abba my full attention.

"God commanded Moses to live in tents or booths for seven days every year as a reminder that our ancestors lived in the desert for forty years."

Dohd continued, "It's called Sukkot, the festival of the booths. Ezra said he couldn't find a record of the last time it had been celebrated."

I had to ask, "So why start now?"

"Good question, wee one. We celebrate because Yahweh doesn't want us to forget. Those who forget history repeat the mistakes of their ancestors. That's what happened to the last kings of Israel."

Dohd continued, "Your Ab is right, Adira. Those kings stopped trusting Yahweh. They forgot that's what caused Moses to wander around the desert for so long."

Abba's voice grew deep as he transitioned into storytelling mode, "You see, after just fifteen moons, Moses and the people found themselves on the banks of the Jordan. Yahweh told them the land was theirs. They simply had to cross the river to take it.

"Moses sent twelve men as scouts. For forty days, they traveled through all of Canaan. But when they returned, only Joshua and Caleb believed they could take the land. The other ten spread fear among the people. Only Joshua, Caleb, Moses, and Aaron had faith to believe Yahweh could take the land from the Canaanites, so the whole nation had to wander in the desert for forty years—one year for every day they had scouted the land. Of the adults in the crowd that day, only Joshua and Caleb got to cross over forty years later."

Dohd finished, "For forty years our ancestors lived in tents and lean-tos, so for seven days each Tishrei, God asks us to do the same. He wants us to remember to trust His promises. The festival begins two weeks from today!"

"You'd best get those couriers sent, brother."

"Everyone in Israel will celebrate this feast!"

Mid-Tishrei 444 B.C.

Dohd sent the couriers out on the second day of Tishrei, and by the tenth, even more people from all over Judah began to pour into Jerusalem. All around the city, tents went up. Roughly constructed booths could be seen on nearly every rooftop in the city. I wondered how many more folks the town could hold.

The streets buzzed with excitement, but after four moons of sleeping under a wagon and two more living in that little shelter, I wasn't anxious to give up the comfort of the governor's residence for a week.

"I'm not looking forward to living in a booth for a week, Miriam," I told my friend as we carried water for our final indoor meal.

"I wonder why Yahweh chose the beginning of the rainy season instead of Av or Elul for this festival?"

"I'm still not sure I would classify this as a festival, but I agree. The nights have already begun to cool, and the rains could begin any moment."

"Well, I guess if we survived the caravan to get here, we can make it through seven days."

"I suppose. But I can see why the history of this feast didn't get passed on for long."

The seven days passed much more quickly than I imagined, and it was nice to see Em relax around a small fire rather than preparing a meal for more than a hundred people each afternoon.

Dohd thanked Em over and over for her efforts in feeding the nobility. A whole moon had passed without relying on the governor's allotment for food. The nobles had huge flocks and herds as well as stocks of wine they could tap into. He'd been able to cut the people's tax in half. Many in the community showed gratitude by bringing the little extra they had.

Each time someone thanked him, Dohd replied with a prayer, "Remember me with favor, Adonai, when you see what I have done."

During the festival, Miriam and I helped the priests with the games they planned for the children, and I enjoyed listening to Ezra share from Yahweh's Word each day. My light blanket kept me warm each night, and praise the gods, they held off the rain. Yet, even as that thought crossed my mind, I could feel myself questioning the truth behind my fading pluralistic faith.

As my friend and I lay alone on the rooftop watching the stars on the final night, I let my thoughts have a voice, "Forty years, Miriam."

"Forty years of what?"

"Moses and our ancestors slept like this for forty years."

"All because they didn't trust Yahweh."

Miriam's reasoning stopped me in my tracks. Even though Dohd mentioned it weeks before, I still hadn't linked my current suffering to a lack of trust. I'd just been feeling sorry for them, but what if the forty years could have been prevented?

"So, you think they brought this on themselves?"

"Isn't that what Sabba and your ab have been telling us?"

I'd been so focused on blaming Yahweh for their trials, I'd forgotten their wandering was a consequence.

Thirty-Five

On the eighth day, we took down the booths and everyone gathered near the Temple. Ezra had read from Yahweh's law each day during the festival, but I didn't understand everything I saw going on today. Some of the crowd wore sackcloth and others had sprinkled ashes on their heads. By the time the sun signaled mid-morning, the noise from the crowd drowned out the voices of Ezra and the priests. I couldn't hear myself think. I turned to hide in my father's embrace, but he'd fallen to his knees with his face to the ground, adding his deep voice to the raucous.

I knelt beside him in an attempt to calm my fear, but the noise just grew. Finally, I just concentrated on Abba's voice. "Forgive me, Yahweh, I have sinned. I am not worthy."

Focusing on his comforting timbre allowed me to truly hear what was going on around me. Although they didn't speak in unison, each person cried out the same, "Mighty God, forgive me. Forgive the sins of our fathers and their fathers."

Some confessed specific sins, others just cried. Part of me wanted to escape, but something held me there. The sun climbed as the crowd continued. By midday, the rumble waned. I felt relieved for a few moments, but gradually the low roar grew again. Tears streamed as I sat next to my kneeling father, but mine stemmed from fear and confusion rather than cleansing of conscience.

When, in mid-afternoon, the crowd grew quiet, the Levites shouted, "People of the One True God, stand and praise Yahweh."

All around the people rose, and one of the eight men who'd been translating for Ezra opened a small scroll. He and the others took turns praying.

"Blessed be the Name of the Lord. Be exalted above all."

"Lord, who chose our Father Avraham and promised him this land we possess, we praise You!"

"Almighty, who brought our people out of Egypt, we praise You!"

For a long time, the priests kept reminding Yahweh of all He'd done. Was He a forgetful god? Or perhaps these priests were remembering? My mind wandered, still unsure of what was happening.

The voice of one of the Levites brought me out of my own thoughts, "Despite our failings, You, Yahweh, have remained righteous. Even when our ancestors turned their backs on You, You remained faithful. See us, Lord, slaves in the land You gave our forefathers. Today, we make a covenant with You. Holy Lord, we set our seals to this promise."

I watched as Dohd raised his seal and fixed it first to the parchment. Abba's eyes misted as he moved forward to take his turn. Twenty-two priests, sixteen Levites, and forty-four leaders, including Ab, each dipped their seal into a waxy spot on the scroll.

When they finished, Dohd sent out a challenge. "I invite all of you who've separated yourselves from the nations that do not worship Yahweh to bind yourselves to this covenant we've made."

Men throughout the crowd shouted their affirmations, "We promise not to allow our children to marry those from nations who do not follow Yahweh."

In unison, the crowd cried, "Amen."

"We will not buy or sell on Shabbat, even when foreign merchants come to our gates."

"We will give what is due for the work of the temple."

"We will bring the firstborn from our flock to the temple and redeem our firstborn sons."

After each statement, a resounding "Amen" rose from the crowd.

I'd never seen such a grand festivity. The sunset blazed a bright orange, purple, and pink. Em said it looked like Yahweh celebrated with us.

Jerusalem buzzed with excitement for weeks, and many families stayed in the city after the celebration. Then life settled down. I found comfort in the routine of the everyday. But change seems to have become a big part of my mundane life.

Thirty-Six

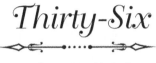

Jerusalem winters require bigger fires than Susa winters. I pulled my cloak tight as Dohd closed the door behind the courier. He glanced at the message and passed it to Em. "This one is for you, Chava."

A letter for my mother?

"This is Natalia's hand." I could see tears threaten as Em broke the seal. She scanned the parchment before she read it out loud.

"From: Natalia. To: Abba and Em.'

"Queen Esther has grown ill. The physicians don't expect her to last more than six moons. Her head eunuch told me I'll be released immediately after the days of mourning. I'm writing to see what you'd have me do.'

"Avraham is well. He will be writing soon, he has some exciting news for you, but I'll leave that for him to tell."

Natalia was released! Would she join us in Jerusalem?

As tears of joy began to flow, even Jok and Jon got in on the hugs. Abba's eyes glistened behind his big smile. "We'll have her send a courier on the day of the queen's death. If I return with the young man, I can be in Susa before the time of mourning ends."

"That will be a hard ride, Hanani. There's a reason the couriers are young."

Abba grinned, "I know, my beloved. But I've ridden with them before. I'm not that old yet."

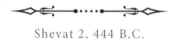

Shevat 2, 444 B.C.

For the next weeks, even Jok and Jon kept an eye out for the king's couriers. They rarely came to Jerusalem more than once or twice a month, but we kept hoping. A note from Avraham finally arrived with the Shevat snows.

"What does our son say, Hanani?"

"He says Natalia is well, and the queen still lingers." I opened my mouth to ask Abba to finish the letter when I noticed the teasing glint in his eye.

"Husband," Em said with a smiling sternness, "our son did not write to tell us about the queen."

"Oh, yes, he also mentions he's betrothed."

Em's face beamed, yet I saw some concern there I didn't understand.

"The stable master has asked him to become his son-in-law."

"Anna?" I chimed in. "She's Natalia's age. I think she's pretty."

"You're right, Adira, she played with Natalia when they were young." Em turned to Abba. "Is he pleased?"

"Seems so. They will be wed next Kislev."

I wish I could read Em a bit better. I expected her to be ecstatic. And while she looked happy, I could tell something was amiss.

Abba quickly cleared things up for me, "Good thing so many have moved into Jerusalem and need houses right now. I may need to make some extra money to take my wife to Susa next year for a wedding."

Thirty-Seven

Tishrei 1, 443 B.C.

The year passed quickly. I hated leaving Dohd and Miriam behind, but I didn't want to miss my brother's wedding. We traveled with a merchant caravan heading back toward Susa for the winter. No walking during this trip. These traders covered the miles in less than two moons.

Kislev 15, 443 B.C.

Yahweh provided perfect Kislev weather for the wedding celebration, and the full moon took the place of torches. Avraham looked so happy, and Anna would balance our brother/sister ratio.

We stayed the winter with Ab's brother while he worked on a building project inside the palace.

Shevat 25, 443 B.C.

No one imagined Queen Esther would hold on for so long, but Natalia cared for her for two moons after Avraham's wedding. We spent our last seven days in Susa sitting shiva and hearing more stories about the beloved queen.

Adar and Nisan, 443/442 B.C.

Another merchant caravan heading for Anatolia provided safe passage as far as the Karbhak River. There we joined a group coming from Nineveh to complete the journey.

My sister and I spent the two-moon trip catching up. I felt bad for her. At eighteen, she was well past betrothal age, but she'd come to adore Queen Esther. Even if she'd been released, Natalia hadn't been able to bear the thought of leaving the queen in her final days. On the other hand, I relished the idea of having my sister to myself.

Thirty-Eight

With Natalia home, everything was perfect, but my dream life crumbled just after I marked my fifteenth year.

We'd just finished the evening meal when Ab broke the news. "Natalia, your mother and I have spoken to Hallohesh. His son, Shallum, has asked for your hand. We won't force you to marry; however, this could be a good match. Hallohesh leads one of the half-districts of the city, and Shallum worked harder than all the others his age when we rebuilt the wall."

Natalia grew noticeably quiet. I knew she was trying to find the right words to tell Abba she didn't want to marry. She wouldn't want to hurt our parents, but she hadn't even had time to settle in yet. "I've met Shallum, Abba. He was in the market the last time Adira and I shopped."

So that was the name of that handsome man. He was too old for her. I must have taken longer choosing vegetables than I thought.

Em smiled, "So this is not a surprise?"

"Oh, no! It's very much a surprise. I've only spoken to him once." Natalia paused and turned just a bit pink. "But, Em, I'm not disappointed."

Ab smiled. "I will get the contracts ready. His father and I will set things in motion, and I'll tell him he can call on you when he likes."

I met my brother-in-law-to-be over the next evening meal. And while I tried very hard not to like him, before we cleared the dishes, he'd won me over.

After dinner, Shallum and Natalia took a walk. Miriam and I had been appointed chaperones, but we held back, trying our best to give them some privacy while still obeying my parents. Fortunately, a nice breeze cooled the warm Tammuz air, and the full moon gave the evening a romantic glow. As I watched my sister walking with a man for the first time, every stroll I'd taken with her flooded my memory.

"You haven't heard a word, Adira." Miriam's voice interrupted my thoughts. "What's the matter?"

"Just feeling sorry for myself, I guess."

"Wishing you were the one betrothed?" Miriam teased.

I stopped and stared at my friend, stunned for a moment. We admired handsome young men every time we went to market, but we'd never mentioned betrothal. "No!" I said emphatically. "Wait—do you?"

"Well, maybe—a little." Miriam's face turned bright red as she answered. "But if that's not it, what had you in a trance?"

"I'm selfish. I thought I'd have my sister back for a while. But here we are, not even two moons have passed, and she's with Shallum."

"You still have a year before they'll marry. That's plenty of time."

We walked the rest of the way in silence watching my sister's betrothed be the perfect gentleman. He didn't even try to take her hand.

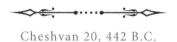

Cheshvan 20, 442 B.C.

Miriam was right. Shallum only whisked his bride-to-be away for a few hours two or three times a week. So, Natalia and I got to enjoy some wonderful sister time. Thankfully, Natalia didn't mind including Miriam in our escapades. After two years, my friend had become my second sister.

Of course, having two sisters I loved so much caused a struggle deep within. I couldn't tell anyone about my childish bent. Sometimes I wanted one or the other all to myself, and I still wrestled with losing Natalia to Shallum. No matter how much I rationalized or tried to tell myself I was being ridiculous, I couldn't escape. My life couldn't be any better, yet peace eluded me.

Everyone else seemed so content. Miriam and Natalia never complained. Nat talked constantly of Shallum and their future, and Miriam was enthralled with her busy life. She watched over children for several large families and helped in her uncle's merchant booth, receiving payment in the form of food and scarves.

Maybe that's what I needed, some kind of work to keep my focus off my selfish thoughts. I would talk to Ab the next time he broke his fast.

Cheshvan 21, 442 B.C.

I rose early to catch my father before he left for the day. "Abba, what do you think about me taking on some work?"

"Is my wee one bored?"

I no longer cringed when he used his term of endearment for me. "Well, Jok and Jon don't need me anymore. They'll be going with you to learn to build within a year. And Em only needs my help to prepare the evening meal." I paused for a moment, but before he could reply, I blurted out, "Abba, I spend too much time feeling sorry for myself, and I'm tired of it. I need some sort of distraction."

My father smiled, "Perhaps you are not my wee one anymore. Only someone maturing can see her own flaws and discover a possible solution. Let me see what I can find for you."

I put both arms around Abba's chest and held on. His loving laugh temporarily removed all my discontentment. This is how it should always feel. Abba's arms held so much peace.

Thirty-Nine

After each evening meal, our family moved into a cozy common room, leaving the nobles to entertain themselves. Family time had always been important to Ab and Em, even when they served the king. Jok and Jon were finally able to retell Israel's ancient stories.

Occasionally, Ab and Dohd would update us on the progress of the fortress' interior wall. Though the outer wall had been built in record time, construction on the inner wall moved painfully slow.

Tonight, Shallum stoked the fire as we each found a cushion. Winter always brought chilly weather to Jerusalem. Even after two-and-a-half years, I couldn't get used to these temperatures.

Ab surprised me when he said my name. "Adira, I think I may have found a position for you. It won't pay much."

I didn't care about the compensation. I just needed to get out of my own head.

Ab continued, "A widow living near the Water Gate lost both of her sons in battles fought during the temple rebuild long before we arrived."

"She has no daughters-in-law, Hanani?" Em asked.

"Though both had wives, they had no children. The women's

kinsman-redeemers still lived in Susa, so she released the girls to remarry. She has no one. She needs a companion and caregiver. What do you think, Adira?"

Remembering Natalia's position with Queen Esther, I had to ask, "Where would I live?"

"For now, you'd be here every night. I told her you needed to be home early enough to help Em prepare the evening meal. It would only be four days each week, but as she ages, she may need more help."

"That sounds perfect."

Gratitude filled my heart. My parents have always given us choices. Many young girls in Susa didn't have that luxury. Two of Natalia's friends had married before their fourteenth summer to give their family a better standing in court. Others had been forced to work under cruel masters because they paid much better than their kinder counterparts.

Despite Ab making sure his children always had pleasant places to serve, we'd never gone without. My parents would credit Yahweh; however, I think their kind nature and integrity made them popular wherever they went.

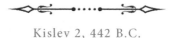

Kislev 2, 442 B.C.

Salome waited for me outside her small home the next morning. Hers was one of ten that lined the Street beyond the Water Gate. From the outside, the homes looked like one long building. Only the doors gave away the number of families who lived there.

My new mistress was wonderful. We spent the first morning just getting to know one another. Salome's parents had returned to

Jerusalem under Darius' rule. Even older than Queen Esther, she remembered getting the notice that the Persians would be slaughtering the Jews. She had met and married her husband here in Jerusalem. And though she'd lost her sons during the middle of King Xerxes' reign, tears still fell when she told me about them.

"Do you find it difficult to go to the temple since you lost your sons because of it?"

Salome looked surprised. "No, my child. It's even more precious. The temple reminds me how courageous and full of faith my sons were. They fought for Yahweh's house. Its completion was more important to them than their lives."

Salome rarely went further than her front stoop. Her frail legs wouldn't hold her light frame for any length of time. So, before I finished the day, I gathered eggs from the nests in the little courtyard behind her house, cooked a small meal for us to share, and filled her water jars from the nearby pool.

Though she'd told Ab she only needed me every other day, I returned on the off mornings to empty her chamber pot and get her clean water. I hated thinking of her drinking day-old water. Or worse, she might try walking to the spring.

Each workday, I prepared enough bread and stew for the following day. During the first week, Salome let me make bread my way, but by week two, she couldn't hold back her years of experience. I followed her suggestions out of respect, but after the bread came out even lighter than Em's, I whispered, "Can I share this secret with my mother and sister?"

Salome laughed, "Since I received it from a very old lady sixty years ago, I suppose I can't really claim it."

Spending time with Salome did the trick. I felt useful, and my charge's sweet spirit made the work light.

In addition to shopping, I also traded her eggs at the market. "Don't trade them for less than one small basket of vegetables per dozen," she instructed.

"My husband, Mattityahu, set up this fence for the chickens fifty years ago," she explained as we gathered eggs one morning. "He was wise even when we were young. I don't know how I'd have survived these twenty years without my little chicken farm."

Most afternoons we just visited. I loved her stories as much as Ab's. Growing up in Jerusalem, she had watched men use ropes and gadgets as they moved the massive stones one on top of the other to build the temple.

Salome shared Ab's faith, too. Each day she told me how Yahweh had been with her through the years. I felt myself beginning to trust the God of Israel, but the times I hadn't seen Him work cast a shadow over all their testimony.

Forty

Tammuz 15, 441 B.C.

I entered my sixteenth year without fanfare. As Natalia's wedding date approached, Miriam and I talked of little else. Fortunately, my friend had enough enthusiasm for both of us. I still hadn't embraced the idea of my sister leaving my room.

"Soon we'll be betrothed." Miriam beamed. "I've seen grandfather talking to Aaron's father. Last night he asked me if I knew the boy, so I expect an announcement soon."

Miriam continued to talk about Aaron. He'd become the center of all our conversations recently. I wished I could share my friend's outlook, but I didn't feel ready for marriage. I knew I should. Every girl my age was fixated on finding the perfect match. Praise Yahweh my parents didn't rush me. Was Yahweh truly looking out for me?

"Adira!"

"I'm sorry, Miriam."

"You zone out every time I talk about our upcoming betrothals."

"I didn't think you noticed. You seem so excited."

"Of course, I'm excited. Aren't you?"

"Not really."

My friend's mouth fell open. "You've never said a word."

"Why should I spoil your dream with my fears."

"Fears? What do you fear? Your ab would never force an unwanted match on you."

"I know. I'm just not ready for marriage. I like caring for Salome. And I don't want children."

I laughed at the look of horror on my friend's face.

"No, no, no." Miriam remained confused while I tried to compose myself. "It's not that I never want children. I just don't want any next year."

"Yahweh will work it all out, my friend."

I hoped Miriam was correct, but I continued to have some doubt about Abba's God. As much as I loved Miriam, I'd never let go of being ripped from Yasmine and my home. No one knew the dark secrets of my heart or that I blamed Yahweh for my misery. I didn't like the way things were changing. Natalia getting married. Miriam talking about betrothal. Little did I know all the upheaval I'd faced so far would become inconsequential before the next full moon.

Part Four
Truly Slaves

But while all this was going on,
I [Nehemiah] was not in Jerusalem,
for in the thirty-second year of Artaxerxes king of Babylon
I had returned to the king.
Nehemiah 13:6

Success is to be measured
not so much by the position that one has reached in life
as by the obstacles which he has overcome.
Booker T. Washington

Forty-One

Natalia's wedding day arrived, and with it came all the heat of Summer. As Em put the finishing touches on my sister's robe, Miriam and I went to gather blossoms for the bridal chamber. Everything near the city had withered since the rainy season had passed. Hopefully, the large grove of trees just east of the Horse Gate would provide enough shade for flowers to flourish.

Baskets in hand, Miriam and I headed out. With no clouds in the sky, the light breeze felt wonderful. The day promised to be perfect for a wedding.

Wedding and betrothal conversations filled the air as we chose the best of the blossoms until I heard a stick break on the other edge of the grove.

"What was that?" Miriam whispered.

"You heard it, too?" The thick trees prevented us from seeing anything.

"Yes—and that was no deer." Miriam moved closer to me.

"I think we have enough. Let's head back."

Before we'd taken three steps, two men popped out from behind trees. We tried to run the other way, but two more stood waiting. How had they snuck up on us?

I started to scream when a hand from behind covered my mouth. I tried to bite my attacker, but he held tight. Another man picked up my feet, but when I started kicking, the one who had my mouth laid my head down none too gently to help his friend.

As soon as his hand left my mouth, I started screaming. But even with Miriam joining me, our cries couldn't reach the city, and we were just far enough into the grove no one could see us, not even the gate guards. As soon as they had our ankles tightly bound, they jerked us to our feet and tied our wrists behind us. I tried to fight them off but quickly realized my struggle would likely land me on my face. They worked fast then flung us over their shoulders.

The flowers we'd collected lay trampled beneath our assailants' feet. Tears rose as I realized our broken baskets would be our families' only clue to what happened.

"Where are you taking us?" I screamed.

"Please, please just leave us alone," Miriam said through her weeping.

But the four men remained silent.

On the other side of the grove, a caravan waited. Within seconds they added blindfolds and gags. Our struggling did nothing but wear us out. They set us in the back of a covered wagon between barrels of what smelled like freshly dug potatoes.

No matter how I moved, the wood rubbed my knuckles, and I couldn't nudge my skirts back down over my knees. When the caravan began to move; Miriam and I leaned in against each other, the only way I could let her know I was glad they hadn't separated us.

Powerless to do anything else, I began to soak my blindfold.

Where were they taking us? The slave markets? The bride markets? I wanted to talk to Miriam, to wrap my arms around her, instead, I scooted a bit closer. Horrific scenes played in my mind. I saw us wasting away chained in a dark dungeon. Would we be auctioned off like lambs?

Miriam's sniffles brought me back to the present, and I leaned into her a bit more. Other sounds, previously muffled by my imagination, reminded me to think more rationally.

Abba and Dohd would come looking for us. Em would send Jok and Jon to retrieve us, expecting to reprimand us for taking so long. And when my brothers returned with only the broken baskets, Ab and Zabbai would follow the tracks, and we'd be rescued.

Oh no, poor Natalia. I'd ruined her day. Instead of going to the bridal chamber, she would sit up worried, and her new husband would join the search. If they took horses, they could easily catch the caravan. The thought calmed me a bit.

Without being able to see the sun, only my hungry belly and the need to relieve myself gave me any indication of time. When the wagons slowed, I hoped our captors would at least allow us to address the latter of the clocks.

Someone grabbed my feet and pulled. No one spoke. I nearly fell over when they unleashed my ankles. Miriam's muffled moans told me at least we were still together.

"Relieve yourself if you need to," a man's voice broke the silence.

Stunned for a moment, I didn't move. Relieve myself? Blindfolded with my hands tied behind my back? While men watched?

"You don't need to go?" The man said as he grabbed my arm.

I jerked away. Okay. I had to do this. Being rocked around in a wagon scared for my life was bad enough without needing to go. I spread my legs as wide as I could and squatted slightly wishing I could lift my skirts. I heard Miriam's relief hit the ground, then mine.

Humiliated, and certain I'd soiled my robes, they drug us back to the wagon. Feet tied again, they returned us none too gently to our spot between the barrels.

They must have been watering the animals and eating because the wagon didn't move right away. My dry mouth made me wish I was as valuable as a horse.

Exhausted from the afternoon heat and the stress of the day, I had no idea how long I'd been sleeping when the sounds of shouting and the jerk of the wagon stopping woke me.

First, I heard horses, and then, "We're looking for two girls." *Abba*!

"We haven't seen anyone since we left Bethlehem this morning," an unknown voice lied.

Miriam and I were helpless. We tried kicking the floor of the wagon and screaming through the gags, but impatient horses stomping and someone moving barrels outside drowned our feeble attempts.

"Have you seen other merchant trains today?" That was Dohd's voice.

"One caravan left Bethlehem ahead of us, and we passed some wagons headed south out of Jerusalem."

I heard a horse just outside our wagon, so I banged again.

"What was that?" Was that Shallum's voice or Miriam's uncle?

"I didn't hear anything," the stranger's voice lied again.

Miriam and I both kicked and banged again. The tight gags muffled our screams.

"Oh, that? We have lambs in that wagon. They grow restless."

"Well, if you find two girls, bring them back to Jerusalem, and I'll see you are handsomely rewarded," Dohd promised.

Why don't they open the flap on the wagon?

"We'll do that, sir. Who should we ask for if we find them?"

"Just ask for the governor," Ab finished, and then we heard them ride away.

Tears threatened again as the wagon pulled out. Why had Ab given up so easily? Would we ever see our families again? I felt Miriam scoot closer.

The rocking wagon accented the bruises, and my belly had long forgotten to tell me the time. Without any fluids, my second clock's cries were minor. I don't know how much time had passed when the sounds of a city rose.

As the wagons slowed, fear of what might happen mixed with a cry of relief from my jostled bones.

"No, we can't risk it." That was a new voice.

"But they haven't had anything all day." I'm not sure why a women's voice surprised me. Wives often traveled with merchants.

"They'll be fine."

"They probably need to relieve themselves."

"Not in the city, Jochebed." The man's voice was firm. "They'll be fine until tomorrow. If they soil themselves, we'll clean it up after we've driven out of the city."

We were to be confined to the wagon all night. No way to move, nothing to eat or drink.

I attempted to stretch out, but my cramped legs moved only half a cubit before they hit something. We wouldn't be lying down.

Forty-Two

"This is the wagon." A whisper outside the wagon startled me awake.

"How many swords protect it, Hanani?" Dohd and Abba were here! We would be rescued.

"I saw at least twenty men this afternoon, Nehemiah. The four of us are no match for that number."

Four? Who was with them?

I considered trying to scream through the gag, but I was afraid I'd alert my captors to Ab's presence.

"It looks like some chose the serai instead of sleeping under the wagons. Did they honestly think we'd give up when the tracks didn't match their story?" That must be the fourth man.

"Lambs indeed. I've never known lambs who don't bleat."

"Quiet," Ab said, "surprise will be our only hope."

A strange voice came from the other end of the wagon, "And you don't have that hope."

The scuffling made it impossible to tell how many fought. The clang of swords and yelling filled the air. Horses' hooves added to the mix, and I prayed one of the gods would take care of my family.

Suddenly I was ripped from the wagon. Do they have Miriam too? Was it Ab?

When the man flung me over his shoulder, I realized the truth. *Where is he taking me?* I almost rolled off his shoulder when he rounded a corner.

"Break it up. We will not have this in our streets." We were still close enough to hear the soldiers get involved in the fight.

"But my daughter is in there."

"Search the wagons."

"We have no one hidden in these wagons, sir." That sounded like the man who'd mentioned Jochebed earlier.

"Where did you take them?" I'd never heard Ab's voice grumble low like that before.

"We told you, we don't have the girls."

"The wagons are clear, sir."

"Then why did you lie about the other merchants? Tracks told the truth," Ab growled.

"I do not lie. You just don't know how to read tracks."

"Enough of this!" I think that was the soldier. "There will be no more disturbance tonight. Do you understand?"

"Yes, sir." That was Dohd.

Everything grew silent. I wanted to make some noise so Abba and the soldiers might hear, but what could I do dangling over this man's shoulder?

Finally, the sound of footsteps then horses riding away stole what little hope remained. Our fate was sealed.

Someone approached. "Hide them in the stable. Cover them with straw and sleep in front of them. Do not defile them. Virgins bring a good price in the Persian bride market."

As I heard the man walk away, the woman's voice returned. "Let's get them to the stable. Then we'll let them relieve themselves."

"But, mistress. . ."

"What he doesn't know won't hurt him. Come, let's get them out of sight."

Forty-Three

Av 4, 441 B.C.

In the stable, someone untied our feet and hands. I reached for my mouth.

"Touch that or the blindfold, and I will have the men mark you with the sword where it won't be seen in the bride market," Jochebed spoke again.

She led me several cubits and directed me to relieve myself. Free to lift my robes, I squatted hoping the men weren't watching.

But they must have been because as soon as I let go of my clothing, a large hand grabbed my arm and drug me to the other side of the stable. My thigh took a beating as he maneuvered me into a wall. I assumed he put me in a stall.

"Both of you, sit down."

I reached for Miriam and held on as we obeyed the man's command, but he jerked us apart as he rebound our feet and hands.

"Lie down."

I complied and felt the straw cover my body.

"Not their faces," Jochebed scolded. "If they can't breathe, they won't be worth much tomorrow." Her harsh tone surprised me. She'd seemed to have compassion on us when she spoke to her husband.

Exhausted, I fell asleep quickly, though the ropes didn't let me sleep sound. My vengeful stomach woke me long before they came to collect us. The lack of light leaking through the blindfold led me to believe we were on the move before dawn.

As we rolled away from the city, all hope of ever seeing my family again rolled with it. I would be back in Babylon before the winter rains fell, set to be sold to the highest bidder in the bride market. Perhaps I'd been hasty not wanting Abba to find me a husband. Anything would be better than this.

Forty-Four

By the time we stopped, I could feel the sun high in the sky. Although our hands remained bound, even while we squatted, our captors took off our gags and blindfolds. I'd hoped that meant we'd get something to take care of our dry mouths and empty stomachs, but as they fastened our ankles to the wagon, one of the servants had to convince the master of the caravan we might not be alive to be sold in the market if he didn't give us at least a few sips.

And limit it to a few sips, he did. The tiny bit of cool water just made me long for more. I realized, even without the gags, Miriam and I still hadn't spoken. I guess they knew they'd stirred up enough fear to keep us quiet. The noise of the wheels gave us the courage to finally have a whispered conversation.

"Are you hurt, Adira?"

"Just bruised. How 'bout you?"

"The same. What is this bridal market they keep talking about?"

"Em told me about it long ago. Before the time of King Darius, men could sell their daughters to the highest bidder. Though Darius outlawed them, a few still operate in the tiny cities of Persia. I'm certain they intend to sell us as wives."

Miriam gasped. I could hear her dreams of betrothal crash at her feet as the rocking of the wagon let the idea settle in.

"I hope your family wasn't hurt trying to rescue us."

"Well, I heard Ab and Dohd talking after the fight. So, I think they survived."

"Do you think they'll feed us?"

"I was wondering the same thing, but from that lavish amount of water they gave us at the last stop, I'm guessing it's going to be a while before we see food. I'm just glad they finally let us talk. I feel better at least hearing your voice."

"I agree," Miriam said as we leaned into each other and fell asleep.

⬦⪜ •••••• ⪛⬦

Av 8, 441 B.C.

For three days our captors kept us in the back of that wagon, getting out two or three times a day to relieve ourselves. On the second day, they offered us bits of bread, but we had to eat from Jochebed's hand. My wrists felt raw from the constant pull of the ties. When we passed by a town or another caravan came close, the gags came back out.

On the third day, I could smell it.

"Miriam," I whispered, "we're approaching the sea."

"How do you know?"

"Breathe deep. You'll smell it. I can't wait to feel the breeze. It's so stifling hot in here."

As the servants drug us out of the wagon by our feet, I saw it. The water stretched for miles before us. Memories of sitting on the bank with Abba more than three summers before flooded my mind. I'd passed my thirteenth year on these shores.

Jochebed arguing with her husband brought me out of my reverie. I couldn't make out what they were saying, but soon a servant brought back the gags and blindfolds. At least we'd been allowed to take in the sea.

Dread filled my being as I heard footsteps approach. "Girls." It was Jochebed. I breathed a little easier. This woman had done her best to care for us as much as she could. "I've talked him into allowing you to bathe."

They untied our ankles and led us a short distance to what must have been the Jordan just south of the sea. For the second time since we'd left Jerusalem someone freed our hands, but my sense of freedom was short-lived when the warning not to try anything came with a sword point placed carefully under my chin.

The blindfold made it difficult to take off my outer robe and make my way to the water. Jochebed led us, and the sneers and snickers made me grateful I didn't have to see the men watching us bathe.

I drank in as much of the cool water as my body could hold then cleaned myself as best I could with an audience. Only the memory of that sword tip kept me from lifting the blindfold long enough to take in the beautiful scenery.

We put on our underrobes and sat by the warm rocks to dry. One of the men handed me a small loaf of barley bread. I inhaled the first few bites. Then I realized this might be the last I'd see for a few days. I considered saving some to put in the folds of my robe, but once they tied my hands again, it would just tease me, so I savored the last few morsels.

I felt almost human on the walk back to the wagon, though the clean water and fresh air made the smell of my robes even more noticeable. As they tied our hands and legs, I wondered how long it would be before we would be able to walk without restraints. Thankfully, they removed the blindfolds and gags. It was two days later before it dawned on me—we hadn't even put up a fight.

Forty-Five

Miriam and I shared memories and cried about the life we'd lost as we traveled on this seemingly endless journey. The days passed so monotonously we lost track of time. When the wagon stopped for what we'd soon find out was the last time, they blindfolded and gagged us again, and a strong arm led me down a damp walkway. No light made its way through the blindfold. Someone removed the rope restraints, and I wondered if Miriam was still with me. I tried reaching out to find her, but a man pushed me back against a cold wall and put my ankles and wrists in iron shackles.

As I listened to the footsteps fade into nothing, I guessed they'd chained me in a cell of some sort. The only sounds in the thick silence were my own breathing and that of what I hoped was Miriam. Fear paralyzed me.

My stomach ached with hunger, and the damp mixture of mold, dirt, urine, and vomit didn't help. I guessed half a day passed when I decided to chance it.

"Miriam," I whispered.

"Yes," her reply sounded like she'd be crying in silence.

"I think they're gone."

I pulled against the chains and discovered I had enough slack to gently expose one eye. One torch several cubits away provided the only light, still, I winced at the brightness. "We can take the blindfolds down. If we leave them around our necks, we should be able to get them back on before they see us. We should hear them coming."

Another tug at the chains proved the cell's stone walls held the shackles in place.

Though the space was small, for the first time since the night we spent covered in straw we could stretch out to sleep. The dirt had captured every smell, but that didn't stop us from laying our heads on it. I figured it would be a long time before I saw a sleeping mat again. I might as well get used to it. Too exhausted to worry about what tomorrow held, Miriam and I stretched our arms toward one another and held hands as we fell asleep.

Forty-Six

The Next Day, 441 B.C.

Boots kicking our feet wakened us the next morning. For weeks, we hadn't seen anyone but Jochebed and a few servants, but these men looked more like guards than merchants.

"Eat," one of them said as he tossed us two small barley loaves and a ladle. He sat a small bucket of water between us. "Wash up and relieve yourselves. Get rid of those blindfolds around your necks and make yourselves look presentable. We can't have you looking like that. We'll be back."

We'd barely finished their instructions when they returned. They removed the shackles but tied our wrists and then bound us together at the elbow. Running would be difficult like this. But just as quickly as the thought entered, I realized we had no place to run. We didn't even know where we were.

"What will happen to us?" I asked the guard.

"The market master will decide where you'll bring the best price."

I looked at Miriam. Tears filled her eyes. *Would we stay together?* I doubted it, but it sounded like the market master held the keys to our future.

We crossed a courtyard with a large platform at one end. Around the perimeter, shackles secured waist-high lined the walls, a few already in use. Men milled around inspecting those chained as if they were judging sheep for sacrificial value.

To my surprise, the guard led us to a small room on the other side of the complex where a short plump man waited. Miriam caught his attention first. I'd always envied her soft features; however, today I thanked the gods my nose and chin were a bit square and my complexion not as smooth.

Our head coverings had been left behind with the flower baskets in Jerusalem. I cringed as the man I thought must be the market master ran his fat fingers through Miriam's long straight hair. Raven black, it complimented her sun-touched skin beautifully.

"This one will bring a better price in the bride market." Miriam and I both gasped. "Hold her until next week but take her to Ghazal so she can get cleaned up. An Egyptian robe and some kohl and she'll bring a nice price. The better they look, the more they pay.

He turned his attention to me as they untied the rope around our elbows. I wanted to hug Miriam one last time. My heart screamed as I watched my best friend be led away. Both of us had wet cheeks when she turned to mouth goodbye.

When the plump man reached to touch my brown curls, my sorrow turned to rage. "Don't touch me."

He simply smiled as he ran his finger down my cheek. I wanted to spit on him, but my dry mouth couldn't muster anything. Instead, I pulled my head away, but he jerked it back. "They told me you'd been compliant on the way here, and we wouldn't have any trouble with you. But you're a little feisty, aren't you? I kind of like that."

Doing my best to mask my horror, I stood tall, giving me a slight height advantage. He'd have to get on his toes to look me in the eye now.

Laughing, he said, "Take this one to my residence. My wife has been asking for a new kitchen slave. I like her spirit." He walked toward the door, but just before he exited, he turned back and looked me directly in the eye. "We'll see how long it takes to break it."

Staying on the donkey with my hands tied was difficult; however, being in the fresh air without a blindfold made it bearable. I breathed deep and took in the scenery.

As we rode away from what looked to have been an old caravanserai, my heart hurt for Miriam. In a week she'd be someone's bride. I looked back wishing I could say goodbye and wondering if I'd ever see my friend again.

Forty-Seven

Though time had no meaning anymore, the cool breeze and hot sun held fall in their grasp. I heard a river to the west, and the willows that lined our way confirmed it.

"Could you tell me the date?" I asked the man who led my donkey. But he didn't answer.

For the first time since I'd been taken, my fear felt manageable though my future remained a mystery. Perhaps being able to see removed some of the terror. Since the servant wouldn't talk, I was left to my thoughts.

Did my family think I was dead? Did Natalia marry? I know I spoiled her day, but surely, they'd gone on with it by now. Tears spilled as I realized I'd probably never know. The fear that had been my companion since Natalia's wedding day was replaced with self-pity. I would never know my nieces and nephews. Ab and Em would never see my children, and if I had children, they'd be born into slavery. Would I be allowed to marry, or would the master of the house just use me and toss me aside? I shook that thought aside as I recalled the short plump market master.

The donkey's gait quickened as a great wall came into view. A house of stone towered behind the gates, and I could see the tops of several other buildings. Not large enough to be a city or town, I guessed this fortress might be my new home. All around the structure, men and women worked in the fields, and that river I'd heard could finally be seen wrapping around the manor and watering all her crops. On the horizon to the east, I could see what might be a small town.

On the other side of the gate, barns and outbuildings decorated the landscape, making the main house look even grander than I'd imagined. The guard helped me off the donkey and led me to the back of the house where a well sat on one side of a great courtyard surrounded by trees and greenery. Hints of flowering bushes meant springtime would be lovely. At least if I'd be trapped behind these walls, I could enjoy some beauty.

Inside the back door, five girls who looked to be younger than Jok and Jon prepared midday meal in a large kitchen. Whatever cooked on those three firepits reminded my stomach of how little it had been given since we'd left Jerusalem. I'm certain if I hadn't been so dry, my mouth would have been watering.

Just then, a woman about my mother's age entered the room carrying supplies.

"Elizabeth, here's a new one for you." So, the man did speak. "Master told me to bring her right over."

"Thank you, Parsa, will you unbind her?" Elizabeth turned to the girls, "Leila, show her where to bathe. I can't have that smell in my kitchen. And find her something clean to wear."

The oldest of the girls moved, but Parsa stood like a statue. "Elizabeth, you know if I unbind her hands, I'll have to put on the ankle shackles."

"Do what you must Parsa," Elizabeth floated around the kitchen working as she talked. "She's of no use with her hands tied."

Elizabeth stopped in front of me for a moment, "I'm sorry about the chains, but until he can trust you won't run, the master insists. Fortunately, you can still walk in them."

"Where would I go, g'veret?" Parsa attached the shackles to my ankles as I continued, "I don't even know where I am."

"I agree," she said with a bit of a smile, "but the master makes the rules." She turned to get back to work, but hesitated for a moment, "And what is your name?"

"Adira bat Hanani of Jerusalem."

"As soon as you get cleaned up, Adira, return here. Leila, don't be gone long. We have work to do.

Parsa released my hands; then I followed Leila into the courtyard.

The young girl led me to a very small building hidden behind all the others. She opened the door to reveal a hammam just big enough for two people. Water flowed through a fire and into a small pool that overflowed into a pipe leading back outside. Even in Susa, I'd never seen anything like it. I must have let out a gasp.

"Don't get too taken with it." Leila sounded quite hardened. "It's the only pleasant thing about this place."

"After what I've been through, this is luxury." I slipped out of my clothes and into the wonderful warm water, "Can you tell me where I am?"

Leila handed me a basket of soaps and oils. "You've been purchased by the estate of Tiridata ben Majidi. The town you see in the distance is Hamath."

"How far from Damascus?"

"I don't know. I've heard of Damascus, but I was born in Hamath. My parents died when I was four, and Master bought me from some poor cousins. At least that's what they tell me. I haven't been further than that gate for the last nine years."

"I'm so sorry," I said as I dried and put on the fresh clothes. "What month is it?"

Leila looked at me as if she thought I'd lost my mind.

"I've been tied and blindfolded in the back of a wagon since they took me from Jerusalem. The days just run together after a while, and I can't remember the last time I saw a moon.

She still looked a little puzzled, "Today is the full moon of Tishrei."

Two moons in the back of a wagon. It seemed like an eternity.

Leila handed me a brush from her basket before she headed back for the kitchen. "Elizabeth will expect your hair brushed out, and I'll find a head covering for you. Now, hurry."

Walking with ropes on my ankles had given me good practice for walking in the ankle irons. The dragging chains made a great deal of noise. I definitely wouldn't be sneaking up on anyone soon.

All eyes turned my way when I entered. Leila delivered the promised head covering, and Elizabeth put me right to work. Being in the kitchen put me at ease. This had been my home since infancy.

Elizabeth seemed nice. She reminded me of Em as she flitted around giving instructions. I wondered how many ate at this table and if the kitchen help got any scraps. Though my stomach had gotten used to eating almost nothing, seeing all this food stirred it up again. Judging by the size of the other girls, I decided not to get my heart set on filling my belly tonight.

When the time came to serve, each of us carried one or two plates of food. It didn't take long to understand why Elizabeth's voice was the only one we heard in the kitchen. I'd thought it odd no one else ever spoke, but the atmosphere of the dining room explained a lot. A large table sat in the center of the room, and on this night, the cushion at the head of the table remained empty. I assumed the short plump man usually sat there. A tall heavy woman had the cushion to the right, and ten noble-looking men and women talked in hushed tones in the rest of the spots. Twelve children ranging in age from five to fifteen lounged silently around two other tables, and one of the women looked as if she would be adding to that number soon.

"What is that clanging?" The tall woman yelled.

"That's the shackles your husband requires on our new slaves, g'veret," Elizabeth answered.

"Take her away. I do not want to see her again until she's released from her shackles."

Elizabeth nodded for me to leave.

My new mistress looked surprised and pleased when she returned to the kitchen and found the work area being cleaned. She and the younger girls made several more trips carrying serving bowls to the dining room. Leila and the other older girl must have been charged with seeing to the noble's needs while they were in the room because they didn't return.

I found water in a few buckets and heated a little to begin to wash the platters. Though many washed with water straight from the well, Em liked it a little warm. She said it got things cleaner.

"Come, get something to eat and meet the rest of the help,"

Elizabeth said after Leila and her helper returned. "We'll finish up after we eat. You've conquered most of the kitchen. The girls will be pleased."

We split the leftover food seven ways. Elizabeth made sure the three younger ones had a bit more than we who were older. I hadn't noticed the cushions in the corner before. They looked as though they needed thrown out, but they made for a soft seat as we sat down to eat.

After everyone had a plate of food, Elizabeth began to make the introductions, "Girls, this is Adira. She'll be living with us now." Then beginning with the oldest and going down, "You've met Leila. This is Hannah and her sister, Yael. And the two youngest are Huma and Talia."

Each girl greeted me as she was introduced except Hannah. Even as the rest chatted freely, the young girl didn't even raise her eyes as she nibbled her food.

"Hannah, you look like you might be the same age as my younger brothers," I said, trying to draw her out. "They'll mark their tenth year soon."

Silence filled the air.

The young girl glanced my way as Yael whispered to her.

"Hannah doesn't talk," Yael told me. And with that simple statement, everyone resumed the meal as if I'd never spoken.

After we finished the clean-up, Elizabeth gave everyone instructions to be back by first bell, "Thanks to Adira cleaning the kitchen as we served, you'll have a few moments of free time this afternoon."

As the rest of the girls scattered, Elizabeth gave me a tour. I'd share one of the small serais I'd seen in the back with the other five girls. The basket of oils and soaps as well as the hairbrush were community property.

Our serai bordered the stables. The neighing brought back memories of visiting Avraham while he cared for the king's horses. I wondered about my brother and his bride. The last message Ab read said a baby would be born after Passover. My heart wrenched and tears threatened as I realized I'd never see the wee one.

"Try to stay out of sight of the master and mistress," Elizabeth told me. "Since you work in the kitchen, you shouldn't have to deal with them often, but when you do, keep your head down."

"Yes, g'veret."

"I appreciate your respect, Adira, but you may call me Elizabeth.

As we passed through the hedgerow that hid the servant serais from the garden, I spotted the woman who'd banished me from the meal. I lowered my head and turned on the path toward the kitchen.

"You! Wait!"

I stopped but didn't turn.

"Elizabeth," the mistress sounded angry. "Where did this wretch come from?"

"Your husband sent her along with one of his guards this morning."

"Come here." I obeyed her command. "What is your name?"

I kept my head down. "Adira bat Hanani of Jerusalem, g'veret."

"Look at me!"

When I raised my head, I saw her eyes. They looked so empty. No life, no love, just black pools.

"Did my husband say why he kept you?"

"He told the guard you'd asked for more kitchen help, g'veret."

"I had hoped for someone a bit younger." She nearly spat out the words. "You will stay away from my husband."

"Yes, g'veret."

So, her fear and mine were the same. When he stroked my cheek this morning, I prayed he didn't want more than just kitchen help. I tasted the churns of my stomach at the thought.

"Do not forget your place. You may go." She turned to her kitchen manager, "Keep an eye on that one, Elizabeth."

"Yes, g'veret," Elizabeth answered as she hurried me down the path.

Forty-Eight

As I lay on my mat that night, every emotion from the last ten weeks caught up with me. Had I really been here only one day? So much had happened. The master of the house had confirmed my suspicions when he came to talk to Elizabeth after the evening meal. The looks he sent my way . . .

My thoughts turned to Miriam. Oh, my poor friend. I wept again at the loss. I already missed her as if it had been moons since we'd been together.

And that's when it hit me.

I'd been so intent on listening for wild animals or our captors, I'd never taken time to mourn my family like I missed Miriam right now. With that realization, more grief poured in.

Fear had consumed me, but since tomorrow offered some sense of familiarity, that deep voice sharing the stories of Israel flooded my mind. I could see Em serving the nobles the meals she once prepared for queens.

My gentle tears quickly turned into full-out weeping as I imagined Jok and Jon trying to get Dohd to wrestle with them after dinner. I sobbed at the thought of Natalia's wedding. And what about my wedding?

Quickly my grief turned to anger as I mourned my future. Where was this Yahweh Ab went on and on about? How could he let this happen to Miriam? My friend believed Yahweh was the only God. And why didn't He protect the daughter of someone as devoted as Hanani ben Hacaliah? Even if I didn't deserve to be rescued, how could this God Abba described allow my parents to suffer and worry? The only person I knew who had faith greater than Ab was Dohd. After all they'd done for the temple and the holy city, couldn't Yahweh protect a member of their family?

Anger and grief took turns as I drifted in and out of sleep.

Tishrei 15, 441 B.C.

All those years of waking early in Susa, and more recently staying vigilant for every sound around our wagon caused the movement outside the serai to break into my restless sleep. Slowly I rose to peek out one of the two high windows. Relief slowed my racing heart when I saw Elizabeth heading for the main serai.

Walking hunched over with my leg chains in my hands to avoid waking the other girls, I headed for the door.

When I entered the kitchen, Elizabeth looked surprised to see me, "You're up early."

"I spent many years in charge of our fast-breaking when we lived in Susa."

"Susa?" Elizabeth questioned. "I thought you were from Jerusalem."

"We moved to my ancestral home three years ago so Dohd

could oversee the building of the wall."

"So, the stories are true. Jerusalem is a fortified city again, and the king appointed a new governor. I wondered. You can't believe all the news the merchants bring."

"It's all true. The crews rebuilt the outer wall in less than two moons, and Dohd, once cupbearer to Artaxerxes is now governor."

Elizabeth dropped the bowl she'd just picked up. The wood echoed as it hit the stone floor.

The color drained from Elizabeth's face, "Your uncle is the governor?"

"Yes, I live, or lived, in the governor's quarters. Dohd has no family except us. I'm so sorry, g'veret. I think the past few weeks of not being allowed to speak has made me chatty this morning. What can I do to help?"

She gave me a few instructions, and then we worked in silence until she gave the bell one sharp ring. "You'll need to pay close attention to the bell. I can only let it toll once to call you girls to the kitchen or the mistress gets testy. She's threatened to keep the help in the kitchen all day to avoid hearing the bell more than once. And she won't tolerate me leaving my duties to go find someone."

"She seems harsh."

"You won't want to cross her. Yesterday was one of her more pleasant days."

As we finished preparations, the master came into the kitchen. Giving me that same look as last night, he asked Elizabeth, "Why doesn't the new girl serve us?"

"Your wife doesn't want to hear the chains clanking on the floor."

"Well then, we'll just have to trust this butterfly will not flit away." His smile made me want to run.

As the other girls began carrying dishes into the hall, one of the guards came in to remove the shackles. "Only one day in the irons. The master must really like you." His gaze made me feel violated. Then he left with a hearty wink.

Free to carry serving dishes, I picked up a large bowl and took it into the hall. I placed the bowl on the table furthest from the master and turned to leave, but his voice stopped me.

"Wait. You will take this young girl's place." He pointed at Hannah. "You will remain in here and serve us personally."

The mistress attempted to convince him I needed time to learn my place before being given this honor, but he'd have none of it.

These nobles never served themselves. Leila and I poured wine and placed cheese and bread on their plates. Too good to touch the serving platters, they gave orders during every course of the meal.

The master's hand wasn't the only one that lingered over mine and several made advances toward Leila. No wonder Hannah didn't speak.

After we'd cleared the tables and the nobles no longer needed us, Elizabeth served us the leftovers. Before I could take a bite, the mistress came in and called for me. I followed her outside, head down, toward the stables.

"I thought I told you to stay away from my husband."

I wanted to argue, tell her I'd done nothing, but I knew it would just make it worse, so I remained silent.

"I noticed you flirting this morning, and I won't have it. Remove your outer garment."

I jerked my head up. "Excuse me, g'veret?" They'd given me nothing to put on under my outer robe.

"You heard me. Remove your garment." She nodded toward a stable hand. "He has been given instructions. Today will be ten lashes, but the next time will be more."

The poor boy looked more distraught than me.

I could feel my face burn bright red as I disrobed.

"Kneel here and hold that rail." Her instructions came quickly. I could tell she'd done this before.

Slowly I knelt, clinging my garment to my chest as long as I could. Thankfully she'd let me keep my skirts.

"Okay, boy."

His hesitation almost cost him.

"Do you want to kneel next to her?"

And it began. The pain seared through my entire body. Never had I felt such agony. By the third stroke, I could feel the blood dripping.

When the torment stopped, the mistress screeched, "Four more! Can't you count?"

I thought I heard sobs from the young stable hand, but I didn't have time to worry about that. The final four lashes brought my attention back to me.

After the last lash fell, the mistress turned to walk away, but not before reminding me not to cross that line again.

Modesty forgotten I fell to the ground, finally allowing the sobs and screams to rise. I had refused to allow the mistress the satisfaction of seeing or hearing my cries, but I couldn't hold it in any longer.

The stable boy must have run to the kitchen because Elizabeth and Hannah were there with cool water and rags before I realized he was gone. They washed my wounds and bound them tight to stop the bleeding and keep my garment from rubbing against them.

How often did this kind of thing happen? Everyone seemed to know exactly what to do.

Elizabeth led me back to the kitchen. She wanted me to eat, but my stomach couldn't handle it. When I tried to stand and help, she insisted I lay on the cushions. I didn't even put up a fuss. I just laid on my stomach and fell asleep.

The bustle of lunch preparations woke me, but when I attempted to stand, pain ripped through my back to the rest of my limbs.

"Stay still until we're ready to serve," Elizabeth instructed. How did this woman stay so kind in such a horrible place?

I served in fear, using quick movements to avoid contact. This meal passed without much trouble, but I knew it wouldn't last.

Forty-Nine

I spent each day wondering when I'd next be punished for the master's wayward hand or sleazy looks. Fortunately, the routine of the kitchen gave me a bit of comfort. Like Susa, we did not rest on Shabbat, though Elizabeth did invite all the girls to join her for a special prayer time between the breaking of the fast and midday meal every seventh day.

The master didn't fear his wife, and he certainly didn't care about my pain. The looks kept coming, and twice the mistress called me to the stables. I felt as bad for the boy with the whips as I did for myself.

I'm sure she meant to weaken me, but each attack made me angrier. The pain and humiliation made me determined not to allow her to see me crumble.

The morning after the third lashing, I couldn't sleep, so I joined Elizabeth in the kitchen.

"How are you doing this morning?" she asked.

"Each beating hurts less than the last."

"I'm so sorry you have to endure them."

Elizabeth didn't deserve the emotions her sympathy aroused.

"Why should you be sorry? The mistress isn't sorry. The master isn't sorry, and he's the one causing it. Yahweh doesn't seem to be sorry. He doesn't step in. I'm not sure He's even strong enough to stop it."

"So, are you mad at Yahweh because He doesn't intervene or because He's a weak God?"

I stopped and stared at Elizabeth. The only sound was her knife hitting the board as she continued to slice the cheese.

"You have every right to be angry at Yahweh," Elizabeth continued calmly, "but you need to decide what you believe about Him."

"I'm still not sure if Yahweh or Ahura Mazda is the real god." Where did that come from? I hadn't mentioned or thought much about the god of Persia since my first year in Jerusalem.

"Well, you're not mad at Persia's god."

Elizabeth was right. My inner rage was aimed at Yahweh. Did I finally believe in Abba's God?

Elizabeth laid down the knife and took my hands, "Have you prayed about this, Adira? You can tell God you're angry. The great King David did. He said, 'How long will you forget me, Yahweh? Why do you hide your face from me?' and 'Why do you stand so far away? Why do you hide when I'm in trouble?' 'Yahweh, why have you forsaken me? Why don't you hear my groaning? Why don't you answer?' But even when Israel's great king prayed those prayers, he ended them with, 'I trust in your unfailing love. I will sing because Yahweh is good to me.' Let me pray with you."

I could only nod.

"Creator, Yahweh, your child needs you. Adira wants to believe, but she needs to know you are the great and mighty God I know you to be. Show her, Yahweh. Amen"

"Adira, I don't understand why Yahweh allows these kinds of things to happen, but I know He has a plan for you. My great-grandfather read the letter from Jeremiah when it came to the exiles. He told me it said God has a plan and a future for each of us. Do you know the story of Joseph?"

Again, only a nod would give my answer as memories of Abba's deep voice flooded my brain.

Elizabeth gently held me as the tears flowed—tears fueled by anger, memories, and a longing for Emi's comforting arms.

We heard the girls coming down the path, so I quickly wiped my eyes and picked up my knife. Hannah quietly grabbed the milk bucket, and Leila took the basket for eggs as the rest of the girls busied themselves with the routine preparations.

Fifty

I managed to make it to the next full moon without more lashings, but one night when I was the last one to leave the kitchen, the master's steward stopped me.

"Adira, the master would like to see you."

What had I done now?

I followed him through the great hall and up the stairs. *Why would he be taking me to the family's private quarters?* As soon as the question formed in my mind, I knew the answer, and panic set in.

The steward held the heavy door as I entered, expecting to find the master waiting.

"Master has asked me to fill his bath for you. He left this for you to put on when you're done."

He pointed to a gauzy robe that looked like it had come from Egypt.

"Would you like me to send one of the maids to assist you?"

I stood in shocked silence for what must have been too long.

"Miss?"

"No," I said, realizing he expected an answer. "I'll be fine on my own."

After I was sure the heavy door was secure, I looked for a way out, but servants lined the corridor, and the window offered no escape. I had little choice. I undressed quickly and slipped into the vat. The warm water felt lovely, but I didn't want to be in here when the master arrived.

A basket of the best soaps and oils sat next to the bath. They looked so inviting. I missed having sweet-smelling fragrances. Regardless, I refrained from succumbing to the temptation. I refused to do anything extra to entice the large bald man.

The robe was lovely, more beautiful than anything I'd ever seen in Susa or Jerusalem. Natalia had described one similar that Queen Esther had given her to set aside for her wedding night. The garment's light airy fabric left little to the imagination.

When I finished, I found a cushion in the corner furthest from the door in the darkest part of the room. The door opened. I hope to the gods he didn't see me sitting here. No, not the gods. After my talk with Elizabeth, I decided to give Yahweh a shot at being my one God. And though I still wasn't sure what that meant, I closed my eyes and began to pray, "Yahweh, this is not what I imagined for my first time. I know I shouldn't have waited until now for my first real prayer, but I need your help. Oh, Yahweh, please send help."

When I opened my eyes, the short bald man stood right in front of me with his hand extended. He spoke softly, but my thoughts were louder. He pulled me toward the bed. I'd never seen one raised off the floor.

I sat down next to him, and he gently moved my hair from my neck.

"Adira, I've imagined this night since you came to the market."

He made it sound like he met me while I shopped for fruit. His caress made my skin crawl. I hadn't felt this powerless since the day they carried me off.

Just as he pulled the robe off my shoulder, a knock sounded.

"Go away. I told you I'm not to be disturbed."

He ran his hand across the skin he'd just exposed when the knock came again.

"I'm sorry, Master, this can't wait."

A wave of relief washed over me as the large man stepped into the hall.

The conversation was too muffled to make anything out.

"She's what?" the master bellowed, and the steward's hush brought the conversation back to a muffle.

Only a few seconds passed before he came back in.

"Get out!"

I stood and headed for the door.

"Take your clothes!" Rage filled his face.

I picked up my ragged robes and walked out.

To my surprise, Elizabeth waited on the other side of the door.

"What are you doing here?" I whispered.

"I woke, and Yahweh told me to check on you. When the girls didn't know where you were, I had my suspicions."

I put both arms around her neck, "I don't know what you told him, but thank you!"

Fifty-One

Cheshvan 16, 441 B.C.

I expected the mistress to take me to the stables after everyone broke fast the next morning but banning me to the kitchen was my only punishment. For me, it was a gift. I worried about Hannah and Leila, but I could do nothing to help them.

The moons crawled across the sky. On the new moon of Kislev, each of us received a ragged wrap. The weight felt cumbersome. Why would anyone wear clothing this heavy? As the calendar moved to Tevet and Shevat, my question was answered. I'd never experienced this much snow. Walking to the serai and the barn became difficult. The dustings we'd had in Jerusalem didn't prepare me for this kind of winter.

I took my turn milking cows and goats and gathering eggs and settled into a comfortable routine. Morning quickly became my favorite part of the day. I loved spending time talking to Elizabeth.

The cold of winter seemed like it would never end, but Spring did finally arrive; and with it, a steady stream of merchants. Each time a caravan came through, I listened for familiar voices. I don't know what I'd have done had I heard the merchants who took me, but for some reason, I just wanted to know who they were.

One morning as I milked, I overheard the master talking to one of the merchants. I couldn't make out every word, but what I did hear terrified me. I finished quickly and apologized to the cow for being so rough. Then I slipped out of the barn and hurried back to the house.

"Adira, what is it?'

"Elizabeth, the master spoke to someone about selling me."

Elizabeth's eyes looked up from the stew she stirred. "Are you certain?'

"I heard him say, 'that wench from Jerusalem.' He said I was nothing but trouble and not worth what he'd paid them."

I could tell Elizabeth wanted to assure me I was wrong, but we both knew I was the only one in the house from Jerusalem.

"Elizabeth, I can't go back with those men who took me from my family."

"All we can do is pray." She immediately stopped and took my hands, "Great God in heaven, protect Adira. Keep her out of that merchant's hands. Keep her safe and show her the plans you have for her."

Her prayer calmed me, and relief flooded my being when I heard the caravan begin to move. My short, "Thank you, Yahweh," surprised even me.

Later that evening, I still felt pensive and distracted.

"You're still in a mood," Elizabeth noted as we cleared from the evening meal.

"I'm sorry. I thought I'd be happy to hear those merchants leave. Instead, I just feel angry."

Elizabeth silently continued to clean. She always seemed to

know when I hadn't shared the whole story.

"I've been anxious to see the faces of my captors. Every time I think about them, I feel rage. Today my fear made me completely forget I wanted to confront them."

"What will you do when you know what they look like?"

"I don't know." I felt deflated. "I just want them to pay for what they did. I hate them so much." The admission surprised me, though I'm not sure why. I'd often thought of ways justice might be served. Their camels could be frightened and run off a cliff, or bandits could meet them on the road. Nearly every day since my abduction I'd considered ways the gods might repay them.

Elizabeth allowed me to be alone with my thoughts for a few moments. Then she spoke, "Hate is a powerful emotion, Adira. Unfortunately, its power doesn't extend to the one we hate. And even though it never affects them, the emotion will eventually consume us. When you hate, it's like your attacker still has you tied up."

I took in her words, but how could I just abandon this feeling? Now that I'd said it out loud, I realized the hatred inside encompassed a lot of people. My attackers led the list, but the master and mistress came in a close second. Even those men who'd opposed Dohd fed the monster inside.

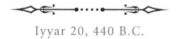

Iyyar 20, 440 B.C.

Spring also brought field hands to the manor. They slept in tents and cooked over fires, but a few came in every day to get provisions. The days became even longer as we baked extra bread and made more cheese. Two more calves were weaned early so we could get more milk.

All the work left little time for me to wallow in my anger and hatred, but it did allow me to consider Elizabeth's warnings. Do I want to give those people all that power?

By the time the hands had planted the last field, the first fields planted produced crops. Two women came in from Hamath every day to help. Some of the produce made it into the dark cellar bins while servants took the more perishable to market. By the time the workload had eased up, the marking of my seventeenth year had passed as well as the anniversary of my arrival.

Just when the daily routine had returned to a manageable pace, one of the merchants barged in. "Which one is Adira?"

Elizabeth stepped in before I could speak. "This is my kitchen. What is your business with my help?"

"She belongs to me now."

A collective gasp filled the room as he held up his bill of sale.

"Let me see that." Elizabeth pushed her authority as far as she could.

I considered running, but where would I go?

Elizabeth tried to convince him he didn't want me, but finally, I stepped forward.

"I am Adira bat . . ."

Elizabeth interrupted before I could finish, "Give her a minute to gather her things."

"I didn't pay for any extra belongings, just the clothes on her back. Let's go—now!"

"Can't she even say her goodbyes?" Elizabeth was doing her best to stall him.

The merchant looked a little defeated. "I'll wait right outside this door. Don't make me come drag her out!"

The girls all gathered round scheming ways to hide me.

"I have to go. Hiding will just delay the inevitable and bring trouble on us all." I hugged each of the girls. When I got to Elizabeth, I held on tight.

Just before she released me, she whispered, "You must tell everyone your name is simply Adira. I know you're proud of your heritage but being the niece of Jerusalem's governor could prove dangerous."

"Why?"

"I don't have time to explain, just trust me."

Outside, I followed the man to the wagon. He pointed to a spot in the back near two other women. Their dress told me they were the merchant's wives, and one looked to be with child. The two talked in hushed tones. I didn't care. No sense in getting to know people I'd probably never see after the next city.

At least my eyes were left uncovered this time, so I knew we were heading east. Back toward Babylon. Five years ago, that's all I'd wanted, life in Susa. Now, I just wanted my family, a family Elizabeth had warned me to hide.

Fifty-Two

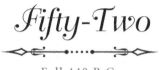

Fall 440 B.C.

Each day we stopped in another village or city. The merchants sold their wares, and I was put on display; however, the conversation always ended with, ". . . she'll be worth more in Nineveh."

I'd heard stories of the great city. Ab had told us of Jonah. He'd described the city as magnificent, but upon our arrival, I could tell it had lost some of its shimmer since the capital moved to Babylon then Susa. Jonah had spent three days walking the streets. Looking at it now, I'm confident I could explore the deteriorating town in a day.

Artaxerxes and his predecessors had banned slave and bride auctions; however, the court never moved any further north than Ecbatana, so the slave markets reigned here. My life would be controlled by whoever managed to be the highest bidder.

Men from all over Persia crowded the open arena the next morning, and my new owners replaced my ragged robes with a gauzy covering similar to the one Tiridata had given me. "You'll bring more if those men can see your curves."

I vomited twice as I changed, and I'm sure the fire of embarrassment showed on my face.

As the guard herded me toward the platform, I could hear the market master begin to introduce me. "Next for sale is a young, strong virgin we call Mara." I stopped. Who was Mara?

The guard pushed me forward, "Get out there, Mara." He stretched the new name and gave me an evil grin. I'd lost not only my dignity but my identity.

I stood in a daze as the bidding droned on.

When they ushered me back to my holding cell, the guards gave me hearty congratulations, "You brought the highest bid of the day, little lady." The laughter and celebration made me sick all over again. I was no more than an animal to these men.

The holding cell smelled of urine and vomit. It was just as well no one had thought to feed me all day.

One by one I heard the cell doors open and close. The wooden shelter grew quieter with each grind of the lock until finally, I realized the noise had completely stopped. Darkness settled in. Had they forgotten me? Surely no one expected me to sleep in this damp stench. With no mat or blanket and only the see-through robe to cover me, I huddled in a corner to keep warm.

Fifty-Three

Cheshvan 11, 440 B.C.

"There must be one more here." The sound of a woman's voice and footsteps brought me out of my restless sleep. "My husband showed up drunk last night with this bill of sale and no slave. Do you know how much he paid for this wench?"

"I assure you the place was empty when I left last night, g'veret."

I didn't know whether to try to hide or to stand and say something so they could find me.

"Well then, what is this?" A short woman a little younger than Em stood at the opening to my cell. "Look, she can't stop shivering. If she'd frozen to death, you, sir, would owe me a lot of money."

The lady was right. I'd grown so accustomed to the cold I didn't even notice my quaking.

"Well, as it is, g'veret, you owe me one night's board."

"Really? I see no mat, no blanket. Did you feed her?"

The man tried to stammer something.

"Exactly as I thought. I will not pay board when you offered no boarding accommodations."

After the man unlocked the door and left, the woman hurried in and gave me her wrap.

"You poor thing. The papers say your name is Mara. I'm Derora." I tried to correct her, but my lips would not cooperate.

"Can you get up?" With her help, I did. The first few steps were painful, but soon the movement offered a bit of warmth.

We walked to a waiting wagon where she bundled me in blankets then crawled in next to me.

"I left before dawn this morning. I didn't know what they'd do if no one claimed you. Those holding cells are horrible."

The woman named Derora just kept rambling as the driver slapped the reigns.

"It's been a long time since I've been in one, but I'm sure the stench hasn't improved."

Confusion must have shown on my face. "You're wondering why the wife of your master was ever in a holding cell." She laughed.

"I am Rajif's seventh wife, purchased at a bride market before you were born. My parents died, and my uncles didn't want an extra mouth to feed. They sold me just after I marked my thirteenth year. I'm little more than a slave as far as his other wives are concerned but being his spouse does have clout in the slave market.'

"At least last night wasn't as cold as normal." Derora's nonstop chatter brought a bit of comfort. "It has been so warm, especially for Cheshvan. Yahweh must have been watching over you."

The blankets and the rising sun gave me back my speech, "Where are we going?"

"Rajif has a large estate between Resen and Calah, though you probably haven't heard of either. Both met their demise with Nineveh almost two hundred years ago. We'll be there before the afternoon meal."

My stomach started to protest.

"Oh my, how long since you've eaten?"

"I had some cheese and bread about dawn yesterday."

"I'm so sorry. Here I am chatting away and didn't even think about you being hungry. I packed a small basket. I had no idea how long it might take me to find you. Fortunately, Yahweh took me right to your holding area first. He told me I'd find you there. That's why I insisted we search even when the guard said he'd released everyone."

The fruit and water tamed my stomach as she continued. I smiled and wondered if she ever kept still.

"I'm talking too much," she finally said. "I'm sorry."

"Oh no, please. I'm enjoying a little normal conversation for a change."

"Well, let me hear about you. What happened to your family?"

"They all live in Jerusalem. Except my brother. Avraham still cares for the king's horses in Susa."

Derora gasped, "But your papers said you were orphaned and had been sold to give you a home."

"They also said my name was Mara."

"So, I take it that's not right either?"

"No, I'm Adira bat . . ." I paused remembering Elizabeth's warning.

"Adira bat what?"

I should have known my curious new friend wouldn't settle for my hesitation.

"At the last place, I served under a kind woman. Elizabeth told me I should just be Adira."

"Why?"

"She didn't have time to tell me. The merchant who bought me waited outside."

"And why did they call you Mara?"

"I have no idea. I didn't discover my new name until I stepped onto the platform."

"Well, until I find out why someone felt the need to give you a new name, I think we'll introduce you as Mara. Just to be safe."

Derora paused and pointed to a small walled village surrounded by fields and groves, "There it is. Your new home."

Fifty-Four

Cheshvan 11, 440 B.C.

A young man about my age pulled open one door of the gate allowing ample room for our horse and cart to enter.

"Is this the new slave, g'veret?" he asked.

"Yes, Asshur."

"They want her in the kitchen right away. Master promised Amin help yesterday when he left, then brought nothing back."

"After I get her settled in, I'll bring her to the kitchen."

"Amin expects her in . . ."

Derora cut him off. "Asshur, please explain to Amin, she'll be there soon."

The young man bowed his head, "Yes, g'veret."

As he walked away, I took in the view of the enormous courtyard. What I'd thought was a village from the hill was an estate.

"My husband tells me I'm too familiar with the servants," Derora laughed. "Follow me."

She led me to a small serai the largest manor I'd ever seen outside the palaces of Artaxerxes.

"You'll share a room with four other girls. In addition to the kitchen, you'll work in the laundry, and come summer, they may have you work in the fields."

The room looked clean. On the wall, fifteen iron pegs served as clothing hooks, thin sleeping robes hung on four of them. "I'll get you some extra robes and a sleeping gown. Rajif likes his wives to show off his wealth, so Shiva and I—Shiva is wife number six—bring our cast-off robes to the slaves. Rajif is so wasteful."

"Wash off the road dust," Derora pointed to a basin of water on a small table in the corner, "and I'll find you something more presentable to wear. I'm guessing they gave you that robe for the auction."

"Yes, g'veret."

She quickly returned with two robes for day and one for night. Between the water and the clean garments, I felt almost human.

Amin made sure that feeling didn't last. The moment Derora stepped out of the kitchen, he started.

"We needed you here hours ago. I don't have time to train you now. You will not be late in my kitchen. Do you understand?"

"Yes, reebon." I focused on the floor.

"You'll work with Ziba today."

A young girl stepped forward and handed me a large pail of slop. Using both hands, she picked up a second and headed out the door.

"Don't be at that pig pen all day!" Amin yelled behind us.

After Derora's chatter, Ziba's silence left a hole.

"I'm Mara," I introduced myself after we got rid of the weight of the slop from the buckets. The name felt strange on my lips.

"Amin doesn't like us to talk. He says idle chatter keeps us from our work."

I got the feeling the phrase had been drilled into the young girl's mind. She looked to be a few years older than Jok and Jon, though they would be a year older now. I blinked back tears.

Ziba's responsibility included cleaning up after everyone else. We collected discarded utensils and emptied buckets of scraps.

I wondered how many people this kitchen fed. The staff rivaled that of the king. Three women kneaded dough while five others cut vegetables and sliced cheese. Three men assisted Amin with pots over six fires lining one outside wall of the room. Two more young girls washed dishes from the last meal as the rest prepared for the next.

I'd obviously missed midday meal. Fortunately, the portions I'd eaten in the Tiridata's house had prepared me to keep going on very little food. I hadn't seen my reflection in a looking glass or a pond in so long—I wondered if my face looked thin.

Each time I carried a bucket outside, the sun hung lower in the western sky. This time of year, it set so early. The animal pens sat on the highest part of the estate, allowing for a grand view of the purple and orange sky. Jerusalem lay in the direction of that sunset. My family would be sitting down to dinner soon. I wondered if it was Shabbat. I'd lost track of days. Soon Ab would begin to share the stories of Israel and Yahweh. Who would have ever thought I might one day long for Jerusalem?

The bell outside the kitchen brought me back to the present. We hurried back to the house where Ziba picked up a platter and handed it to me. Picking up a second, she led me through a large door into the great hall. More than forty tables with five or six cushions each littered the room.

For an hour, Ziba and the girls who'd been washing dishes handed me platter after platter as we carried them to and from the great hall. Once again, my stomach complained.

On one trip into the kitchen, I noticed those who'd been kneading carried larger platters with choice food through a second door on the other side of the kitchen. Did a second grand hall lay on the other side of that door?

When we brought the last empty platter back to the kitchen, I hoped we'd get to eat, but Amin had other ideas.

"Ziba, you and the new girl start with the slop buckets and dishes." He sent the other girls back in to scrub the two dining halls while he ate with the men and older women.

As we washed platters, I noticed sounds of chatter begin to fill the room. While I couldn't make out the hushed tones over the clank of pots and goblets, the tension eased with the broken silence.

With the cleaning done, Ziba motioned toward a small table in the corner of the room. Only five of us remained unfed, but the quantity of food didn't look like it would stretch.

When I started to say something, Ziba shook her head. Apparently, conversation was limited to the seasoned kitchen staff.

It was late when my new friend led the way to our room. The others we'd shared a meal with joined us. Still, no one said a word.

"I'm sorry for the silent treatment," Ziba explained after she closed the door. "No one speaks outside this room unless Amin or a noble speaks to us."

My face betrayed my thoughts.

"I know it sounds ludicrous, but Amin has ears everywhere, and breaking any of Amin's rules brings lashes."

"He can do that?"

"He can and he will. He uses the whip himself. I think he delights in it."

"Isn't he a slave, too?"

"He's a paid servant, and he enjoys making certain we understand there's a difference."

As we changed, Ziba made the introductions, "Mara, this is Mahsa and Mahin. They sleep there." She pointed to the two mats closest to the hearth.

"Sisters?" I asked.

"Twins," the girls said in unison.

"And this is Sarah."

"Are you from Israel?" I asked this young girl with a Jewish name.

"I don't know. My parents died before I can remember, and I came here to be with my aunt. She's one of the master's wives, but she didn't want me, so when I was six, she moved me to the kitchen."

I gasped. I couldn't imagine any of my family ever relegating me to slavery.

The twins couldn't have been more than ten, but their dark skin and deep brown eyes promised they'd be beauties one day. Sarah looked to be just a little older.

Sarah added a log to the fire as Ziba blew out the lamps and we settled down to sleep. Though exhausted, my mind raced. I missed my parents so much it hurt. I'd lost all hope of them finding me when I left Tiridata's estate, and now that everyone thought my name was Mara . .

.

Fifty-Five

For the next two weeks, we began before dawn and worked well past sunset, stopping only to break our fast and eat a meal before bed. I saw Derora a few times when she stopped in to give Amin instructions, but she only sent a nod my way. I'm sure she didn't want to put me on Amin's bad side.

Of course, I did that myself soon enough.

Amin's rule of silence was difficult for me. Nearly every day I caught myself just before I said something—until I didn't. It was a simple, "Can I help you with that?" to one of the older kitchen slaves that brought a gasp from around the room. Amin just stared at me.

All day I wondered how I'd avoided punishment, but after the evening meal, I realized I was wrong. As Ziba and the twins took their place on the cushions, Amin spoke above the hushed tones of his table.

"You may finish cleaning."

So, no food this evening would be my punishment. I'd gone without food before. It was better than the lashes.

I finished the kitchen while everyone ate, then Amin sent the rest to their serais.

"I think the floors need an extra scrubbing tonight."

Still better than a lashing.

As I scrubbed, I remembered life in Susa. Sabba told stories of cruel slave masters, but they'd always been just stories. Artaxerxes and his father had made it clear slaves could be treated no worse than a paid servant. I started to wonder how much negotiating Ab did to get permission to move us to Jerusalem. Ab and Dohd longed for the freedom of Jerusalem. Every Passover my father made certain we understood the hardship Israel faced under Pharaoh, but like my grandfather's memories, I saw them more like bedtime tales rather than history.

By the time I finished, I was tired and hungry. I considered curling up on the cushions beside the table, but unsure of what rule I might violate, I headed to my serai.

Fifty-Six

The nights grew cold, but unlike my former master, Rajif provided no additional blankets. The fire in the small room helped, but with only one piece of wood each night, the room cooled considerably before morning.

Each night, we chatted a few minutes before we fell asleep from exhaustion. I discovered Ziba had lost her parents. They'd been slaves of Rajif and had died of the plague before she turned four.

All five of us welcomed the heat of the kitchen fires each morning. We rose well before dawn to begin our daily routine. Amin arrived just before the sun. Prior to his arrival, we had to collect the eggs and milk. The generous animals provided at least ten dozen eggs and sixteen buckets of milk. Amin checked the milk vat and egg bin as soon as he arrived to make sure we'd accomplished our assignments. By the time he got to the kitchen, the first run of bread would be rising, and yesterday's milk would be in cheesecloth.

Morning after morning repeated itself. I lost track of days; Shabbat existed only in my memory. Fortunately, the new moons and the weather allowed me to measure time.

At least once every moon, someone crossed Amin. Mahsa

dropped a knife and scrubbed the floor alone. When the bread didn't rise properly, the one Amin called Hettie received ten lashes.

So, when I spilled a bucket of milk on my way back to the kitchen, I wondered what my punishment might be.

I didn't look up when Amin entered the kitchen. I hoped he wouldn't notice just one bucket of milk missing from the vat.

"Why is the milk low today?"

I kept slicing cheese as I spoke, "I tripped and spilled one bucket, reebon."

His footsteps echoed in the silence.

"You know you have to be punished for this?" I could feel his breath on my neck. "Since you've been here less than six moons, I'll go easy on you."

"Thank you, reebon."

But I wondered what 'easy on you' meant. Perhaps I'd just have to scrub the floor tonight. The punishment began the moment I sat to eat. He had one of the servants remove my plate from the table.

"Since you're not going to break your fast yet, you might as well get the kitchen cleaned so we can start preparing midday meal."

"Yes, reebon."

The rest of the day moved on as usual until evening milking time.

"I think you can milk on your own tonight. Plus, you can check the chickens, too."

I started with the hen house. Checking all those roosting nests alone would take time. Most laid their eggs at night, but each evening we found another couple dozen.

In the barns, I headed toward the goats. Eight trips to and from the barns should take care of it.

The nannies were restless. They could feel the storm coming.

"Come on, girls. I'm in enough trouble as it is. Help me out here."

"We talk to the goats now?" A voice laughed from the other end of the barn.

Fear gripped me. Would the barn hand tell Amin I'd broken the silence? "I'm sorry. I didn't know anyone was here."

"No need to apologize. I like to tease." I looked up when I heard the footsteps round the stall gate, but just as quickly I lowered my eyes again.

"I am so sorry, reebon. I didn't mean to disturb you."

Where had this handsome noble come from?

"You didn't disturb me. I'm just taking the shortcut through the barns from the stables and hoping I didn't miss the evening meal."

I kept my eyes on the goat. "They were still serving when I came out; you'd better hurry."

The boots headed toward the door, then turned back.

"What's your name. Just occurred to me I haven't seen you before."

"Ad . . . Mara"

"Admara, how unusual."

"No reebon, just Mara."

I kept staring at the now fully milked goat wondering how to proceed.

"Well, I hope to see you again, Admara."

"Have a good evening, reebon."

I dared to look up as I heard him walk away. Though all I could see was his wavy brown hair and confident gait, the smile and lovely brown eyes that had held my gaze for those few moments when I thought he was a barn hand lingered in my memory. I watched until he walked around the house toward the main entrance.

By the time I finished, everyone had eaten. Hettie and the twins were almost done in the kitchen. I picked up the slop buckets to deliver them to the pigs, but Amin stopped me.

"Leave one here."

Only Amin remained in the kitchen when I returned. I grabbed the scrub buckets. I could see he saved the floor for me.

"Wait. Come with me and bring the slop bucket."

He led me down the stairs to the root cellar. I'd been down here before. Urns of potatoes and beets lined the walls.

Amin pointed to the cushions in the corner, "This will be your sleeping chamber for the next three nights, and you'll eat from the slop bucket to help you remember to not be so wasteful." He took a step toward me. I tried to back up, but my leg bumped an urn. "Unless you'd like to share my sleeping chamber," he whispered.

I swallowed back the bile, "This chamber will be just fine, sir."

He leaned in just a bit more, but I turned my head away.

He stomped up the stairs. "Get up here and scrub this floor," he yelled.

Halfway to the well, I realized Amin must have limits on his power. Perhaps Rajif didn't allow him to violate us without permission. Or perhaps he prefers to imagine his victims as willing participants. The thought made me shudder.

By the time I got to my cool, dark sleeping chamber, my stomach welcomed anything, even the slop bucket. I moved the pomegranate rinds to see if I might find a scrap of bread or a corner of cheese. A piece of cheesecloth lay beneath the rinds. That's odd. The cheesecloth should have been washed out to be reused. I lifted it out to wash tomorrow. I'm sure Amin counted every piece.

But I soon discovered the cheesecloth didn't make its way to the bucket by accident. Wrapped inside were two pieces of cheese, a piece of fruit, and a small loaf of barley bread. One of the others knew what the remaining slop bucket meant. I ate half the treasure and saved the rest for morning.

On each of the next two evenings, a piece of cheesecloth hidden under rinds protected a meager meal. I wished I knew who'd taken the risk. I wanted to show my appreciation.

Sleeping in the cellar could have been worse. I missed the few minutes of chatter with Ziba and the girls before we fell asleep. Honestly, the sound of any voice other than Amin's would be welcome. Especially the deep voice of the stranger from the barn.

Fifty-Seven

Shevat 3, 440 B.C.

A heavy snow had coated the courtyard since the middle of Kislev, and each person who entered the kitchen brought slush and ice. On top of our other duties, Ziba and I were now charged with keeping the floor dry. So, when Mahsa slipped on a puddle spilling the contents of the bread tray, everyone knew Amin's wrath would soon follow.

Just after we finished serving midday meal, the head kitchen steward called, "Ziba, Mara, Mahsa, please see me outside."

"You won't need those," he said as we picked up our wraps.

Amin waited near the hitching posts. He instructed us to pull our robes down to our waist and hold on to the rough wood, but before anyone could disrobe, I interrupted.

"Master, this was my fault. I missed the water on the floor. Allow me to take all the lashes."

Ziba started to speak, but I stopped her. "I beg you, please don't let these two be punished for my carelessness."

Ziba sighed. I saw Mahsa's silent tears fall to the ground.

"You two get back to work," Amin yelled.

Amin walked up to me and ran the back of his hand across my cheek. "We could arrange for you to avoid these lashes altogether," he whispered.

I looked up, and for the first time since I'd met him, I locked my eyes on his. "I'll take the lashes."

His eyes filled with rage as he stepped back.

"Disrobe, then!"

I pulled my robe down so my back was exposed and held the folds over my front.

"Hold on to the post," Amin growled.

"I prefer to take my lashes this way."

"You'll have extra if you disobey."

I stood my ground, "Do what you must." I surprised even myself. The last eighteen moons had toughened me.

It was hard to keep from falling without holding on to the post, but I was determined not to expose myself. Amin's anger came through every strike.

"Ten for Ziba," he hissed.

"Ten for Mahsa."

Now I could feel the blood running down my back.

"Ten for your mistake."

I refused to let myself pass out.

"And ten for your insolence."

With the last strike, I fell into the snow.

"You have ten minutes to get back into the kitchen."

The last thing I remember was thinking how good the snow felt on my wounds.

When I came to, I knew my ten-minute limit had passed, but I just stayed there with my eyes closed as the snow enveloped me.

Perhaps if I laid here long enough, death would take me away from all of this. My family had already mourned their loss. I thought of Ab, Em, and Dohd. They were all so strong. What would they do right now? I knew they'd never give up, but I just didn't want to do this anymore. The hunger, the cruelty. It was too much. How did my parents stay so steadfast?

The sounds of Ab and Dohd praying filled my head. Their voices wove together playing a harmony only I could hear. Every prayer I'd ever heard reverberated in my memory, calling me to join them.

"Yahweh, God of my father and mother, God of my Dohd Nehemiah," I whispered. "Hear my cry. Heal my wounds or send me to Sheol. I can't do this anymore. It is good they changed my name. I've never felt I lived up to Adira. Never did I feel strong, noble, or powerful. Mara fits. My life has become bitter. Yahweh, if you are as real as my parents believe, rescue me."

A soft hand touched my shoulder just as I finished. I opened my eyes to find Derora kneeling in the snow beside me.

"Mara, what happened?'

I tried to sit up, but pain seared through my back. "I crossed Amin."

"Oh, my dear. How many lashes did he give you?"

A look of horror crossed her face as I whispered, "Forty."

"Forty?!" She threw her wrap over me and stood. "Let me get some help."

She quickly returned with two strong men and a canvas.

"Take her to my room," Derora instructed.

"G'veret, the master would not approve. We don't want any

trouble."

"You did not cause this trouble."

The pain was excruciating as the men lifted me onto the canvas, but I didn't feel it for long.

Fifty-Eight

Shevat 4, 440 B.C.

The creak of the door woke me. *Where am I?* When I tried to roll over to see who was there, I remembered.

"You summoned us, g'veret?" The hushed voice sounded like Ziba's.

"Yes, Ziba. I don't want to wake Mara, but I'm trying to figure out what she did to deserve forty lashes."

A sobbing Mahsa spoke, "Nothing, g'veret. It was all my fault."

Ziba's voice comforted the young girl. "Hush, now. It wasn't your fault. G'veret, someone brought snow in on their feet. Mara and I try to keep it cleaned up, but we missed a spot, and Mahsa slipped and spilled a tray of bread."

"He intended to give us all lashes!" Mahsa's sobs increased.

"Mara volunteered to take them all for us."

"She did what?!" Derora's shock filled the room.

"Just what I said, she took all our lashes."

"And more," Mahsa cried out.

"More? What do you mean more?"

"G'veret." Ziba's voice again. "Amin sent us back to the kitchen, but we couldn't just leave her."

"Oh, but I wish we had." I hoped Ziba was holding Mahsa. "Poor, poor Mara." I wanted to console the tiny girl, but I didn't have enough strength to open my eyes.

"We heard Amin offer to spare her the lashes in exchange for . . ."

"In exchange for what, Ziba?" Even Derora's hushed tones couldn't hide her anger.

"Well, g'veret," Ziba paused. "You know . . ."

"I understand."

"Then he gave her all our lashes and ten extra. We ran to the kitchen so Amin wouldn't catch us watching, but I saw her fall just as we opened the door. That's why I asked Sarah to bring you the message. I didn't know who else to tell."

"You did well, Ziba. Here, take this tray and pitcher back with you so Amin will know you brought my dinner as I asked. Don't worry, I'll take care of Mara."

I wanted to call out to Ziba and Mahsa to thank them for sending help, but the slight movement made everything start to spin.

I flinched as pain brought me out of sleep the next time. Someone was cleaning my wounds.

"I'm so, sorry. I didn't mean to wake you." It was Derora. "I'm almost done."

I could tell she tried to be gentle, but every touch brought fire to my back. "That stable hand in Hamath didn't prepare me for this," I groaned.

"What?" Derora walked around to face me.

"I was beaten a couple of times in Hamath, but I . . ." I paused to breathe through the pain. "I always felt worse for the stable boy they forced to beat me than I did for myself." I took another deep breath. "I think he must have held back."

"Oh, you poor dear."

A knock on the door interrupted.

"Derora." a man's voice came with a knock from the hallway. Derora's soft footsteps gave way to the creak of the door. "Amin reports you're hiding one of his kitchen slaves," the man continued. "You know I give the stewards full reign of their area. Return her at once."

"Really, Rajif? Would you like to see what he's done to your property? Remember, I saw the bill of sale." Her voice grew closer. "You paid a hefty price for this one."

"Amin thinks you're overreacting because you have a soft spot for her since you had to rescue her and she's a . . ." He gasped. "Amin did this?"

"Yes, all because a young girl slipped on wet snow and spilled some bread. I'd like to care for her until she's healed."

"Yes, that will be . . ." *Is the man gagging? How bad does my back look?* "I will speak with Amin."

Fifty-Nine

Some Days later in Shevat 440 B.C.

I don't know how many days passed as I slipped in and out of consciousness. Each time I woke, Derora held a cloth soaked with water or wine to my lips. Ab and Em and my siblings laughing as we listened to Ab's stories filled my dreams, and in between, I heard Derora's prayers and the deep voice of the barn stranger.

When my eyes managed to stay open for more than five minutes, my stomach complained because I hadn't fed it, but the slightest movement promised to bring up even the water and wine. With every rise to relieve myself, I either passed out over the chamber pot or filled it with vomit.

One day I finally sat on the side of Derora's raised bed for more than a minute. She immediately asked Ziba to bring a small basket of bread and cheese.

"How long have I been here, g'veret?"

"Six days."

"I'm so sorry to have troubled you for so long."

Derora smiled, "It was no trouble to care for such a brave woman."

I could feel the color rush to my face. "I felt a lot more fear than courage, g'veret."

"You took lashes for those young girls and resisted Amin's advances."

"Since his first flirtation, I wondered why he never forced himself on me. More than once his look made me fear his intentions."

Derora smiled gently. "My husband is a kind man. He could never beat servants himself and doesn't know how to keep them in line. To keep his stewards happy, he gives each one a free hand with their staff, but he draws the line at forcing themselves on women. I told you he bought me at a bride market, right?"

"Yes."

"He needed a wife who could give him a son, but he wooed me before he had relations with me. He often gets drunk when he buys kitchen slaves because he hates the way Amin treats them, but he's too weak to challenge Amin's tactics."

"How long before Amin will expect me back in the kitchen?"

"Never," Derora answered as she carried the empty food basket toward the door. She sat the vessel out in the hall.

My shocked face brought a light laugh. "All of my husband's wives have personal slaves. The first two have six each. I have none. I can't bring myself to own another human. The household slaves take care of my room. Rajif constantly asks me to take on one slave to keep up his wealthy appearance, so I told him I would take you."

Relief flooded my being and tears flooded my eyes. "Thank you, g'veret. Thank you, so much."

"I think we'll get along well. Now, you need a few more days rest before you begin your duties."

She was right. Eating had taken everything out of me.

The sound of several people moving about woke me, but when I finally found the strength to sit up, I saw only one young girl filling a large tub.

"Look who's awake," Derora said as she entered the room. "I think your wounds have healed enough you can stand a bath."

A proper bath sounded lovely. A small basin of cool water had greeted me every morning before my lashes.

The warm water stung, but it felt wonderful too. Derora gently washed my back while the young girl bathed the rest of me. I felt a bit embarrassed, but it took my full energy to stay upright in the tub. Though exhausted, the warm water they poured over my head and having my dark curls scrubbed refreshed me. I missed being clean.

By the time they put the linen robe around me, I could barely walk back to the bed. "We'll get you some oils after you've rested."

"Shouldn't I have a mat in the corner, g'veret? I can't keep sleeping in your bed." *Where had she been sleeping?*

"We'll worry about your spot in my room after you have enough energy to walk to the dining hall and back."

I didn't have the strength to argue. She covered me to keep my wet head from giving me a chill. A conversation would have been nice, but as I breathed in the smell of fresh lavender, I felt myself relax wondering when they had time to change the bedding.

"Em?" A familiar deep voice interrupted my dreams.

"Avraham?" Had my brother come?

Derora's voice returned me to reality, "Shhh, that's just my son at the door. Go back to sleep."

Sixty

Adar 2, 440 B.C.

Each day I grew stronger. "I think I'm well enough to give you your bed back."

"Are you certain? You still sleep most of the day."

"You've been too kind already."

"Alright, tonight I'll take the bed, and you can have the cushions in the corner. But we'll give you one more week before you start to serve."

The next morning, Derora brought me two lovely robes and began asking about my past. "How long have you been a slave, Mara?"

"Merchants snatched me and my best friend just after I marked my sixteenth year, so I think it's been a year and a half."

Derora asked more questions, and I told her my story. She made me feel so comfortable.

"It sounds like Yahweh has been watching over you."

"It doesn't feel like it."

"I'm sure it doesn't. The sting on your back is too fresh. But as lovely as you are, I'm surprised you haven't been passed from man to man or sold to a brothel. A virgin with your features is worth a lot of money."

I hadn't thought of that. I'd only wondered why Yahweh hadn't allowed Ab and Dohd to find me. *Had my father's God been protecting me all this time?*

"My Ab and Dohd are men of prayer. I know they've been praying since the day I disappeared. Is this how Yahweh answers prayer?"

"Exactly. Yahweh doesn't always take us out of our situations, but he always walks with us through them. When I knew I was going to the bride market, I cried out to Yahweh to give me a kind man. He brought me to Rajif. Not only is he kind, but we've also grown to love each other, and he gave me three sons and a daughter."

"I'd never looked at prayer that way. I always thought if everything didn't go exactly as I wanted it to, Yahweh wasn't any more effective than Ahura Mazda."

"You're not alone in your thinking. But even in the story of our people, we see that when they entered the Promised Land, God didn't remove all the inhabitants so they could have peace. Instead, he went with them into every battle as long as they followed him."

"Ab used to tell us the stories of Israel. I miss his strong voice." Derora's story finally registered with me. "Wait! You have children?"

She laughed. "Yes, dear. They are the primary reason the other wives don't care for me. All six women come from nobility while I come from the bride market. Three are barren, and the others have four girls between them. My sons will inherit the estate."

"But why haven't I seen them?"

"My daughter Rebekah lives in Susa. Rajif secured a good marriage for her in Artaxerxes court. I miss her, but she and her two babies will visit in Tammuz. My oldest two sons live in Babylon and serve in the king's army. Laban's last letter says they expect a child soon. My youngest has the business head. Michael runs the estate with his father. He's off making deals right now. He'll drop in for a few days, then be gone again for weeks. But planting season starts in Nisan. You'll get to meet him then."

Sixty-One

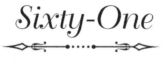

Adar 5, 440 B.C.

After a couple days of rest, I began taking on a few duties. Derora still wouldn't let me leave the room for fear I'd faint with no one nearby. I first ventured outside the chamber for food. Derora asked Damaris, the girl who'd helped me bathe, to look after me. While g'veret headed to the nobility's great hall, my new friend led me to where the servants and slaves ate.

As Ziba sat the serving bowls on our table, her eyes brightened. Kitchen servants and slaves may not be permitted to start a conversation, but my new position allowed me to introduce her to Damaris. Ziba immediately seized the opportunity. She busied herself filling goblets as we chatted.

"Mara! We've missed you! Will you be coming back?"

"I've missed you, too. I'm in the service of G'veret Derora now."

"We were afraid you'd die."

"So, I've been told."

"I'll let everyone in the kitchen know you're fine. They've all been so worried." She filled the last drink and moved to the next table.

The twins followed with the bread. I squeezed their hands as they passed by. It would be good to see them each day.

Nisan 5, 439 B.C.

Derora expected little. I felt more like a companion than a slave.

"This must have been how my sister felt when she served Queen Esther," I shared as we walked in the flower garden one Shabbat in Nisan.

"Your sister served Queen Esther? I thought you were from Jerusalem."

"Yes, but . . ."

"Em!" A deep voice interrupted from across the complex, and we both turned toward the sound.

"Michael!" Derora couldn't contain her joy.

I, on the other hand, needed a moment to recover. Exceedingly grateful his eyes were fixed on his mother as he crossed the courtyard, I could feel color rush to my face.

This was her son? I had assumed he was one of Rajif's sons the day I met him in the barn, I just hadn't put two and two . . .

"Admara?" His smiling face finally saw me as he hugged his mother.

Realizing I'd been staring, I lowered my eyes, "Just Mara, reebon."

"You two know each other?" Derora looked confused.

Michael laughed, "Not exactly. I startled her as she milked the goats back in Kislev. You remember—when I dropped in from Damascus for a day or two."

I could feel his eyes on me. I stared at the ground, still, my face heated.

"I didn't realize he was your son, g'veret."

"I'm afraid I was quite rude that day. I asked your name but didn't give you mine in return. Forgive me."

"An apology isn't necessary, reebon."

"Oh, come on, call me Michael. I'll be home from now till the last harvest. If you're serving Em, I'm sure we'll run into one another."

"Yes, reebon." I continued to focus on my feet—more to hide my glowing face than out of respect.

"Seriously, I'm Michael."

"Ok. Michael."

"Walk with me, son." Derora saved me. They chatted as I walked behind admiring his strong shoulders and curly brown locks.

What is the matter with me?

I'd had friends, including Miriam, who talked endlessly about every cute boy they saw, but I'd quickly grown bored of their game. Until now.

Sixty-Two

Sivan 14, 439 B.C.

The weather stayed cool through Nisan, Iyyar, and Sivan. I had to light fires in the mornings as well as the evenings. Derora worried about the fruit trees, but Michael assured her Yahweh had kept the killing frost away.

Thoughts of Michael consumed me. Despite the number of boys Miriam, Natalia, and I had teased one another about, none had caught my attention like this man.

My newfound faith brought me to prayer many times each day, and more than one included a cry to Yahweh to stop the feelings. A nobleman could never care about his mother's slave.

By Tammuz, the harvest filled the yard outside Derora's window. As I mended her day gowns, I could see Michael inspecting every barrel. He directed Amin to the fruits and vegetables he could move to my previous sleeping chamber then bartered with merchant after merchant as they loaded wagons with the fresh produce.

Michael towered over most of the merchants. And watching him hoist those barrels made it obvious he did more than just supervise in the fields. Even under his short loose robe, I could see his arms and back define and tighten as he lifted the merchants' heavy purchases without assistance.

"That window seat is a lovely place to do the mending, isn't it?" I nearly dropped the robe out the window.

"Yes, g'veret. I'm so sorry. I didn't hear you return."

"And the view is magnificent this time of year."

Do I hear a hint of laughter in her voice. Does she know how I feel about Michael?

Michael hadn't been to see his mother since he dropped by in the garden. I'm sure they took the evening meal together, but he'd been too busy for any leisurely visit. No, it had to be my imagination brought on by a guilty conscience.

"Amin always requests extra help from the household slaves as he prepares fruit, vegetables, and grain for winter storage. He asked for you specifically."

Fear gripped me.

Derora sat down next to me. "Mara, he won't be able to touch you. You belong to me now. And as much as I detest that phrase, it will protect you. He will treat you with the utmost respect or face my wrath. He'd like your help because you know your way around the kitchen, and you work hard. I think he regrets his hasty decision.'

"The only reason I didn't tell him no is because you'll have a chance to see your friends for a few weeks. Plus, your status will allow you to disregard his no-talking rule. You can feel free to chat, and the worst he can do is send you back. It will only be three or four hours each afternoon through the end of harvest."

My fear turned to excitement. Derora was right. I missed my young friends.

Sixty-Three

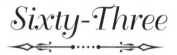

As I entered the kitchen the next day, I could feel the light mood. A soft buzz filled the room. I quickly found a place near Ziba and the twins. We salted some things and others found their way into clay pots filled with vinegar. Some days, I ran the millstones, and on others, I helped with the everyday kitchen chores. The physical work felt good. I'd grown lazy serving Derora.

One day near the end of the season, the twins invited me to gather eggs with them. I grabbed a basket and headed toward the barnyard. I must have been enjoying the conversation a bit too much because as I rounded the corner of the goat shed, I ran right into one of the nobles. My basket and I both landed in the dust. The startled twins ran ahead, and as I tried to gain composure, a familiar voice squelched my apology.

"I believe that may have been just as much my fault as yours." He reached out a hand. The tingling warmth surprised me as I accepted his offer. I pulled away as soon as I was on my feet.

Michael retrieved my basket as I dusted myself off. "Thank you, reebon."

"Admara," I know I should correct him, but it was so close to my real name, and it felt like a secret between the two of us. "When will you start to call me Michael?"

"Thank you, Michael," I said with a smile and my eyes lowered.

I nearly melted when he touched my chin.

"Feel free to look me in the eye. I'm sure my mother doesn't approve of your lowered head. And you really shouldn't hide something Yahweh created so perfectly."

His teasing smile brought one of my own. "I will do my best to remember, Michael," I said adding a bit of emphasis to his name. "I should probably go help the girls gather the eggs now." I tried to excuse myself, but his finger still held my chin.

The few seconds of silence drew my eyes to his lips, and I wondered if he might try to kiss me. I realized I'd let my imagination run away again when he slowly lowered his hand. "I look forward to running into you again soon, Admara. Perhaps not quite so literally next time."

As we each turned to leave, I laughed and fought the urge to take one final peek.

At least the hard work kept my mind off Michael. I enjoyed my service to Derora, but it gave me too much time to think. "G'veret, now that I'm completely healed, shouldn't I keep your chamber clean to relieve the other household servants a bit?"

She looked surprised, "I've never heard a slave offer to do more work."

"Forgive me if I spoke out of turn."

"Oh no. It's not that. I'm serious. No slave or servant I've ever known has ever asked for more work."

"I guess I'm just used to keeping busy. I've been caring for the house, the midday meal, and my younger brothers since I turned eleven. Helping with the harvest reminded me how much better I feel when I'm productive."

"Did something happen to your mother?"

"No. She left early each morning and didn't return till almost time for the evening meal. She cooked for the queens and the concubines in Artaxerxes' court. That's why my sister was chosen as one of Queen Esther's personal maidservants."

"Tell me more about your family."

"I'm sorry. I shouldn't be going on like this. You're just so easy to talk to. Elizabeth, the kitchen steward at the last place I served told me I should keep that to myself."

"You can tell me. You once told me Mara wasn't your real name."

"Yes, I'm Adira bat Hanani."

Her face showed she didn't understand the need to be secretive.

"I believe Elizabeth wanted to keep people from knowing the name of my dohd."

"Who is your uncle?" She sounded gravely concerned.

"Nehemiah ben Hacaliah, former cupbearer to King Artaxerxes."

She shook her head in understanding, "And current governor of Jerusalem."

"Yes. You've heard of him?"

"Mara, your uncle has made quite a name for himself in Artaxerxes' empire. We heard he rebuilt the entire wall of Jerusalem in less than two moons."

"Well, the outside wall and the gates. They were completing the inner wall when I was taken."

"Your friend Elizabeth was right. Until we can find the right time, you mustn't tell anyone."

"I've never understood why."

"Someone made a grave mistake kidnapping the niece of the governor. Now everyone who owns you is in danger of losing their estate or even their life. I'm guessing that's why your last master changed your name at the market."

"But Ab and Dohd would never retaliate like that."

"Even my Rajif would never believe he was safe if he knew your identity. He'd either sell you or kill you to protect himself."

A gasp escaped, and I pulled my wrap closer.

Sixty-Four

Winter 439 B.C.

My third winter away from my family passed uneventfully. This year I stayed warmer when I had to go outside thanks to Derora's cast-off robes. She let me take four wraps to Ziba, Sarah, and the twins.

Michael stopped to visit his mother each time he came home, but I always found excuses to leave the room. I never imagined I'd feel physical pain knowing I could never be with him. Fortunately, the water pitcher needed to be filled often and trays had to be returned to the kitchen.

Nisan 438 B.C.

With Spring came the merchants. They traveled the southern road during the heavy snows, so by Nisan, all the wives looked forward to the wagons in the courtyard.

During one visit, Derora sent me to get her fresh oils. She enjoyed the ones that came from Babylon. As one trader allowed me to smell the variety of fragrances, I felt someone walk up behind me.

"I'll get that, Ahab," my heart leapt at the sound of Michael's voice. "I assume it's for my mother."

I nodded.

"Do you like this?" He held up a large amethyst on a gold chain.

"It's lovely. Your mother will approve."

"What about you?"

"I've never worn any kind of jewels."

"What about this?" He said as he lifted a polished bone bracelet with silver and gold inlays.

I gasped. It was beautiful.

"This too, Ahab."

Michael settled with the merchant, and I took Derora's oils.

"Will you walk with me in the garden?"

"I really should get back." *Before my racing heart explodes,* I finished silently.

"You can blame me."

"I have a lot of work to do, reebon." I lowered my eyes with the title of respect.

"I insist." He sounded irritated.

We walked into the flower garden in silence. Only a couple of the plants had buds. He walked toward a bench and motioned for me to sit.

When he sat next to me, I found it difficult to breathe.

"Mara," he began with a serious tone. I missed the nickname. "What have I done?"

I looked up surprised. "What do you mean?"

"You avoid me every time I come home. I can see Em at meals. She almost always eats alone unless Ab joins her. None of the other wives will even sit with her. I'm sure she wonders why I've been stopping by her chamber so often."

He'd come to see me. I looked down to hide my smile.

He let a few seconds of silence pass. "So, I'm not to know what I've done? Is it the teasing? I can call you by your correct name if you want. I just thought. . ."

"Oh, no!" I interrupted, "It's not that." I couldn't let him stop calling me Admara.

"What then?"

"I am a slave." I couldn't say his name or look at him.

He took my chin again and raised my face to see his smiling eyes and lips. Oh, those lips. *He should stop doing that; I can't keep my composure with his finger there.*

"My sweet Admara." He grabbed my hands. "So, you've been avoiding me because you think my status won't allow us to be together."

Though I smiled, tears threatened, so I answered with a nod.

He slipped the bracelet on my wrist. "Will you accept this gift as a reminder I plan to convince my father to release you to me?"

"Didn't you buy that for your mother?" I choked out the words.

"No, Em would have preferred the amethyst." He smiled, and as he stood to leave, he kissed my forehead.

I obviously didn't hide my disappointment well, because he laughed softly as he said, "I will save your lips for the day I can tell you Ab has freed you."

Sixty-Five

Tammuz 2, 438 B.C.

The heat of my nineteenth summer came well before I marked the year. For weeks, the warmth made it worse than any I'd felt in Susa. Though small storms came through almost every afternoon, the cooling effect was short-lived because the rain just increased the humidity. Derora and I walked to the river to cool off most mornings.

While the combination of heat and humidity brought discomfort to humans, it made for a great growing season. From dawn to dusk, Michael worked in the fields, and each afternoon, I worked alongside Ziba, Sarah, and the twins.

I hadn't seen Michael except in passing until one afternoon the rain lasted longer than usual.

"Amin, may I borrow Mara for a short while?" The voice made my heart race.

"She belongs to your mother, Master Michael. What you do with her is no concern of mine."

Taking off the apron that protected my hand-me-down elegance, I followed Michael to the garden. I wondered if he'd talked to his father.

"I guess this must be our bench," he laughed as he waited for me to sit before joining me.

"Admara, I've missed you so much. The fields haven't given me a moment's peace this year. And I don't know if you've noticed, but Ab hasn't returned from his spring buying trip. He headed to Jerusalem this year to trade, and that's a long journey."

"I know that too well!"

He looked confused. "Really?"

"Yes," I laughed, "I come from Jerusalem."

"I guess I don't know much about you, do I? When did your parents die?"

"Ab and Em still live in Jerusalem with my sister and two of my brothers and perhaps a niece or nephew by now."

"They had to sell you?"

"No, but it's a long story. Someday I'll share it with you."

"Well, then, tell me something else about yourself."

"There's not much to tell."

"Sweet Admara, I want to know you better."

"Okay. Let me think." My mind raced as I tried to remember a time when I could do as I pleased. "I love to wade in the cool river on hot days, no matter how unladylike and childish it is!"

And I love the sound of your deep laugh. My thoughts continued.

"I have to get back to the fields, but I wanted you to know I haven't forgotten my promise." And with a soft kiss on my forehead, he escorted me back to the kitchen.

Sixty-Six

Rajif returned from his journey just after I marked my nineteenth year. On the evening of his return, he visited Derora. I don't think he even noticed me mending on the window seat.

"Derora, I have exciting news. I've found a good match for Michael." My heart sank. "One of the leading tradesmen from Damascus has a daughter marrying age."

"Have you told your son yet?"

"No, he's working late in the fields today. I'll tell him tomorrow, but I wanted you to know."

Was it the setting sun or the tears that made the mending difficult to see?

Rajif pulled Derora close, "I've been gone for moons. Perhaps you'd join me in my chamber tonight?"

"I would love to, my lord," Derora smiled.

And just as abruptly as he'd entered, Rajif was gone.

Derora sent me to have the tub and hot water brought to her room. I worked in silence as I helped her prepare.

"My Michael," she said wistfully, "finally marrying. It seems like yesterday his sisters came crying about the snakes and frogs he brought into their room." She laughed. My mistress had no idea the pain she inflicted on my heart. "He always loved being outside. During a growing season like this, I'd drag him to the river every night to get rid of the mud and grime. He started going into the fields in his tenth season and took over the production of the fields by the time he turned sixteen. Marriage . . . I've tried not to think about my baby getting married."

My silent prayer of self-pity blocked the rest of her chatter. *Yahweh, I thought you'd finally shown me a way out of this life. Why did you bring Michael to me only to rip him away? Almighty God, I'm not sure my heart can handle another loss. Please save me from this hurt.*

I wondered if the Creator minded that all my first real prayers have been selfish cries.

I escorted Derora down the corridor to Rajif's chamber then returned to cry on my cushions in the corner.

Since there was no one to hear, I prayed out loud between the sobs. "Yahweh, God of Ab and Dohd, I know I should be more grateful. I've heard Em pray. She always offers so much praise, but honestly, I don't see much praiseworthy right now."

"Look harder."

Where did that voice come from? I sat silently for a few minutes waiting to hear it again. My imagination must be running wild tonight.

"I'm a slave. When I should be home enjoying nieces and nephews and perhaps married myself, I sit here nothing more than property."

"You are much more." There it was again, almost audible, yet I felt it deep within.

"Yahweh, hear my cry like you hear the prayers of Dohd Nehemiah. Grant me freedom like you freed my people from Egypt. Grant me success like you prospered the armies of King David."

It was in the remembering of Ab's stories I found words of praise.

"Yahweh, I praise you for the victories of Israel. I praise you for bringing your people back to Jerusalem. Thank you for the kindness of King Cyrus and his descendants. Thank you that life in Susa was so good I didn't realize I was a slave. I praise you for Ab and his knack for telling the ancient stories, for Em and her lessons, and the love of my sister and brothers."

My heart started to fill as I began to realize the truth, "I am so grateful that you delivered me from Amin and my last mistress. I praise you that even though I'm a slave, I wear fine robes and sleep on satin cushions."

And somewhere in the praise, I found peace.

"Yahweh, I don't know how you did it in such a short time, but I feel my pain lifting. Creator God, I love Michael. My heart still aches for him, but I praise you for the peace you've given me to outweigh the pain."

"Because I love you more than you can imagine!" *Could that be the voice of Yahweh?*

"You love me?" Tears began to fall again. "Yahweh, you love me?" The room felt full as if large arms engulfed me. And though I was the only one in the chamber, I sensed I wasn't alone.

"Thank you, Yahweh. Thank you for loving me. I praise you for allowing me to feel your presence and hear your voice. I trust you like Dohd. Even when the enemies surrounded us, determined to stop the building of the wall, he always believed you walked with him. I understand now. I trust you to guide me and be with me even if I never find a husband, even if Michael marries another, even if I never see Ab and Em again."

The sobbing was different now, it came with a feeling of peace bigger than I can describe. Though I might have to endure more lashes or face death like the friends of Daniel, I knew Yahweh, the One and Only God, would be with me. Somewhere amid the tears and praise, I fell asleep. And though it had been late when my eyes finally closed, the next morning, I felt more rested than ever before.

Sixty-Seven

Rajif and Derora must have broken their fast in his chamber because I didn't see her until just before midday meal. Derora told me they'd slept so late they missed their opportunity to tell Michael the good news.

On the following day, my mistress and I celebrated Shabbat together. We prayed, and she shared a Psalm before she asked about the difference she saw in my countenance. I hadn't considered it might be noticeable.

"I had a long talk with Yahweh while you were gone the other night. I found so much peace. I'm sure this is the way Ab, Em, and Dohd know Him. They tried to show me all my life."

Derora surprised me with a huge hug. "I've been praying Yahweh would allow you to truly see Him." She laughed as she pulled away. "I'm sorry if I startled you! But I'm so happy for you, propriety and decorum will just have to be set aside."

A pounding on the door interrupted our conversation, but before Derora could answer, Rajif burst in.

He spoke to Derora, but he stared at me. "Our son has returned from the field, but he's not willing to accept the marriage arrangement

I've made for him. Do you have any idea why?"

"None, my lord," Derora answered honestly.

"The question was for your maid."

I lowered my head even more.

"Well?" he roared.

"Yes, reebon."

"Mara?" Derora sounded shocked. I felt so bad for her.

"Forgive me, my lord, if I've been inappropriate, but we've only talked, nothing more."

Rajif took a step toward me. "Why would you seduce a nobleman?" I'd never seen him so angry.

I stared at my feet. "I honestly did not try to seduce him, my lord. We simply enjoyed a few conversations. I can make certain it never happens again." I bit back the tears.

"You need to make sure your slave knows her place, my love. You give her too much liberty." His anger spilled onto Derora before he stormed out.

I remained very still with my head bowed as I waited for Derora's wrath.

But instead of chastising me, she began to pace. "How did I not see this?" She stopped for a moment and directed her thoughts my way, "Do you love him?"

"Yes, g'veret." I hoped she'd allow me to leave before the tears spilled.

She picked up her pacing, "Do you believe he loves you?"

I couldn't speak without tears, but a knock at the door rescued me.

"Em?" It was Michael. I wondered if Derora could hear my heart race.

"We'll finish this conversation when I return," my mistress sounded tired rather than angry.

"Em, I want to see her."

I wanted to press my ear to the door to hear Derora's side of the conversation, but I stayed where she'd left me.

"Is she alright?"

Derora still spoke too hushed to hear.

"I do not need to go for a walk." Michael's reply, on the other hand, could have been heard at the other end of the house.

"Keep your voice down and walk with me." Derora's firm voice was barely audible, but the sound of footsteps moving away from the door told me he listened.

I had held on to the hope that when Michael talked to his father, he'd convince him we should marry. I'd known better. A noble couldn't choose a slave for his first wife. He had to try to have sons through a proper arrangement. And since Michael was the product of a wife from the bride market, propriety became even more important. I'd spent enough time in Artaxerxes' court to know protocol trumped love. I'd told myself this countless times, but I'd let Michael's promise and a kiss on the forehead convince me this time would be different.

Sixty-Eight

The moon had risen high in the sky by the time Derora returned.

"I sent him to his chamber." I didn't realize my hope he'd be with her would be so obvious.

"Mara, what were you thinking?"

I had no words.

"Some masters would have had you whipped or stoned for this. Fortunately for you, Rajif doesn't have it in him."

I helped her with her outer robe.

"I told Michael he needed to stay away from you and accept this marriage arrangement to protect you. I hope you'll respect him enough to do the same. He would be devastated if you were punished for this."

"Yes, g'veret."

She said nothing as she blew out the lamp and crawled into her own bed leaving me standing in the dark.

Sixty-Nine

I didn't see Michael again until the heavy snows kept him from traveling. We didn't speak, but the sorrow in his eyes matched the heaviness in my heart.

By the next planting season, I had accepted there would never be a Michael and Admara.

Derora tried to spare me wedding details, but I overheard her making plans to travel to Damascus after harvest. Michael was betrothed. Another chance at happiness had been ripped from me, and after a few days of feeling sorry for myself, I realized I hadn't been praying.

With planting season in full swing, Michael would be in the fields, so I asked permission to go to the garden. I needed time alone to pray.

"Yahweh," I began, "what do you have in store for me? I thought it was Michael, but there must be something else. I praise you for allowing me to serve Derora. You've been good to give me as much freedom as someone in my position can have. Bless Michael and his future family." Though the thought brought tears, the prayer gave me release, and the more I prayed love for this family yet to be, the more peace I felt. I conversed with my Creator until I knew I trusted Him completely again.

I could hear Rajif's voice long before I reached Derora's chamber.

"As long as she's here, Michael won't agree to this marriage, and I've already accepted the man's pledge."

"Surely there's something else we can do, Rajif."

It's done, Derora. She leaves with the merchants' caravan this afternoon."

What! He doesn't mean . . .

"But, Rajif, I've grown very fond of her."

"Yes, and so has your son!" He growled. "Let her take anything you'd like to give her, but not enough that she could buy her freedom. Send her to the courtyard as soon as you've finished midday meal."

When I heard the door open, I slipped around a corner so Rajif wouldn't see me. As soon as the footsteps faded, I hurried to Derora.

"What should I prepare to take with me, g'veret?" Derora looked up from her weeping as I entered the room. I wanted to make this as easy on her as I could.

"I overheard Rajif." I swallowed hard to keep from crying but watching her grieve made it difficult. "It's alright, I understand. The master just wants what's best for his son."

Derora rose and pulled me close causing my own grief to spill out with hers. "Oh Mara, I prayed Rajif would change his mind, but he has to keep up appearances." We wept together until Derora restored her practical self.

"Take two nice robes and these oils and perfumes. Perhaps if you have some personal possessions, the merchants can get you a better position." She handed me a basket. Make certain you have a shawl and a blanket. And here, put this papyrus and charcoal on the bottom. Write if you have the chance. Tell me how you're doing."

"Thank you for everything, Derora."

I laid the bone bracelet on a chest in Derora's room before walking out to the merchants' wagons. The beautiful piece would just taunt me.

The merchants apparently expected guards to bring me out in chains. I enjoyed seeing their look of surprise as I joined them on my own.

The man who helped me into the back of the wagon apologized as he put shackles on my ankles. "You understand, they said I have to put these on."

"It's all right. Do what you must."

As the estate grew small in the distance, I wished I'd have said goodbye to Ziba, Sarah, and the twins. What would Michael think when he discovered I'd been sold? And I couldn't help but wonder where I'd be when I marked my twentieth year.

Seventy

Iyyar 20, 437 B.C.

I quickly realized I'd be covered in bruises by days' end. The rocking and bumping of the wagon never stopped. Even with my hands free, I couldn't keep myself from being thrown around. I'm sure the day I left Jerusalem wasn't much different, but I'd been four years younger and frightened more than I could imagine.

When we stopped for the night, the amount of food they put on my plate surprised me—cheese, bread, and stew enough to fill my belly. I'd never experienced a satisfying meal while tied up in the back of a wagon. When the sun set, I appreciated the blanket Derora had insisted I put in my basket. The Iyyar night grew cold.

For the first week, no one spoke to me. Even when we stopped at estates and small cities, they kept me hidden in the back of the wagon. My only contact with anyone was when I ate or relieved myself.

This caravan definitely didn't travel the main merchants' route. Not even the trip from Jerusalem to Damascus had been this rough. Each day we had one or two stops, and each night we slept outside the gates of the next estate. The wagon that had become my lodging seemed to be used for storage. Produce and grain, as well as clay pots and bronze pans, filled the front. I sometimes wondered if any of the mystery crates held knives, but I figured they kept those out of my reach.

After a few days with no one to talk to and nothing to do, my mind turned to everything I'd lost. As I made the mental list, I felt myself sink. Each item pulled me deeper—friends in Susa, Sabba, and Avraham. Then I lost Natalia, Ab, Em, and Dohd. Tears filled my eyes as I recalled my adventures with Miriam. I missed Elizabeth, and just when I thought I'd found a home with Derora, my own bad decision ripped that away too. All my dreams of a life with Michael crashed around me, and for the first time, I simply grieved my losses. The solitude became a gift. It gave me time to let go of the tiny pieces of my past I'd been clinging to.

With no distractions, I found myself in constant prayer, and in a span of two days, I released so much. I let go of bitterness and resentment. Ever since Elizabeth explained the constraints brought on by hatred, I'd been praying about it, and even felt it diminish, but this time that heavy burden washed away with my tears. Feelings I'd never had time to process as I struggled to survive surfaced, and I recalled others I'd pushed to the back of my mind as I served day and night. Sorting through it all, I began to see my life through a new lens.

Each memory brought a new prayer, more questions for the Almighty. And though no answers came, the mourning and prayers brought peace. For the first time, I was honest with myself and Yahweh about my fears and doubts. By the third day of my constant reflections, my prayers began to sound a bit like Dohd's. He talked to God in a rich and deep way, and even when we all sat with him, he prayed as if he were the only one in the room.

While Ab made trip after trip to Jerusalem, Dohd had served the king, rising to the most trusted of all positions, cupbearer. But his position also meant he was always on call, required to be in the king's presence at a moment's notice. Despite my uncle's restrictive schedule, his prayers had always been full of faith and praise.

Looking back, I finally understood the miracle of the king releasing Dohd to journey to Jerusalem and the enormous blessing of the ruler funding the trip. My dohd, the slave, had become governor. How does that happen? Just as quickly as the thought crossed my mind, I heard Abba. "Joseph," the deep voice said. "And Daniel."

Abba would point to my own few years as a slave. I had risen to being treated like a daughter in Derora's service, nearly a daughter-in-law.

But that part of my life was over. Like Joseph, I would start over again at the bottom and wait for Yahweh to raise me up. It took thirteen years for Joseph. Father Avraham waited twenty-five years on his promised son. *Praise Yahweh, Ab shared those stories so many times.*

Now, I would wait for Yawheh's next big move.

Seventy-One

As best I could tell, we'd been traveling northwest for ten days when, for the first time, they pulled me out of the wagon inside a city. I couldn't tell which town, but it was nice to see the sun longer than the time necessary to eat or relieve myself.

"Don't run! When we catch you, we'll teach you how to do what you're told."

Where would I go? I had no idea where we were, and the iron chains on my ankles would definitely slow me down. Just as I was about to ask what they planned to do with me, a short plump man appeared from the side of the wagon. His robes looked like those of a noble, but the dirt and wear gave him away as a wannabe. A woman with her head bowed low followed.

"Take her to the hammam to get her cleaned up. She'll bring a better price if those dark curls are clean."

The obedient woman walked me to and from the hammam without a word. Only the sound of my shackles broke the silence. I asked her name and where we were, but she didn't even look at me. If she hadn't followed the short man's instructions so quickly, I might have thought her deaf.

Despite the company and the stares from the locals as I entered the water, the hammam was exceedingly refreshing. Praise Yahweh Derora had given me the small basket of oils and a fresh robe.

When we returned, the short, plump man gave me my instructions. "You'll help Thalia sell the kitchen wares today. You won't need that head covering."

I'd never thought about so many men buying pots and pans and ladles. Only a handful of women visited the makeshift stand, yet we'd almost sold out of the kitchen supplies. Each time the short plump man checked our money box, he looked quite pleased.

As I chatted with shoppers, I discovered we were in Carchemish. It must have been a rather large city with so many people flooding the marketplace. Several men looked me over like a heifer at an auction. One even touched my face, until Thalia stepped in.

"No touching until you've talked to the master."

"What if I intend to buy?" Even his voice sounded sleazy.

"Talk to the master."

He walked toward the lead wagon but never returned. As we packed up the little we had left, I overheard the reason why.

"I'm surprised this one didn't sell, Jurjis." *So that was the little man's name.*

"Oh, I had plenty of offers, but I think she might be more valuable if we don't sell her."

"I don't follow."

"Have you ever seen us sell so many kitchen wares in one morning?"

"They did seem more popular today."

"I think it was the pretty face. I'm going to try her with Margat tomorrow and see what happens."

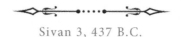

Sivan 3, 437 B.C.

Margat looked tired when she came to retrieve me from my secluded wagon the next morning. I soon learned the reason. Besides the baby in the carrier on her bosom, five other children under the age of six hopped in and out of her wagon and ran circles around the caravan.

Fortunately, Margat took care of the more luxury merchant items, things like instruments and fine bracelets. Beautiful necklaces hung from hooks on half the wagon's side, and Egyptian scarves covered the table that dropped from the other half.

"Jurjis puts me here so I can care for the children. The grain, produce, and kitchen wares always stay busier than this wagon."

Margat was interrupted by two men looking at scarves.

"These come from Egypt. You won't find any finer," Margat began her sales pitch.

"Which do you like?"

"Well, I . . ." Margat started to answer.

"No, the curly-haired one."

"Me?" I answered.

"Yes, which should I get for my wife?"

"I'm sure she'd like any, sir."

"Which would you prefer?"

"I like these wide ones." And I held one over my head to give him the full view.

Both men spent considerable time going back and forth between scarves, asking my opinion with each one.

"I should help someone else while you decide." Four more men had crowded our little stand.

"No, wait. I'll take this one." He made a terribly low offer, and I looked at Margat for confirmation. Her thumbs up prompted me to ask a third more as Thalia had taught me the day before. After a little more dickering, both men agreed on a price.

"Will you wrap them for me?"

"Of course," I answered.

Over and over the scenario repeated itself. Jurjis produced two more crates of scarves and jewels from my sleeping wagon.

"You do well, Mara. A few more days like this and I'll trust you enough to remove those shackles."

That night, as I reflected on the last couple of days, I laughed. I'd never been the beauty. That had been Miriam. Obviously, those men liked what they saw, and it helped the business.

My evening prayer was filled with praise. "Thank you, Lord, for a place with plenty to eat and little to fear." I fell asleep with hope the shackles would be gone soon.

Seventy-Two

Two days later, we left Carchemish with one less wagon and no leg irons.

They moved me to the wagon with Jurjis' family. It didn't take long for me to miss the quiet of my solitude. The next to the youngest picked me to be his friend. Javis spent much of the journey curled up in my lap while his older siblings played quietly. Each time we stopped for meals or relief, all five ran hard, releasing all their stored-up energy.

The trip became easier on the bones once we hit the Royal Road. Jurjis drove the team for his family, while his partner, Abhur, and his two sons drove the other three.

On the first day riding with Margat, I learned more than I wanted to know about every member of our caravan. "Abhur's wife died when the boys were young; I never knew her. She passed a couple of years before my father contracted my betrothal to Jurjis. Thalia is married to his older son, Deebar, and the younger one, Tahir, prefers the single life."

Only two years older than me, Margat and Jurjis married just after her fifteenth birthday. She'd given birth to Priya before their first anniversary. Rashud came just eleven moons later, and the twins followed suit. No wonder Margat looked exhausted.

A full moon passed before we reached Isparta. Margat kept watch over the children while Jurjis gave me free rein over his tables. We'd sold everything from the wares wagons before a week passed. Some of it went to traders who provided Jurjis with silk from the far east and the specialties of India. By the full moon of Tammuz, I marked my twentieth year, and our small caravan headed south once again.

Seventy-Three

By Av's full moon, the road began to look vaguely familiar. When we stopped in Nineveh, I looked for Rajif. I doubt seeing him would have made a difference; still, I prepared to plead my case. I considered writing to Derora, but I figured if Jurjis saw me pass a letter to a courier, I'd be wearing shackles again.

By the time the weather turned cool, the caravan had made it to Susa. I scanned the crowd daily for Avraham or his wife, but never saw a familiar face. So much time had passed since I shopped in this bazar. My friends probably had families by now.

Alone in my wagon the second night, I prayed, "Yahweh, I've changed so much since I lived here. Forgive me for my fascination with Ahura Mazda. I know you are the one and only almighty God. Praise you, Yahweh, for Ab who constantly tried to help me see the truth. I can't believe how easily I gave in to everything my friends told me. Yahweh, if Avraham still lives in Susa, please help him find me."

Seventy-Four

Winter 437 B.C.

I'd never been south of Persepolis before, but fortunately, the further we journeyed, the warmer the nights grew. Jurjis and Abhur had filled the wagons again, forcing everyone to sleep under them.

The two men had discovered the better I looked and smelled the better the sales, so they sent me to the hammams in Elam at least weekly. Abhur said I kept the men distracted. Whatever the reason, I enjoyed the fresh soaps and oils at my disposal. Abhur's younger son, Tahir, found an old bronze mirror in a junk pile and gave it to me. After I polished it, I found the reflection shocking.

The curls that had plagued me when I envied Miriam's straight locks now laid on my shoulders in soft deep brown waves. I couldn't believe how I'd grown into my oversize lips and sharp slanted nose. I recognized them from my childhood, but they didn't look nearly as awkward.

"You look as though you've never seen yourself before." Margat's voice startled me, and I laid down the brass piece, embarrassed.

"I haven't taken time to study my reflection since my sixteenth summer. Derora's oils have really tamed these wild curls."

"I'll have to get your secret. I think Priya will end up with hair like yours. I can't keep it under a head covering, the mitpachat just slides . . ." Margat stopped abruptly as the color moved up her cheekbones.

"It's alright. I've grown accustomed to men looking at me like I'm a harlot. Jurjis and Abhur will not let me cover my head. Fortunately, Yahweh knows better. A girl who smells sweet and looks like a harlot sells more in the bazar. I've learned to live with it."

By winter's end, the merchants had replaced the fifth wagon and filled the other four with fruit, vegetables, and beautiful Egyptian wares those in the north would be missing after the long winter. Jurjis said we'd reach Nineveh sometime before the new year started.

Seventy-Five

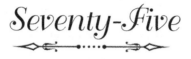

Adar 437 B.C.

On the way north, we only stayed in Susa one day; and though we didn't overnight at any caravanserais, we made sales at several who needed to fill their supply cupboards.

We stopped for a day in Ecbatana before continuing our trek. Each day took us one day closer to Nineveh and Michael. I knew Jurjis usually visited Rajif twice a year, and he'd already missed the fall stop.

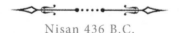

Nisan 436 B.C.

In Calah, I expected to see someone from the estate, but not even Amin showed his face. One day Abhur's sons loaded oils, jewels, and fabrics on a small, borrowed cart and headed east.

"When do you usually stop at Rajif's estate?" I finally asked Margat.

"We won't. Deebar and Tahir went to pick up the winter grain, but the caravan won't stop."

"I thought you visited the estate twice a year."

"Part of your contract includes never bringing you closer than Calah. Rajif didn't even want you here, but Jurjis insisted our livelihood couldn't skip this city."

And just like that, my chances of seeing Michael vanished. I'd thought he'd come after me last summer. The final remnants of that dream fell to the floor like shards of glass. He'd probably married by now. It was time I forgot about him.

No matter how I tried, my brain couldn't convince my heart. I held back my grief until I laid alone under the wagon; then six moons of holding out hope crashed around me. I sobbed into the small pack Derora had sent with me, hoping it would muffle my uncontrollable tears.

"Yahweh, I hurt. This pain comes from my heart. I don't know how much more I can lose. Will I ever be loved again?"

"I love you, daughter." That voice brought so much peace. "You can never lose me, Adira." I buried my head to soften the noise, though these tears held a touch of joy at hearing my name.

"You know the real me, don't you, Yahweh? I praise you! I praise you! You've not forgotten me. You always go with me. Even if I never see the people I love again, I have you. I will trust you."

As I prayed, the tears subsided. I lifted words of praise until exhaustion overtook me.

Though she didn't say a word, the pity on Margat's face told me I needed to find some cold water for my face. I decided in that moment I'd cried my last. I didn't want anyone to look on me with pity again.

We traipsed through Persia and Anatolia following last year's itinerary closely. Jurjis bought an extra wagon and took on another apprentice.

"Sales have doubled this year," he told Margat at evening meal.

"How many years do you think we'll have before Mara's beauty fades?"

He talks about me like I'm not here. I wonder what he'll do with me when I don't bring in the top sales anymore. "It doesn't matter, does it, Yahweh? Even when my beauty fades, you'll be with me." Fortunately, I had discovered my parents' secret to contentment. My peace grew daily.

Seventy-Six

As summer drew to a close, our caravan headed back toward Babylon. Abhur had purchased even more from the craftsman in Anatolia this year, certain the men of the south would pay top dollar.

Our wagons entered the massive city with Tishrei's full moon. Though Nineveh had once overshadowed her, Babylon now made every other major city look small. The cautiousness Em had instilled in me in my thirteenth year remained. I'd never seen so many people, so many traders. I stayed close to the wagon for the entire week, grateful Jurjis splurged for one room in the guest serai for Thalia, Margat, me, and the children. The men would guard the merchandise.

On the fifth day in the great city, Jurjis disappeared for a few hours. Upon his return, he instructed us to pack up tight when we closed the wagons today. "I've made a trade for some Indian spices, but we have to go to Susa to pick them up."

After Margat and I secured our wagon, I went to help the apprentice. I wanted to get to Susa. I held out hope I might see Avraham. Would he recognize me?

Twelve days later I sat next to the apprentice as we entered a familiar gate. Last year we'd been on the south side of the city; this year the palace complex lay just ahead. The hammam Natalia and I visited before we left laid just beyond those trees, and to the south, I could see the path that led to the king's stables.

The stables. Avraham should be there. Did I dare?

In five years, I'd never once considered an escape. Where could I run that my master wouldn't find me? But now I could get to Avraham. Why hadn't I thought of this last year? Of course, we'd entered from the southern part of the city, so nothing looked familiar. Tonight, I would sneak out.

Jurjis sent me to the hammam to get rid of the road dust while everyone else got things set up in the bazar. By the time I returned, curiosity had several customers waiting for us to get the wares out.

I found it difficult to stay focused on the trades. My mind continually returned to my escape plan. After five years, this life would be over. I'd stay with Avraham until we could find a caravan he trusted to take me to Jerusalem. A letter to Ab and Em would be the first order of business. I'd longed to send them a note since Derora had given me the papyrus, but I knew Jurjis would find out, and I feared that might end his kindness.

Night couldn't come soon enough. Though the late Tishrei air had a chill, it still felt warmer than Calah.

I pulled my wrap close, acting as if I needed to relieve myself. Fortunately, everyone slept soundly. I picked up my small pack and quietly walked toward the stables. With only a sliver of the moon to guide me, I thanked Yahweh this had been my home for thirteen years.

A lamp burned in the stables. The door was bolted, so I knocked softly. My excitement drained when a boy about six years my younger opened the door.

"Is Avraham here? Or could you tell me where he lives?"

"Avraham?"

"Yes, the stable master."

"The stable master is Simon. I think he trained under an Avraham, but he left long before I became an apprentice."

My heart fell, "Do you know where he went?"

"No, but Simon might. You could ask him in the morning."

"Could you wake him? This is urgent."

The boy walked toward the last stall where the stable master's room had always been. His lamp cast a long shadow as he walked. Jok and Jon would be about his age. Could my little brothers be that tall?

"She said it was urgent, sir." Well, at least Simon was awake.

A groggy stable master walked toward me, "What's so urgent you have to wake me in the middle of the night?"

"Do you know where Avraham lives?"

"Last I knew he had settled in Babylon. The army captain recruited him to care for the battle horses. The army stations in Babylon between battles, so he moved his family in the spring so he could see his children more often."

"Children?" My resolve to allow no more tears to fall was breaking.

"Two boys and one on the way when he gave me my room."

I had two nephews and one niece or nephew. Perhaps tears of joy didn't count.

"Are you all right, g'veret?"

"Fine. Yes. Just sorry I missed him."

"He stops in to see me when he's over this way. Gets fresh

horses for the commander. Should I tell him you stopped in?"

"Please. Tell him his long-lost sister hoped to see him."

When I stepped out of the stable, Dabeer greeted me. I considered running, but where would I go? I obviously didn't know anyone in Susa anymore.

Seventy-Seven

Winter 436 B.C.

I slept with both hands tied behind my back and secured to the wagon.

Though I expected a beating the next morning, only shackles awaited me.

Jurjis was almost apologetic as he untied my wrists and put the leg irons on. "We just can't afford to lose you, Mara. Sales have never been so good. You captivate men with your beauty, and women tell me they trust you."

"Where is my pack?" I'll need to be presentable before the market gets busy.

"It's here. Abhur wanted to make sure you didn't steal something."

A glance showed evidence of Abhur's rifling, but it didn't look like he'd taken anything.

We spent the winter traveling through southern Mede again. My robes hid the shackles, and rags wrapped around them kept them from clanking. Customers preferred to buy from a free pretty Jewish girl.

My attitude probably fed their lie. Ab and Em had instilled the necessity of doing my best in every circumstance. We'd been slaves in Susa, still both my parents had always worked hard and never complained. Until I experienced true freedom in Jerusalem, I had no idea we weren't free in Susa. And now, even in leg irons, I carried myself with the confidence my parents had passed on. No one knew I was a slave.

Jurjis and Abhur moved me back to Margat's wagon so she could keep an eye on me, and my master's wife made me her confidante.

"Mara, I'm so tired today."

"Chasing after all those children will do that." I tried to keep the conversation light.

"And I'll have one more to chase by the time we arrive in Anatolia next Summer. Sometimes I wish I could go to sleep and not wake up."

"You know you'd miss your beautiful babies."

"I love them, but I don't know what I'd do without your help. I'm exhausted all the time."

A customer looking for a scarf for his wife interrupted. Margat's eyes held a darkness I'd never seen before, and I began to appreciate the good in my life despite my slavery.

That night, instead of complaining about the shackles and missing Avraham in Susa, my prayers moved to praise. I remembered the songs Ab taught us—tunes written by a shepherd running for his life.

Have mercy on me, my God, have mercy on me,

for in you, I take refuge.

I will take refuge in the shadow of your wings

until the disaster has passed.

God sends forth his love and his faithfulness.

Be exalted, O God, above the heavens;

let your glory be over all the earth.

My heart, O God, is steadfast,

my heart is steadfast;

I will sing and make music.

I will praise you, Lord, among the nations;

I will sing of you among the peoples.

For great is your love, reaching to the heavens;

your faithfulness reaches to the skies.

Be exalted, O God, above the heavens;

let your glory be over all the earth.

"Thank you, Yahweh, that Ab taught us these songs. I praise you that Ab and Em showed me how to have joy even as a slave."

I began to sing the songs of King David as I worked, and the praise caused me to forget my chains. Though I missed Ab, Em, and my family and still shed a few tears for Michael, the burden lifted when I started humming the ancient songs.

"What's got into you, Mara? I wish you'd share some of your potion."

I laughed, "It's no potion, Margat."

"What then?" She smiled slyly, "Have you been sneaking off with Tahir?"

Shock replaced my laughter. "Oh no! Never!"

"You could do a lot worse."

I had never considered Tahir for a match, "My heart belongs to another I can't have, Margat. These chains don't make me a good first wife. Fathers try to find more lucrative matches for their sons."

"Well then, what are these songs you're singing?"

"Ab taught them to us. There were written by Israel's greatest king. Yahweh called him 'a man after His own heart'."

"Your god spoke like that about a man?"

"According to my ab, He did. Have you ever heard stories of Yahweh? Some seem unbelievable, but they've all been recorded in the history of my people."

"Tell me some of these stories that cause you to sing. I could use some joy."

From that day on, whenever we had a break in customers or were traveling, I shared all Ab's stories I could remember, thankful he'd repeated them so often.

Seventy-Eight

Summer 435 B.C.

By the time Margat was due to deliver, I'd told her every bit of Israel's story—from creation to the great flood all the way through to David, Solomon, and the exile. The history lessons seemed to distract her.

We'd reached one of the estates at the end of the Royal Road the day Margat's baby decided to come.

"Master, we need to find a midwife."

"I'm sure you can handle it."

"I've never delivered a baby before." I couldn't believe he'd even suggest it.

"Margat has done this six times before, she'll tell you what to do."

As I made my way back to Margat, I prayed, "Lord, I don't think I can do this." The prayer didn't make me feel any more confident, so I told myself Yahweh would be with me.

I made sure the five older children were together and told Priya to watch over her little brothers. Then I asked Tahir to keep an eye out for them.

"I'm not a nursemaid," came the terse protest.

"I don't need you to be a nursemaid; Priya does a good job with the boys. Just make sure they don't give her a hard time or fall off a cliff and die. Alright?" My voice wasn't very slave-like, but I didn't have time to beg and bargain.

"I'll be working on this wagon. They can stay close." He sounded disgusted, but I had what I needed. I wondered how far I could push it.

"Could you find someone to bring a pot of cold water to Jurjis' wagon and put another by the fire to heat?"

"Is that all?" His sarcasm told me he wouldn't put up with more demands.

Regardless, I kept the tone of authority in my voice, "That's all for now. I'll let you know if I need more after I get Margat comfortable." And with that, I walked off before he could regain his composure. His mouth hanging open almost brought a laugh, but I refrained. A baby on the way may have let me get away with ordering him around, but I'm sure he wouldn't stand for being laughed at.

I found Margat in the wagon next to a napping toddler. After six births this baby wasn't wasting any time.

"Jurjis won't send to Sardis for a midwife."

"I don't think she'd have time. . ." Margat grabbed my hand and squeezed. When she started breathing again, she asked for a clean rag.

I scrambled to find something in the wagon.

"Rip it in half," she instructed.

She took the torn cloth and rolled it into a scroll. Just as I started to ask its purpose, she put it in her mouth and grabbed hold of me again.

After what seemed like too long to hold her breath, she removed her gag and took a deep breath. "Get some hot water." Another breath. "Over there you'll see some linen blankets I used for my other six."

I stuck my head out the back of the wagon just as one of the apprentices delivered the cool water.

"Bring the warm water."

I used the cool water to wipe Margat's sweat-filled forehead, but before I could finish, she put the cloth back in her mouth.

"Shouldn't you be breathing?"

"I can't concentrate on breathing when the pain comes," she answered after the pain subsided. "I think you'll meet my wee one very soon."

"One pot of warm water," came a voice from outside.

"Just sit it right inside the wagon."

"Is everything all right in there?" Jurjis had brought the hot water himself.

"You should meet our child very . . ." A short scream escaped before Margat could get the rag back in her mouth.

"Margat?!" His concern was touching.

"It's time, Jurjis, just give her a few minutes," I told the anxious father.

"Yahweh, help this baby come quickly," I prayed out loud.

And with just a couple of pushes, I placed a beautiful baby girl in Margat's arms.

She gave me instructions on finishing the delivery, but she sounded exhausted.

"As soon as I get this all cleaned up, I'll take the baby so you can sleep."

I picked up a few more rags. Margat had moved the baby from

her arm to the center of her chest. She'd already dozed off.

Fortunately, the toddler had slept through the whole ordeal. His cherub face made me smile. When I glanced back at Margat, I yelled for Jurjis. All the color had drained from her face.

"Jurjis," I yelled again.

I handed him the baby. "See if they have a medicine man nearby."

"What's . .?" He stopped when he saw Margat's color.

"There's too much blood. I'm going to try to stop it, but I don't know what I can do."

Alone with Margat, I cried out to Yahweh. I didn't even know what to pray as I applied pressure.

Jurjis finally returned with a servant from the estate. She stuffed rags inside Margat.

"It's the only thing I've ever seen help." The aging woman turned to Jurjis, "We'll need more rags and yarrow if you have it."

Jurjis handed me the newborn and hurried off.

"Will she be . . .? I couldn't finish.

"I can't tell. I've seen this go both ways." She leaned over Margat's face. "I still feel a faint breath, so the fight's not over yet."

Jurjis returned with the rags, a bowl and pestle, and the dried white flowers.

"Crush this." She passed the yarrow to me as she removed the rags.

She added a little warm water to the flakes in the bowl to form a poultice. She quickly put the mixture on a rag and stuffed Margat again.

"If she survives, she'll need to be kept still for at least a moon."

Poor Jurjis looked so helpless.

"Could we stay here for a few days until she's got enough strength to move to a serai in Sardis?" *Is that my calm voice taking charge?*

"You'll have to take that up with my g'veret. Though I'll tell you she is the kindest woman I've ever served, so I believe she won't mind your wagons."

"I'll go talk to Alexandrous and his wife. His estate has been one of our stops for years. I think he'll be gracious." Jurjis turned to go, still in a state of shock.

"I'm Toya," the woman introduced herself while we waited. She served as head kitchen steward. Her mistress had sent her because she knew how to use the healing herbs.

By the time Jurjis returned, Margat's breathing had become somewhat regular, though her olive skin remained colorless. "Squeeze drops of water into her mouth every few hours."

Jurjis helped Toya out of the wagon. "I'll stop over to check on her after the evening meal."

Just then little eyes began to flutter. How had that toddler slept through all this commotion? Well, he did not need to see his mother like this.

"Jurjis?"

The master poked his head in the wagon, and I handed him the infant. Then I whisked the big brother out of the wagon before he could get fully awake.

"Emi." He cried as we stepped out of the wagon.

"Emi sleeps, wee one. You can see her later."

Jurji laid his head on my shoulder. This one had been named

after his father.

Where had Jurjis gone? Why would he walk away with Margat's condition so grave?

I peeked in to check on our patient every few seconds as her fully awake son struggled to get down to play. The rise and fall of her chest grew more steady with every breath.

"Don't leave my sight," I warned the little one.

By the time the master returned, I'd grown impatient. "Where did you go?" No one would have ever guessed I was a slave with that tone. "And where is the baby?" Now I was frantic.

"She is fine. I've paid Alexandrous' oldest daughter to care for the children so you can tend to Margat. They have a household slave who will nurse the baby.'

"Come, Jurji. You can play with Priya and the boys."

Always happy to be included in his older siblings' adventures, the toddler went without protest.

I stayed with Margat day and night, dripping water into her mouth and making her comfortable each time she stirred.

"Yahweh, I praise you for the healthy baby, but great Healer, I pray you'll send your power to raise Margat from this bed."

Seventy-Nine

The next morning, I heard the other wagons begin to roll.

"No sense in everyone sitting here waiting for Margat to heal," Jurjis told me as he stepped into the wagon.

The man sat down and tenderly held his wife's lifeless hand. I waited for instructions, but soon it became awkward, me watching him watching her.

"I'll step out for a while so you can sit with her, sir."

"No, wait, Mara."

I sat back down, but Jurjis remained silent for a few moments.

"You really took charge yesterday."

Oh, no! I had overstepped. "I'm sorry, reebon. I just . . ."

"No need to apologize," Jurjis interrupted. "You saved her life."

"Toya did that, reebon."

"No, you took charge. If you hadn't thought quickly and acted, she would have died. If you'd behaved like a proper slave, I'd have lost her."

Jurjis continued, "I know I don't often act like I care, and I realize I'm old enough to be her father, but Margat is my life. I don't know what I'd do without her."

"Praise Yahweh she survived."

"Margat told me you've been telling her the history of your people and Yahweh."

"Yes, sir. She heard me singing the songs of King David and asked about them."

"Yahweh. Ahura Mazda. I don't care who she prays to as long as she gets better."

"I will keep asking Yahweh."

"What do you give your god when you ask such a great favor?"

"Ab taught me Yahweh isn't like other gods. He only asks for obedience and devotion."

"But didn't your people offer great sacrifices before they were carried off to Babylon?" So, he knew a bit of the history of Israel.

"Yes, but those were never to appease Yahweh. Those sacrifices paid the penalty for the sins of the people. But when hearts didn't demonstrate sorrow for disobedience, Yahweh rejected the sacrifice. The sacrifice alone won't appease the Creator of the Universe. Ab says that's how our people ended up in Babylon."

"Your father seems quite wise, Mara. When did you lose him?"

"He was alive and well in Jerusalem the last time I saw him."

"Ah, you were sold to pay his debts."

"No, reebon. My family does well in Jerusalem." I considered elaborating but Derora's warning echoed.

"Well, I believe you have earned your freedom today. I could never repay you for what you've done for Margat. We'll get those leg irons off, and should you choose to stay, you'll receive a servant's pay."

Overwhelmed I cried out, "Yahweh, I praise you!" I never thought I'd see freedom again. "Thank you, reebon."

"No need for thanks. You've earned it." He stood and found the tool for the shackles. "Now why don't you take a blanket and rest under the wagon while I sit with Margat. I'll call if I need you."

Free of the chains, I stepped out of the wagon without fear of tripping. There near the rear wheel sat my small pack and basket. Jurjis must have remembered to grab them out of the apprentice's wagon before they left.

I laid my head on my pack and curled up with the blanket. Would I be able to sleep with the sun so high in the sky and all the activity in the nearby courtyard? I didn't wonder very long.

Eighty

Summer 435 B.C.

I loved seeing Natalia laughing. Were those her children running in the courtyard? They'd grown so much! They looked a lot like Jurjis and Margat's family. What a coincidence!

Hands grabbed my waist from behind. Turning I saw it was my brother. I threw my arms around his neck.

"Oh Avraham, I looked for you in Susa. I escaped to find you, but you weren't there."

I buried my head in his chest as he tried to explain, but his deep voice got lost in the crowd noise. I looked up. His mouth moved, but all I could hear was a voice in the distance, "Mara, Mara!"

Why did the voice seem so near? Who here would call me Mara?

"Avraham! It's Adira! Don't you remember me?"

But he was gone. It was all gone.

"Mara." It was Jurjis. "Mara, please wake up."

"I'm awake." I rubbed my eyes to discover the sun had hardly moved.

I rolled out from under the wagon and Jurjis helped me up. "She's burning up and delirious. I don't know what to do."

His words jarred the last of the cobwebs. "Get me cold water, rags, and Toya."

As I climbed into the wagon, I could hear Margat, "No, please don't hurt him." Her arms flailed as she tried to hit something.

"Margat, it's me, Mara." I held her arm and moved her hair from her forehead.

"Shhhhsh, You're safe Margat. You're here with me. Jurjis went to get us some cold water." She tried to pull away.

"Please let go," she cried, still living in her nightmare.

"Wake up, Margat. You're dreaming. Stay with me. You're in a wagon just outside Sardis. Jurjis has been taking good care . . ."

Just then her eyes opened, "Mara!" She tried to sit up. "Ooooh," she cried in pain.

"Stay still. You had some problems after the delivery."

"My precious baby girl." She tried to get up again. "I need to feed her."

"Lie still. You lost a lot of blood. Jurjis found someone to look after the children. You just need to rest."

Margat had calmed just a little when Jurjis returned with Toya.

"Let's get these cold rags on her." Toya took control immediately. "Since she's awake, help her drink as much as you can." She turned to Jurjis, "Keep the pots of cold water coming."

I managed to get two cups of cold water past Margat's lips before she passed out again. Toya checked to make sure her bleeding stayed normal, then covered her in cool rags, even soaking her blanket in the bucket.

"I have to get back to the kitchen. Just keep changing out the cool rags and make sure her blanket stays damp."

All night, Jurjis brought water and I changed the rags, but we couldn't keep the fever away. We took turns dozing, and I prayed every waking second.

On the third day, Margat finally woke. The fever lingered, and she was very weak.

"Mara," she said my name decisively.

"What can I get you, Margat?"

She said it again, "Mara."

"I'm here, Margat." She looked right at me.

"Mara," she said again in a very direct tone. It didn't even sound like she was calling for me.

Jurjis understood. "You want us to name the baby Mara, my love?"

"Yes," she struggled to talk, "babe," a whisper escaped.

She paused for a long time before she took a deep breath and said plainly, "Mara."

And then Margat was gone. Jurjis and I sat by her side willing it not to be true, but as her lifeless hands grew cool for the first time in days, we knew it was over.

Another loss. "Yahweh," my silent prayer came from deep inside. "I trust you. I know you told me you love me, but how much more must I lose?"

Toya opened the back of the wagon. She carried a basket of food. The midday meal must be finished. Jurjis' face told the old woman all she needed to know.

"I'm so sorry."

"Thank you for all your help," Jurjis choked out.

With tears in her kind eyes, Toya sat the basket of food in the wagon and took charge once more. She left for a few minutes and returned with two men who gently lifted Margat out of the wagon and placed her in a clean stall in the stable. Then she went to work preparing my friend for her burial.

Alexandrous cleared the stable as I retrieved Margat's favorite robe from her belongings. When Toya had finished her work, Jurjis brought the children to say goodbye.

We sat in the hay for hours while Jurjis shared stories. Priya and Rashud stayed glued to every word. He told tales of their early marriage and how they met the day before they wed.

Abhur returned the next day just as we laid Margat to rest in a tomb Alexandrous graciously provided. And after Jurjis bartered with the estate owner for an extra goat, we headed back toward the Royal Road to follow the merchant's regular winter route.

Eighty-One

As baby Mara rested in my arms, Javis and his eighteen-month-old brother slept on either side. Sometime on this journey, I'd marked my twenty-second year.

"Yahweh," I prayed silently, "I'm free. Yet freedom doesn't feel much different than slavery."

But I did feel different. I'd lost so much in the last six years, but I'd gained even more. I'd learned the truth about Yahweh. Though I still felt like a slave, within I felt completely free. I have nothing, still, I have my Creator.

My heart felt light. I'd spent six years trying to find a way home. Even when we left Susa, I'd mourned losing what I thought was home.

"Now, I know, Yahweh, You have always been everything I needed."

"Welcome to freedom, Adira."

Joy filled my being. I truly was free.

Eighty-Two

When we stopped in Calah, I asked Jurjis if I could visit Rajif's estate.

"You may do anything you wish, Mara. You no longer have to ask my permission for anything."

When we pulled into the courtyard, Derora look stunned. She ran to greet me.

"Adira!" I loved hearing my name.

"Oh, Derora! I've missed you!" I held her tight.

"What are you doing here? If Rajif sees you, he'll be furious."

"I am free. Jurjis released me! I wanted to see you and Michael."

A darkness invaded her countenance. "Michael is gone. He refused the marriage his father arranged, and he left. He joined the king's army. He writes when he can. Rajif doesn't know. You should stay in the wagon while you're here, my husband still blames you for Michael leaving."

We stole one more embrace before I hid myself in the wagon.

The ride back to Calah saw a few tears but praying reminded me Yahweh is all I need.

Abhur had made some deals in Babylon, so we followed the Tigris south. While I continued selling in the markets, my main responsibility became Margat's seven children.

Nine-year-old Priya stepped into the caretaker role without missing a beat. She took the two youngest boys under her wing, while eight-year-old Rashud kept the twins in line. Except for breaking up the occasional sibling fight and keeping them fed and clothed, they weren't any trouble.

I'd never realized before how quickly children grow. I felt like I asked Jurjis for cloth or robes at least once each moon. He laughed when I apologized for bothering him so much.

"Margat asked for much more. Growing children need new robes. What about you? When did you last get a new robe?"

"The ones Derora gave me were the finest quality, so they've held up well."

"Perhaps we'll get you something new in Babylon." The look in Jurjis' eye bothered me a bit, but I quickly dismissed it. Margat had been gone less than three moons. Surely, he wasn't thinking. . .?

Eighty-Three

In Babylon, I couldn't stop looking for Avraham and Michael. Between customers, I scanned the crowd for soldiers. A few times I thought I saw one or the other, but nothing ever came of it.

Priya started helping in the bazar. The older women loved her. Always polite, she spoke like a miniature grown-up when in sales mode.

"I think she gets better prices than I do," I laughed to Jurjis. "She's a natural."

Margat had taught her daughter the basics of stitching, so after we finished in the market, she helped me with the robes for the growing boys.

"Have you ever considered settling someplace and letting Abhur replenish your stores?" I asked Jurjis one evening.

"Actually, Margat had suggested just that when she discovered Mara was on the way. We teetered between the larger income we could get in Babylon or the small-town atmosphere of Calah. She worried living in Calah would be difficult for you."

Margat concerned herself with me. "Thank you, Yahweh, for giving me Elizabeth, then Derora, then Margat. I couldn't have asked for more gracious g'verets."

As promised, Jurjis brought me a lovely robe in Babylon.

"You shouldn't have, Jurjis. The two I have still hold up well."

"As I figure it, I owe you this robe and more." He handed me a small basket of my favorite soaps and oils. "I noticed you've been letting Priya use your oils for her hair."

"I feel so bad for her. I remember what it's like to be a young girl with curls you can't control"

Jurjis laughed and handed me a small pouch.

"What's this?"

"The rest of your wages for the last few moons."

"Wages?"

"You are not a slave anymore, Mara. Between what you do in the bazar and the way you care for the children, you're worth a lot more than this." He took my hand as he spoke. "You have no idea what a comfort and help you've been since we lost Margat."

I lowered my eyes and moved my hands to straighten my hair. "I'm glad I was here to help with the children. I should get them cleaned up for evening meal." Then I hurried off before he could say anything else.

As I washed four little faces and hands, I wondered what Jurjis was thinking. What would I do if he asked me to marry? Almost twenty-three, beyond marrying age, I'd be a fool to turn him down.

"Yahweh give me wisdom."

"What?" A confused Javis looked up at me.

"I think that hand is clean now," I replied.

As I helped the little ones wash, Priya finished the meal I'd started. I remember doing that for Em at her age. So long ago, it seemed like a dream.

After evening meal, we settled the children in the wagon, and Jurjis and I sat near the fire enjoying the cool night.

"I found some soldiers who know your brother." I hadn't revealed everything about my family, but I had told him about Avraham. "He's out with the troops, and no one I talked to knew he was married. In a city the size of Babylon, it would be a miracle if you found your sister-in-law."

"I appreciate you looking. Any word on Michael?"

"No one at this post has heard of Michael ben Rajif. I'm sorry, Mara."

Later, as I prepared myself for sleep, I accepted the fact I'd never find Michael. My biggest hesitation in considering marriage to Jurjis had been the hope of finding my love. I knew if Jurjis asked, the wise thing to do would be accept.

Eighty-Four

Winter 435 B.C.

We went as far south as Persepolis this trip. As always, we made a higher profit at the villas and caravanserais in between. Jurjis had developed relationships with many of the nobles along the route. His kind and funny nature made him admired, and he treated all the women with the utmost respect.

I had started wearing my mitpachat just after Margat died. I felt the need to set the example for Priya, not to mention, I hated the way men looked at me without it. By the time we reached our southernmost stop, Abhur protested, but Jurjis quickly came to my defense.

"The men like flirting with her, Jurjis. You know sales doubled after you bought her."

"She's free now, Abhur. She could have stayed in Sparta or hopped the first caravan back to Jerusalem, but she stayed to help with my children. If she wants to cover her head, then she will cover her head."

Abhur stormed off, and I quietly laughed, amused my exposed curls could cause such a heated argument.

Eighty-Five

Winter turned to spring, so our caravan turned north one more time. For the third year, I would mark the anniversary of my birth in Anatolia. Many of the townspeople and estate servants knew me by name.

I had obviously misread Jurjis' intentions. A full year had passed, and he'd made no advances. I loved Margat's children as my own but raising them had stirred a longing to become a mother. I had to find a way to curb these thoughts. At twenty-three, if Jurjis wouldn't have me, any hope of marriage was gone. And even if my former master decided to marry me, would he want more children?

Before leaving the area, Jurjis stopped at Margat's resting place. Priya and Rashud grieved with their father. The younger children cried sympathy tears for their siblings.

Jurjis pulled me aside and asked Priya to take baby Mara back to the wagon, "I've talked to Abhur. We'll winter in Egypt this year. We haven't been there for almost five years. It will give us a chance to stop in Jerusalem so I can speak with your father."

Jurjis pulled me close. That explains his silence in the matter. He planned to do things the right way. I should have been excited to have a man treat me with such respect, but as I returned his embrace, I had only one thought, *"I'm going home."*

Eighty-Six

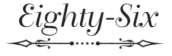

Fall 434 B.C.

The journey to Jerusalem seemed to take forever. I grew more anxious with every mile. Jok and Jon would be men now, and Natalia might have as many children as Jurjis.

Jurjis and Abhur obviously traveled through Damascus often. Every merchant and craftsman who passed our wagon stopped to greet the men.

"Jurjis! Abhur!" A familiar voice called from across the way.

"Vahid, old friend, I'm surprised to see you here. I heard you've been running the eastern route."

"I could say the same, Abhur.

Why did his voice sound so familiar?

"Where is that lovely Margat?"

"She died in childbirth just over a year ago," Jurjis replied. "Let me introduce you to Mara. She's taking care of the children." He lowered his voice, "I'm on my way to Jerusalem to meet her father and ask for her hand."

When I looked up from setting out the kitchen wares, the man's face went white. Jurjis reached out to steady him.

"Vahid, are you alright? You look like you've seen a ghost."

"I . . . uh . . ." I could see him trying to regain his composure. "Pardon me, Mara. You look just like someone I knew many years ago."

Abhur laughed, "An old flame, my friend?"

Vahid couldn't quite get a laugh out, "Something like that. I better get back. Jochebed will wonder where I wandered off to."

"Well, greet her for me," Jurjis said as Vahid abruptly ended his visit.

"He's always been a bit strange," Jurjis told me. "You really spooked him."

"It's weird. I feel like I should know him."

"Perhaps you met him in the market in Jerusalem or Susa. He's been . . ."

"Wait! What did he say his wife's name is?"

"Jochebed."

"That's it! He's the man who took me from my home!" I could feel the rage rise from within.

"Mara, I've known Vahid for more than twenty years. He's never dealt in the slave trade."

"I'm sure that was his voice. They kept me blindfolded. I know the caravan had at least three men and a woman, and her name was Jochebed."

"But even if it was him, what can we do about it? You have to have government connections to get real justice."

Inadvertently, Jurjis reminded me I hadn't found a way to reveal my true identity. Hiding my connection to Dohd had become part of my life. He'd discover the truth when we reached Jerusalem.

As I packed the wares our last night in Damascus, I heard Abhur and Jurjis outside the wagon.

"We have to go to Egypt, Jurjis. I've already made deals with some of the Damascus shop owners."

"Jerusalem could prove to be dangerous, Abhur. I think we should head back to Susa."

"You aren't being sensible. Crossing the Euphrates this late in the year would mean certain death."

"Jerusalem might mean death, too."

I stepped out of the wagon to gather the few remaining scarves. Jurjis looked defeated, and when he saw me, the conversation hushed.

Jurjis seemed cool the next morning as he helped put the children in the wagon.

As soon as we started, I realized Abhur had won the argument. And though I knew I should support the man who wanted to marry me, I silently praised Yahweh as we headed for Jerusalem.

Ten years had passed since I first traveled this road. Caravanserais were still rare, so the men stayed vigilant each night.

The lake at Et Tell gave herself away with her rich smells long before we reached it. The serene body of water I'd sat beside with Ab now rolled in the late Tishrei wind. Fishing boats lined the shores, pulled out of the water to avoid the high waves. The power of the sea amazed me as much as the glasslike water I'd seen ten years before.

As I stood enjoying the beauty, I heard someone approach. Jurjis had come to join me on the shore. I pulled my wrap close, hoping he might try to warm me, but he kept his distance.

"How far from here to Jerusalem?" I asked to break the awkward silence.

"About five days." His abrupt response was typical of his attitude since we'd left Damascus.

"Jurjis, what have I done?"

"What do you mean?"

"Will you look at me? We need to talk."

"There's nothing to talk about."

"Then why are you so distant?"

"I have a lot on my mind. This route is dangerous."

"This is more than danger. You've treated me differently since the last night in Damascus."

"If you must know," he sounded disgusted. "I've been trying to decide how to avoid the calamity that waits for me in Jerusalem."

"In Jerusalem? We'll be safe when we get to my parents' home."

He looked me in the eyes. "Will the merchant who held the governor's niece as a slave for more than a year be truly safe?"

I looked down at the sandy ground. I could feel his stare. "How did you find out?"

"You were right about Vahid. Well, at least partially. He didn't take you. The men he traveled with did. He found out you were the governor's niece after you'd been sold. He thought you'd have been found out by now and killed."

Elizabeth had been right to warn me.

"Haven't you anything to say?"

"What can I say?"

"Why did you let me believe the lie?"

"I wanted to tell you. I started to tell Margat half a dozen times, but I'd been warned more than once that the truth could mean my death."

"But even after I freed you . . ."

"I've carried the fear for so long."

"So, you were just going to let me walk into Jerusalem to face your father? Abhur and I would be killed on the spot."

I looked up and put my hand on his arm. "No, Ab and Dohd aren't like that. They would listen when I explained."

"A lot of good your explaining will do after I'm dead! Make sure you take good care of my orphans!"

Jurjis stormed off leaving me to take in the lake's awesomeness alone. My soul felt like the great body of water. Fear rose and subsided; then doubt took its place. Would I ever see my family? Anger washed up as I considered how my life had been stolen from me. Then fear mounted again.

When Jurjis freed me, I'd thought I was finally safe, but would Jurjis' new knowledge put my life in danger? Should I run? Where would I go? I might be free, but I felt caged. I had to find a way home.

Eighty-Seven

Cheshvan 3, 434 B.C.

Seven days after we left Damascus, Jerusalem appeared on the horizon. I could hardly contain my excitement; I'd be home by nightfall.

Baby Mara slept, so I moved to the front. Jurjis hadn't spoken a word to me since we left the sea, but it didn't matter; I wanted to see the city.

The travel seemed painfully slow, but with every mile, Jerusalem grew larger. Sunset came early this time of year. It would be good to get inside the gates.

We could just make out the guards on top of the wall when the front wagon made a turn.

"Why is Abhur leaving the main road?" I broke the awkward silence.

"We've decided to bypass Jerusalem."

Panic set in. "But what about you talking to my father?"

"Actually, I don't need his permission." The uncaring tone in his voice added to my fear.

What was happening? Jerusalem lay right in front of me. I couldn't go to Egypt. I stood without thinking.

"Mara!" Jurjis yelled and lunged for my skirt as I leaped from the wagon.

Jumping might have been a bad idea. My arm throbbed, but I didn't have time to assess the damage. As I pushed myself up, I realized my ankle hurt, too. But I couldn't stop. If I ran, I could make it to the gates before darkness set in.

The sound of pounding hooves reminded me Dabeer rode on horseback. His mount now stood between me and home. I tried to devise a quick plan to get around him, but reality set in. I collapsed on the rocky soil, the pain in my heart greater than the ache of my bones.

As he dragged me back, I fought with all I had. The struggle ended with the old leg irons as a reward for my efforts. Priya cried as her father hoisted me into the back of the wagon. All but Rashud crowded around me. I could see him fighting tears as he took my seat with Jurjis. Thankfully, the baby slept through it all.

The setting sun hid my silent tears as Jerusalem faded into the distance. We traveled late into the night. They made certain we'd gone far enough I would give up any continued thoughts of escape.

When we finally stopped, I planted myself against a wagon wheel while Jurjis fed the children and settled them to sleep in the back of the wagon. I had no appetite. I knew I should pray, but no words would come.

The man who I once thought might one day be my husband brought me a blanket before he took first watch.

Eighty-Eight

The next morning, Jurjis removed the shackles without saying a word. Priya fed the baby as the twins finished breaking their fast, and I freshened up in the stream nearby.

My arm hurt worse today. It would remind me of my failed attempt at freedom for a good while.

Javis ran to greet me when I returned to the camp. He'd grown so much since my first day in the wagon with him. I could barely pick him up anymore. The children's routine returned to normal, but I'm sure they sensed the tension.

It took a full moon to get to Egypt. The heat made me glad it wasn't Tammuz. Abhur and Jurjis had saved a wagon of goods from India to sell to the Egyptians. We sold out in a few short days.

Memphis left me unimpressed except for the great walls that held back the Nile. Jurjis brought the children out of their wagon to see the tombs of the Pharaohs. The pyramids made the Palace of the Gods in Babylon look small.

With twice as many traders as any place we'd visited, Abhur and Jurjis ran into old friends on every corner. Occasionally I'd be introduced, but my status had quickly devolved to mere servant. I shouldn't have been surprised when Jurjis brought Bita into our camp.

"This lovely is Priya, my oldest," Jurjis introduced the children. "Rashud is becoming a great help in our caravan. Farhad and Farbad are twins, and Javis is almost four. Jurji will be three in the winter."

He took the baby from my arms as he continued, "And this is baby Mara." He held her tenderly for a moment before he passed her to Bita.

"Bita will be caring for the children from now on. I've known her father for years. I haven't seen this lovely girl since her tenth winter. She'll be my wife before we leave Egypt."

I opened my mouth, but no words came. Everything started spinning.

"Mara?"

"You should call me Adira," I managed just before I crumpled to the ground.

<hr/>

Darkness had settled in when I woke under a wagon. Abhur walked by as I attempted to sit.

"Look who's awake," Abhur knelt beside me.

"What happened?"

"You don't remember Jurjis introducing Bita?"

"Oh yes. And I passed out." It all came rushing back.

Abhur smiled a bit too big, "Jurjis didn't expect that."

"So, what does he plan to do with me?"

"I'll let my partner give you those details. His shift begins soon."

Fully awake now, I crawled from under the wagon. I didn't seem to have any injuries from my fall.

The full Tevet moon crept over the wagons. I'd never seen it move so slowly. Finally, Abhur woke Jurjis. As soon as he walked my way, I confronted him, "So what about me?"

"What about you?" He answered nonchalantly.

"How will I earn my keep?"

"You're free to go."

"Go? Where would I go?"

"Anywhere you like. Go back to Jerusalem."

"How am I supposed to get to Jerusalem?"

"That's not my concern."

"So, you're just leaving me on the streets of Memphis?"

"Why should I care?" Jurjis' fury could be heard even in his hushed tones. "You put my family in danger with your lie, and today I discover I didn't even know your name."

"I didn't choose to be called Mara!" I spat.

"That's not the point, Mara—or Adira—or whomever you are. You are the niece of a high-ranking government official. Is it true your uncle was cupbearer to Artaxerxes?"

"Yes. What's that got to do with anything?" I grew angrier by the moment.

"The most trusted man in the empire, and I owned his niece. Do you have any idea the danger you've put us in? Abhur wants me to kill you right here so there's no chance they'll ever track you back to us. If you hadn't saved Margat and meant so much to her . . ."

"So, I never meant anything to you?"

Jurjis grew very quiet. "I thought I loved a young slave girl named Mara."

"But Jurjis, I am that girl."

"When you knew I planned to talk to your father, why didn't

you tell me?"

I lowered my eyes, "I was afraid."

"Afraid of what?" Jurjis grew impatient. "Have I ever treated you badly?"

I considered mentioning the shackles but thought better of it. "Jurjis, I was just sixteen gathering flowers for my sister's wedding when Vahid's men took me. I've lived in fear every day since. Then Elizabeth told me my life could be in danger if anyone found out my true identity. What was I supposed to do?"

"I thought you'd learned to trust me."

"I don't know if I'll ever trust anyone again."

Only the restless sounds of the horses interrupted the quiet of the night.

"I can't risk taking you back to Jerusalem. The penalties for putting a noble's family in jeopardy are great."

"But Ab and Dohd are not like that. I would tell them you treated me well."

"Oh, Mara. You don't understand. When I ride into Jerusalem with you in my wagon, I'll be judged guilty without a trial. I can't put my family in that kind of danger."

"So, instead I'll get left on the streets of Egypt to be raped or sold again, or perhaps to become a prostitute."

"Mara, don't talk like that."

"Well, what do you think will happen to a twenty-three-year-old Jewish girl alone in Egypt," I fumed.

Jurjis' face betrayed his feelings, "I'll talk to Abhur in the morning. It's his family in danger, too. Go to sleep; we'll discuss it tomorrow."

Eighty-Nine

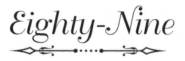

I woke to the sound of arguing but stayed under the wagon.

"Why is she still here, Jurjis?"

"Abhur, we both know what will happen to her if I just send her away."

"And we know what will happen to us if she stays with our caravan. You could always sell her."

"You know I can't."

"I can."

I gasped. Not again. Please Yahweh, I just want to go home.

"Wait, you know she's still got the looks to bring us a profit in the market. We have four wagons full of linen and papyrus. Now that Bita will be caring for the children, we can put her back to work."

They walked toward the fire as Abhur said, "That's not a bad idea, but we'll have to take the Jericho road north."

After I was sure they'd walked away, I crawled out from under the wagon. I wanted to go to the hammam, but my soap and oils were still in the wagon with the children. I had just convinced myself to ask Bita for my pack when Priya poked her head out. Her face brightened when she noticed me. She held a finger to her lips then disappeared.

When she popped back out, she had my pack and headed my way before I could say a word.

"Mara, I missed you." She clung to me.

"It was only one night," I laughed.

"I don't like Bita."

I knelt, "Give her a chance, Priya."

"Do you know she's only seven years older than me? I take care of Mara better than she does!"

"You are a good big sister."

"You have to tell Ab he can't marry her."

"Your father won't listen to anything I say."

"Mara, what happened?"

"Oh, Priya, it's complicated, but the short answer is I was afraid, so I never told your father the whole truth about me; now he doesn't trust me."

"Like your name isn't really Mara?"

"That's part of it."

"Adira is a pretty name."

I smiled, "I like it."

"Can I call you Adira?"

"I wish someone would. You should get back now. I don't think your father wants you to talk to me."

She didn't argue but almost knocked me over as she flung her arms around my neck for a quick squeeze.

"Thanks for bringing my things," I called after her as she headed back. Priya flashed me a big smile before she disappeared inside the wagon.

Ninety

When I returned from the hammam, Jurjis was waiting for me.

"We have to talk. Let's walk."

We ventured toward the city gate as he began, "Abhur said you could stay with us if you agreed to remove your head covering in the bazar and flirt with the sellers to get him a better price."

I hated the thought, but it was better than being left to fend for myself in Egypt.

"And one more thing."

His long pause worried me.

"You'll need to learn to drive a wagon."

"Drive a wagon?! Are you crazy?" Those powerful horses scared me. The picture of that overturned wagon in the Euphrates still haunted my dreams. "Jurjis, I don't think I can."

"Abhur has lined up one more horse and wagon to carry the extra grain barrels. He's already got some great deals in the works, and he figures your flirting should get him an even better price.

"I don't know."

"Abhur won't budge on this. You'll drive Tahir's team. They follow with little coaxing. You can ride with him today to get some training. You'll take over the reins next moon. We still have a few dozen stops before we head toward Jericho."

The horses ended up being gentler and more compliant than I expected. It didn't take long for me to understand why Avraham loved them so much. We became good friends. Their soft noses showed appreciation for every apple, and once we got used to each other, their movements made it seem like they wanted to help me take their bridles on or off.

"We call them Noh and Dah," Tahir told me as he taught me how to care for the mares.

"They have numbers for names?"

He laughed, "Yeah. Ab isn't very creative, and these are the ninth and tenth horses he added permanently to our caravan."

Caring for the team helped ease the pain of watching the children from a distance. After a week they stopped asking for me, and by the time we left Egypt, they seemed attached to Bita.

Despite his newfound animosity, I admired the man. Most in his position would have insisted on an immediate marriage so he could enjoy the full rights of a husband. Jurjis chose to give Bita time to get to know him. At each stop, he bought her a robe or perfume. I'm sure the rest of the caravan thought I'd be jealous. Even I found myself surprised at the relief I felt.

"Yahweh, thank you for saving me from life as Jurjis' wife." My praise didn't stop me from wondering if I'd ever have children of my own.

Ninety-One

We followed the King's Highway east as far as Nekhl. I'd grown accustomed to life without my mitpachat. Why did the men prefer it so? Even with my head covered, my long curls got in the way as I drove the wagon, so I resorted to tying them back while I held the reins.

As we moved closer to Jericho, the road became harder to navigate. I tried to keep the wagon wheels out of the deepest ruts, but my daydreaming didn't help. Jericho was only a long day's walk from Jerusalem. But just the name of the road caused hesitation. Donned "The Way of Blood" even caravans traveled warily. I'd never make it home alone.

The bazar in Jericho teemed with soldiers. In all the stories Ab had told us about Jericho's destruction, he'd never mentioned that the Persian kings had made it a huge administrative center.

The soldiers kept the booth busy. Most of the men flirted while telling me they needed something special for their wives. Thalia and I wrapped countless perfumes, oils, and Egyptian robes for these men. I quickly thanked Yahweh that Abhur had instructed Dabeer to stay close. More than once he'd stopped a soldier from crossing the line. He was escorting one such ambitious man when I heard a familiar voice.

"Excuse me, g'veret?"

"Yes, sir. How can I . . ." My heart stopped for a moment. It couldn't be.

The man in the uniform slowly turned to face me, "How much for this . . . Adira?"

I scurried around the table and threw my arms around his neck, "Avraham!"

"Adira! It is you!" My brother started to return my embrace, but before his arms made it around my waist, he slowly raised his hands.

I stepped back, "Avraham, what's the matter?"

He motioned behind him.

Abhur's son held the point of his short saber in my brother's back.

"Dabeer, let him go." I turned Avraham around. "Dabeer ben Abhur meet my brother, Avraham ben Hanani of Jerusalem."

Dabeer slowly returned his weapon to its scabbard as Avraham carefully lowered his arms.

"Sorry, commander, I'm instructed to protect Mara from advances."

Avraham looked at me, "Mara?"

"It's a long story." I couldn't wait to tell him. "Dabeer, can you take care of my booth while my brother treats me to an afternoon snack?"

"You want me to sell scarves?"

Avraham pulled out two coins and showed them to me. I nodded in approval. "Thanks for looking out for my sister." Avraham handed him the coins "Look, you just made your first sale."

We turned to leave before he could protest.

"So—Mara?"

"I've been Mara for about five years. My first owner changed my name when he took me to the slave market."

"Your owner took you to the slave market?"

"I've been bought and sold three times since you last saw me."

"I'm so sorry Adira. Wait—how could you walk away now?"

"I earned my freedom about eighteen moons ago. Last fall I almost made it home, but that's another longer story. Can you take me home, big brother?" And this time I laid my head against his chest until some other soldiers found us.

"What's this?" The first soldier started, "Avraham cheating on his beloved?"

"I never thought I'd see the day," said the second.

"I guess we don't have to listen to his judgments anymore." The whole group laughed.

Avraham pulled away with a huge smile on his face. "Let me introduce you, boys."

I wanted to laugh. Avraham would enjoy this a bit too much.

"Gentlemen, may I present my sister, Adira bat Hanani, niece of the governor of Jerusalem."

I gave them a half bow as their mouths fell open.

"And for your rudeness to my sister, you're all going to accompany me to Jerusalem tomorrow when I take her home."

Avraham and I took a long stroll. I told him about my situation with Jurjis, and he filled me in on his growing family. By the time we returned to the wagons, Jurjis had heard about my brother's position in the king's army. Frightened for his life, he had my pack with an extra robe and a lovely mitpachat ready for me. I tried to hide my delight as Abhur and Jurjis tripped over themselves apologizing.

"Working with your sister has been a delight, commander. This should cover her winter wages," Abhur handed Avraham a small sack stuffed twice as full as I'd expected.

"I thought she was an orphan when I bought her, sir," Jurjis chimed in. "I only discovered her position last fall."

"Yet you didn't return her to Jerusalem on your way to Egypt," Avraham used his most official voice.

"Fear of your uncle caused me to use poor judgment, sir." I'm sure Avraham's height didn't make the two men feel any better.

"You know the penalty for enslaving a noble?"

"Yes, sir. And believe me, if I'd known when I bought her, I'd have brought her straight to Jerusalem." I'd never seen Jurjis and Abhur nervous before.

"Fortunately for you, my sister has told me of your kindness, and she's especially fond of your children. It wouldn't do to make them orphans. You will go free today."

"Thank you, commander."

"Don't thank me, thank Adira."

It felt so good to be called by my name. I wondered if I'd miss being called Mara. Right now, all I could think about was going home!

Part Five
Journey to Freedom

At the dedication of the wall of Jerusalem, the Levites were sought . . .
The musicians also were brought together
from the region around Jerusalem . . .
I had the leaders of Judah go up on top of the wall.
I also assigned two large choirs to give thanks.
Ezra the teacher of the Law led the procession.
The second choir proceeded in the opposite direction.
I followed them on top of the wall . . .
The sound of rejoicing in Jerusalem could be heard far away.
Nehemiah 12:27-43

The only real prison is fear,
and the only real freedom is freedom from fear.
Aung San Suu Kyi

God's time is always near.
He set the North Star in the heavens;
He gave me the strength in my limbs;
He meant I should be free.
Harriet Tubman

Ninety-Two

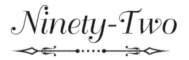

After a good night's sleep in a caravanserai with a heated hammam courtesy of my payday from Jurjis, I felt refreshed and ready to go. First, I stopped to say goodbye to the children.

Rashud didn't look my way, but Priya grabbed my neck and wouldn't let go.

"I'll miss you, Adira." I smiled at the sound of my name.

"I'll miss you, too, Priya."

When she released me, Javis took his turn. The boy seldom spoke, but we'd grown close. "Mara, you leave me?"

"I have to go, Javis. I'm going to go see my Abba. You be good and listen to Bita, okay?"

He shook his head.

I made my way to each of the children. Even Rashud threw his arms around my waist when I tousled his hair. I would miss them, but in a few hours, I'd be back in Jerusalem. I'd couldn't wait to be home and truly free.

Ninety-Three

Avraham and I chatted all the way to Jerusalem.

"We searched everywhere for almost a year, Adira."

"Miriam and I heard Ab in Damascus that first night, but we were gagged, blindfolded, and bound. He and Dohd were just outside our wagon, but we had no way to signal them."

I told Avraham about Elizabeth and Derora but omitted the stories about the beatings and Amin.

"Elizabeth warned me not to reveal my true identity to anyone."

Avraham sighed, "A wise woman. No one wants to be caught red-handed with the governor's niece. Everyone assumed they'd be punished or killed."

I'd get to meet Avraham's children in Jerusalem. He'd moved them there when he'd taken command of the division at Jericho. I asked about the rest of the family, but Avraham hedged. "I think they should each tell their own story."

Normally his vague answer would have worried me, but nothing could bring me down today.

Three times Avraham pointed out men hiding in rocks along the road. "They won't try anything with us. If we win, and we will, we'll put them in prison." I was glad I hadn't tried this trek alone.

As the sun hit its high point, the city walls appeared in the distance.

"It will only be about an hour now," Avraham said. "Men, ride on, we'll catch up."

He let his men get just out of earshot before we started moving again.

"Adira, there is one thing I think you should know before we get home."

I was sure I didn't want to hear what he had to say.

"It's about Em."

"No, Avraham, please, no . . ."

"Not long after you went missing, she became very sick." I felt my throat tighten. "Dohd put the word out, and every healer that came near Jerusalem stopped to help her. She just got too weak."

Silent tears fell.

"I'm sorry, Adira. I considered waiting until you saw Ab, but I thought if you had time to grieve on the way in, you could rejoice with everyone when they see you."

Avraham was right. The others had already had plenty of time to mourn. Today they'd be excited to see me. My tears for Em would only spoil their celebration.

We rode the last few miles in silence. By the time we reached the city, I had composed myself. Despite my grieving heart, I couldn't wait to see Ab and the rest of my family.

The guard at the gate greeted us, "Commander, we didn't expect you back so soon."

Abraham beamed, "I stumbled on a tremendous surprise in

Jericho yesterday, and I had to deliver it personally."

I could feel my excitement rise as we rode through the gate.

The streets teemed with people heading home for midday meal.

"Avraham, is that . . ." a man called out.

"None other."

"Adira?" another man yelled. "Your Ab will be overjoyed!" he added as Avraham nodded.

"Should I know those men, Avraham?"

"Probably not."

"How do they know me?"

"All of Jerusalem knew you'd gone missing. Practically every man took a turn going out with Ab to find you. You're kind of famous in town."

So much progress had been made on the inner wall of Jerusalem's fortress. The rubble that had lined the streets had been removed, and new houses stood in its place. Dohd must be so happy.

When the governor's house came into view, I could no longer control my emotions. Joy, relief, and sorrow overwhelmed me.

A young man carrying water came around the corner of the house just as we entered the courtyard. "Avraham! Anna will be surprised to . . ." The pot hit the ground as his eyes met mine.

Even as a man, I knew those big brown eyes and small left dimple. "Jok!"

His eyes clouded as he helped me off my mount, "It's you. It's really you." And then I got lost in my little brother's arms.

I didn't want to let go, but soon the courtyard filled with noise. Jok released me, but before I could turn around, a familiar voice just behind me whispered, "Adira, my wee one."

As I melted into Abba's strong embrace, I sobbed. This felt like home. My father and I wept together for some time before Natalia reminded us we weren't alone in the courtyard.

"Abba, I hate to interrupt, but midday meal waits." A sniffle interrupted, "And I'll bet Adira and these soldiers would like to eat."

"You'd win that bet, little sister," Avraham spoke for all of us.

Before we could move inside, Natalia took over the task of welcoming me.

Avraham laughed, "Come on, men. I'll show you the way. We're so hungry, we might not even mind Natalia's cooking."

His joking went unnoticed as my sister and Ab held me tight.

"Wait! Where's Jon?" I pulled back to look at the crowd.

Ab laughed, "He found the love of his life. They married just a couple moons ago." Ab looked around, "I don't see Jok, so I expect he's retrieving his twin. Let's get you something to eat before he gets back."

Nothing inside had changed. Em's hand could still be seen in the woven rugs and scenes painted on the walls. Only Ab had known my mother had this hidden talent until we'd come to Jerusalem and scripture and vines began appearing around the doorframes.

Jok and Jon came busting in just as I found a cushion. Food would have to wait. When did these two troublemakers get so handsome?

Jon's embrace felt even stronger than Ab's.

"You must be following in Abba's footsteps, baby brother. Those arms are like to crush me."

He loosened his hold, "I'm sorry, did I hurt you?"

"It feels wonderful," I sighed.

I'd been so distracted by Jon, I hadn't noticed the stranger who'd come in with him.

My brother stepped back for a moment, "Adira, this is Erith, my wife." He beamed and pulled her into our embrace.

Ab broke in, "I think it's time we let your sister eat."

I hadn't finished my first piece of cheese when Avraham's family arrived. Anna was just as lovely as I remembered.

"Don't get up, Adira, eat! You must be exhausted. I'll get my hugs after you finish."

"Well at least introduce me to my nieces and nephews."

Happy tears flowed as I met Caleb, Elijah, Tobias, and Abigail.

"One more should arrive by Cheshvan," Anna reported.

We lingered long after the food was gone, but eventually, Avraham rose, "We have to get back to Jericho. If we leave now, we won't have to ride too hard to get back before dark. Any word you need to send back to the king, Governor?"

"Avraham, I am not the governor."

"Ab, Dohd put you in charge while he visits Susa. That makes you governor whether you like it or not."

"Well, get word to Nehemiah that Adira has been returned to us."

"Will do, Governor!" And with a wink, my brother and his detachment left, but not without one more lengthy hug from the commander.

"I hate to leave, too," said Jon, "but I'm working with the crew finishing the last section of the inner wall. Dohd wants it complete before he returns."

"Let me grab another jar, and I'll walk with you. I'm pretty sure Natalia still needs the water she sent me for, but Adira made me break the jug."

"Back less than an afternoon, and already I'm to blame."

Erith left with the twins as did Avraham's family, and Ab looked torn.

"Adira, I hate to leave, but I've already kept the priests waiting. They have something for the governor to tend to, and I told them . . ."

I interrupted, "Go, Ab. It will be nice to have Natalia all to myself."

"Tonight, it will be just you and me. I think it might be your turn to tell some stories."

"I'll be ready."

It felt good clearing the table and helping Natalia with preparations for the evening meal.

"I wish I'd gotten to say goodbye to Em."

"She never lost hope you'd be found. Friends tried to help her 'face reality' as they called it, but she always said, 'Yahweh will bring her back.'"

"Em always had so much faith."

"Do you remember the time Jok and Jon followed her to the queen's quarters and hid in the pantry spying on her?"

"You mean the day I spent terrified, certain I'd lost my brothers forever."

"I guess that's how it would have looked from your perspective," Natalia laughed.

"I remember being so afraid when I told Em. I thought sure I'd be in all kinds of trouble, but she just held me tight and prayed. She believed Yahweh was taking care of the twins."

"I'll bet Jok and Jon wished they'd gotten off with a hug and a prayer." Natalia laughed.

After a few more, "Remember the time . . ." conversations, I changed the subject.

"Don't you need to go home to take care of your family?"

"This is my home, Adira."

"But, your wedding day . . .?"

"When you and Miriam didn't come back, everyone went looking. Even Shallum helped. He understood I couldn't get married the day you disappeared. He was so patient when I said I wanted to wait for you to be there for the wedding.'

"After a year, Ab and his father agreed we couldn't postpone any longer, but before we could set a new date, Em became ill. Ab and Dohd tried to convince me to go on with the marriage, but Em needed me. She lost the use of her legs and finally couldn't feed herself.'

"By the time she died, Shallum had broken the contract and betrothed to another. It's just as well because now Ab and Dohd need me."

"I'm so sorry, Natalia. If Miriam and I had just paid more attention that day, maybe we could have run. Your whole life would be different."

"Adira, you can't take the blame for any of this. It's fine. I love taking care of Ab."

"But don't you ever wish you had your own children?"

"Sometimes, but Avraham's brood comes by every day. Every now and then I bring them all here just to give Anna a break. It's hard for her with Avraham gone for moons at a time. They've become like my own."

I thought of Priya and Margat's other children. They had given me the same comfort. "Well, I guess these four, almost five, will have one more dohda to spoil them, and Jon and Erith will fill their house in no time. We'll have plenty of nieces and nephews to keep us busy."

"What about you, Adira, don't you want children?"

"I'll mark my twenty-fourth year soon, Natalia. I'm way past marrying age."

I could tell she wanted to give me some encouraging word, but we both knew my only chance at marriage now would be a widower with children to care for.

"Do we have time for a trip to the river? I'd like to get rid of this road dust."

"I'll do you one better. They built a hammam near the water gate last year."

<hr />

Natalia chatted all the way to the bathhouse. She couldn't hide her fondness for Avraham's children. I had missed my sister's enthusiasm for life.

The dust that fell from my garment made me glad I'd brought one of Derora's robes to change into. Riding horseback stirred a lot more dirt than driving a wagon.

I heard Natalia gasp. "Adira, your back"

"What?" I stretched to see what Natalia saw, hoping it wouldn't be a spider or other bug.

"Where did you get those scars?"

Right this moment those scars felt like they belonged in someone else's story. "I got those long ago," I sighed. "Someday I'll tell you about them, but today I just want to enjoy my family." My hand playfully hit the water, and my aim had the desired result. For a few moments, we were young teens again with no scars and bright futures.

The heated water felt good on my tired bones. My muscles started to remind me I'd never ridden a horse that long before. I washed my hair twice to get everything out of my long thick curls.

"What's that?" Natalia asked as I applied Derora's secret oil to my hair.

"One of my kinder mistresses showed me this. A few drops and my wild curls lay down when they dry.

"I think I'll miss watching you try to keep your mitpachat on," Natalia laughed.

"That was once one of my biggest struggles, wasn't it?"

We walked back to the governor's house in silence. I was too tired to talk. Natalia must have noticed.

"You go rest while I finish the evening meal."

I don't remember my head hitting the cushion, and when I woke, darkness filled the room. I must have slept through the evening meal, and I'd missed my visit with Ab. I managed to relieve myself and find some cheese and wine without waking anyone. And that's all it took for exhaustion to set in again. My cushions called my name.

Ninety-Four

Life quickly returned to the routine I loved. Natalia and I shared the household duties, though with Dohd Nehemiah in Susa, the number for the evening meal shrank considerably.

I felt the void Em left most noticeably in the evening. Though Ab had always done all the storytelling, Em had kept him on track, asking questions and adding her own memories when the tales turned to family history rather than Israel's.

I loved being home, but something still felt empty inside. I'd missed so much in those eight years. The family Shabbat emphasized all I'd lost.

Everyone still gathered for Ab to lead us in worship, but the number in the room had doubled since my last family Shabbat. I felt like an outsider. My sisters-in-law and Jok's betrothed were strangers. The niece and nephews delivered the obligatory hugs, but Dohda Natalia got their attention. Each person who added their presence to the room accentuated my invisibility. They'd learned to live life without me, and once the novelty of my return wore off, I felt like an intruder, watching someone else's life unfold before me. No one even noticed when I left the room.

The full Tammuz moon shown bright on the eastern horizon. Though the hours of daylight grew shorter, the remnants of the bright Summer sun kept the stars from appearing. I felt as unseen as those stars in the twilight sky. But why did I feel so sorry for myself?

All my hopes from the last eight years greeted me each morning—freedom and family. It's all I'd wanted. I should be completely content, yet I felt as alone now as I had sitting in that cell before Derora found me.

"My sweet Adira," Ab's voice startled me.

"I'm sorry, Ab, I didn't mean to interrupt your evening. I'll come back in, so you won't miss being with the family."

"Maybe we should just sit here for a few minutes. Natalia has begun recounting the ancient stories. They won't even notice I'm gone."

The sounds of the summer evening filled the silence.

"I've long been amazed at how Yahweh trained the more animated insects and animals to sing during the day while the more soothing share their song at night."

I'd never noticed, but Ab was right. It seemed God reserved the low hums and haunting calls for evening. "They do sound peaceful, don't they?"

I scooted closer to Ab, and he put his arm around me as we allowed the evening songs to calm our spirits.

"I prayed every day Yahweh would keep you safe, wee one."

"I'm glad you never quit calling me that despite all my protests."

Ab pulled me closer.

Twilight gave way to night before Ab spoke again, "What's troubling you, precious Adira?"

Safe in my Abba's arms, all my worries seemed selfish.

"Adira, don't hold those feelings inside. The only way to conquer them is to speak them out loud."

The commanding tone held so much love and compassion. I tried to answer, but words wouldn't come.

"There are no wrong feelings, wee one. But if you don't like how you feel, you need to get it out."

"I feel like a stranger, as if I don't belong here anymore," I whispered.

Ab tightened his hold.

"I thought coming home would take care of everything. I was sure my feelings of discontent stemmed from being in slavery. For a few days, it seemed as though life was perfect, but those feelings of wanting more have returned. I'm sorry, Ab, I feel so ungrateful!"

"Sweet Adira, Yahweh knows you're grateful to be home. But if you watch those who seem satisfied, you'll see contentment comes with maturity, not location."

"Is that what Natalia has? I hear the peace in her voice when she talks about never having children. I realize I'm past marrying age, but I can't bear the thought of wedding an old widower and raising another woman's children. Am I just selfish?"

Ab laughed, "My precious daughter, you've never been selfish. You've given of yourself since Jok and Jon were born and never complained."

"Then why do I feel this way?"

"Probably because you're still not truly home."

"Ab, how can I get more home than right here in your arms?"

"When you were ten, my arms provided the perfect home. Have

you ever wondered how I can go on without your Em? Or what's different about Natalia?"

"I just assumed it was because you're both so strong."

"No, precious daughter, it's because we've both traveled the road home."

"I don't understand."

"I lift my eyes unto the hills. Where does my help come from?"

"My help comes from the Lord. Maker of heaven and earth." Ab had taught us the Psalms of Ascent before we could walk.

"That is my home, Adira. Your Em and I were only able to endure all that time apart when we lived in Susa and I worked in Jerusalem because we both understood Yahweh is truly our home."

I thought about Elizabeth and Derora, though bought and sold like chattel and stolen from all they knew, both lived as though they were free. They had tried to tell me, but I'd never quite understood.

I sat up straight so I could look at Ab, "I met two women over the past eight years who tried to help me understand. Both were so strong despite the first being a slave and the second having been bought in the bride market. They gave me clues, but I didn't get it. Ab, how do I find this home?"

"I think you're closer than you realize. Recognizing you're lost is the final step in finding your way. Just ask Yahweh. He will show you."

We sat quietly together a bit longer under the starry sky.

"I'm turning in," Ab said as he stood, "would you like me to walk you to your room?"

"I think I'm going to take advantage of the warm evening."

Ab bent and kissed the top of my head before he left me alone in my thoughts.

Ninety-Five

Darkness settled in earlier every day. One rare evening only Ab, Natalia, and I shared the table. Ab had worked late again trying to finish his current building project before the snow came.

"Ab, I still wish you were a farmer."

"What? Where did this come from, wee one?"

Natalia laughed, "I'd forgotten our young prayers."

"Okay girls, you got me. Are you telling me you used to ask Yahweh to make me a farmer?"

"So many of our friends' fathers were farmers. And this time of year, they'd always come in early."

"Once they finished the harvest, they may have repaired tools and such, but they never worked late when the days grew short," Natalia helped with my explanation.

"And the farmers never went to Jerusalem," I finished.

Ab laughed, "How did I miss that? Did you girls know I helped in the king's fields before I married Em?"

"Really?"

"Yes, just one summer. Let me just say it's better I trade my skill for our wheat."

After Natalia and I cleared the table, we moved to our cushions by the fire.

"Adira, it's just the three of us. Would you like to share some of your story? You haven't told us much since you came back."

"Ab, I don't think you want to hear it."

Natalia interrupted, "Sweet sister, your pain is our pain, let us carry some of your burden."

I hesitated for a moment, but I could tell they weren't going to let me off as easily as they had the last few times they'd asked.

I began by telling them what happened in the hills when we went looking for the flowers. Natalia filled in the gaps.

"I was so angry when you and Miriam didn't return on time. Then when Jok and Jon came back with your baskets . . . I felt guilty for weeks."

"Why would you feel guilty? We spoiled your day."

"Adira, you did no such thing! Those horrible merchants stole you. They are responsible for all of it."

"I followed the tracks as far as Damascus, but then they all ran together."

"We heard you, Ab! Miriam and I heard you, but they hid us away and lied to you. We were bound, blindfolded, and gagged. We tried to kick and scream, but they made excuses and then put us in a stable in the middle of the night."

"Adira." Ab sounded so sad. "I'm so sorry. If only I'd pressed harder."

"You'd have gotten yourself hurt or killed, Ab!" Natalia chimed in. "Neither of you will feel guilty about these things beyond your control."

We talked late into the night. I told them about Elizabeth and my stay at Tiridata ben Majidi's estate near Hamath, and they shared stories of the many times they looked for me.

"I must have arrived there shortly after you'd been sold. But I didn't meet Elizabeth."

"You were there?"

"I tracked you that far, but none of the servants would talk and Tiridata said he'd never heard of you. Then the trail ran cold."

"Because you didn't know to ask for Mara."

"Avraham said your last owner called you Mara. Where did that come from?"

"When Tiridata sold me, he changed my name to Mara. I guess Tiridata either had to kill me or change my name. I think my story needs to pause here so Ab doesn't fall asleep swinging his hammer tomorrow."

Ab started to laugh, but a yawn interrupted to prove my point.

Ninety-Six

Sharing my secrets did help relieve my burden. I began sleeping well for the first time since I returned to Jerusalem.

Over the next week, I told Ab and Natalia about Derora and my years at Rajif's estate, but the worst parts of those years didn't come up until the next time my sister and I visited the hammam.

"When will you tell us about your back, little sister?"

"It's not a big deal, Natalia."

"It looks like a big deal. What happened?"

"I got out of line a few times."

"That's a lot of scars, Adira."

"Not everyone in Persia treats slaves as well as Artaxerxes."

"You have to tell Ab."

"And watch him mourn even more? Every time I share part of my story, I see him grieve. Even though he did everything he could, he feels responsible for not finding me. I can't watch the pain my scars would cause him."

We finished bathing in silence, but as I put my taming oil in Natalia's hair, she asked, "How long did the pain last?"

"It depended on the severity of the lashes. The last time I almost died, but Derora rescued me."

The words were hard for Natalia to hear, but admitting I nearly lost my life brought a bit more peace.

Ninety-Seven

Winter was filled with preparation. Natalia and I busied ourselves finding the softest linens to make swaddling bands as Jon and Erith's firstborn, a son, ushered in the season, then we focused on helping Jok's betrothed gather all she'd need to start her new home when she and our baby brother married in the spring. Dohd would be home in time for the celebration.

Avraham's detail took the Jerusalem patrol for the winter. Though he had to stay in the barracks near the horse gate with his men most nights, he did manage to make it to dinner at least once a week. Ab insisted I retell my story for Avraham and the twins. I hated the pain I saw in their faces, but with each telling, my nightmares lessened.

Dohd returned with the couriers at the end of Adur. He looked exhausted. He'd aged a lot in the past eight years, or perhaps making the long trip from Susa in five days instead of a few moons had worn him out.

Dohd wept and praised Yahweh as he held me tight the night he returned. "I never stopped praying for you, sweet niece. I knew the Almighty Creator could deliver you."

On the second morning after Dohd's return, Natalia and I walked in on the end of Ab's report.

"I knew I couldn't trust that priest." Dohd seemed upset.

"You had no choice, Nehemiah. Eliashib was next in line for the job, and before this, he'd done nothing to confirm your suspicions."

"I can't believe he would so blatantly bring Jerusalem's enemy into the temple! Did he think I'd let it go when I came back?" Their voices rose as the conversation continued.

"I confronted him, but he had the army commander on his payroll. I wanted to send word, but Tobiah had paid the couriers to read my letters and report to him. I knew such a message would never make it to Susa. At least you understood my cryptic note to send Avraham's unit. Tobiah still has a few shady men, but I think with this new detail, he won't resist."

They must have realized they'd gotten a little loud because they continued in hushed tones. We assumed they made plans to take care of Eliashib and Tobiah, but once we finished clearing the table, Natalia and I lost our excuse to eavesdrop.

Ninety-Eight

Adar 25, 433 B.C.

Dohd and Ab were gone all day. They didn't even return for midday meal.

"Should we take them something?" I asked Natalia.

"Ab won't want us in the middle of whatever happens at the temple today."

"Maybe we should go check on them." I felt so helpless.

"Adira, what are you and I going to do? Ab said he asked Avraham and some of the soldiers to meet him there. You and I would be in the way."

I hated it that Natalia's argument made sense. Unfortunately, it didn't make me worry less.

"Yahweh, be with Ab and Dohd. Protect them. Be glorified in them."

We busied ourselves with evening meal preparations. Since Dohd's return, we had started serving in the great hall again. Nobles filled the room each evening. Natalia enlisted the two girls Em had hired to help in the kitchen when the crowd grew.

Ab and Dohd came in as the girls carried the first platters into the great hall. "Did you see Tobiah's face when we walked up with half of Jerusalem's forces?" Ab turned to me before he finished with Dohd, "Adira, could you have one of the girls get us a basin of water, we need to get some of this grime off before we eat."

Then Ab continued his conversation with Dohd. "He seemed equally surprised when you and I personally carried all his belongings out of the temple and put them in a heap outside the gate." Both men shared a hearty laugh.

"It didn't take long for Shelemiah and Zadok to start helping."

"Pediah and Hana looked pretty eager to get Tobiah out of there too."

"I don't know about you, Hanani, but I'm beginning to notice we worked through midday meal."

"What do you girls have for us? It smells delicious."

Ab and Dohd took their plates into the small room off the kitchen, so Natalia and I let the two girls serve the great hall, and we sat with Ab and Dohd.

"Okay, tell us everything. We started to worry when you didn't come to eat."

"I'm sorry, girls. We should have sent word. Your dohd had the Spirit of Yahweh on him as he cleared out Tobiah's things. Our enemy left to return to Damascus."

Dohd continued, "By the time we had the room cleared out and Yahweh's priests purified them, we'd already missed our meal. About that time the officials I'd left in charge showed up. Tobiah must have paid them well."

"The Levites are back in charge of the temple tonight. They will get their allotments and won't need to neglect their posts to feed their families."

"How could one man cause so much trouble?" I asked.

"One man alone can't," Dohd told us. "If those officials had resisted the bribe, or if even one of the army commanders had stood up to Tobiah, it could have all been avoided. But money corrupts many good men."

"We still have one more problem we need to take care of, Nehemiah."

"What else is going on?"

"You'll see tomorrow. Let's help these girls get cleaned up. The sun has set. It's time to begin our Shabbat."

"Remember what we've done, Lord." Uncle broke out in spontaneous prayer, "Let this work we've faithfully done for your house remain."

Ninety-Nine

Adar 26, 433 B.C.

Ab and Dohd took turns praying and sharing Psalms the next morning. After we had some cheese and bread for our midday meal, we walked to the temple to listen to the priests read from the scrolls. This was my first trip to the temple since my return. Tobiah hadn't observed Shabbat while he led the temple. But I had no idea how bad the city had become.

After eight years of never celebrating a proper Shabbat, what I saw appalled me. Didn't these people appreciate the freedom to worship Yahweh as He asked?

Merchants and traders filled the streets. Men loaded grain, wine, and figs into wagons.

"Has this been going on since I got home, Ab?"

"For almost a year, wee one. Tobiah moved into the temple just after your uncle left, and the guards began welcoming passing merchants almost immediately. Only a handful of us stayed in our homes to honor Yahweh's commands."

Dohd looked even more distraught than me. We continued to the temple and listened as the priests read Yahweh's words. Dohd fell to his knees as soon as we reached the outer court and stayed facedown praying the entire time.

As we walked back home, Dohd stopped in the middle of the market, and yelled at the top of his lungs, "Men and women of Jerusalem, you have disgraced the name of Israel's God. Noblemen, how did you let this happen? You will immediately stop this desecration of the Lord's Shabbat."

One of the fish merchants from Tyre who lived in Jerusalem answered, "And who will stop us?"

The crowd grew quiet as Avraham and two of his mounted guards approached. "Is this the way you address the representative of Artaxerxes?"

"I had no idea, sir." The man fell to his knees.

"Get up and listen to the governor."

Dohd continued, "Don't you know it's this kind of behavior that sent our ancestors to be slaves in Babylon? Will you test the Lord, our God? Go home, all of you! Repent and worship Yahweh."

Slowly the streets cleared until only my family and the soldiers remained.

"Avraham, I want the city gates closed from sunset to sunset next Shabbat. Please station men at the gate. Warn anyone who wants in if they continue to try to sell in Jerusalem on Shabbat, they'll be arrested."

"Yes sir, Governor."

"I'll send some of the Levites to help guard the gates so your men can have a bit of Shabbat too."

Dohd lifted his hands toward heaven, "Remember me for this, Yahweh, show mercy to me according to your great love."

One Hundred

Sivan 25, 432 B.C.

As I headed into my twenty-fifth summer, I grew restless. I hadn't felt this unsettled since I shared my story with my family. One morning as Ab prayed, I felt a stirring in my heart. I thought it strange and ignored it until after midday meal, but the nudge persisted.

Yahweh is this from you?

The thought just grew stronger. I dried my hands, "Natalia, I'm going for a walk. I'll be back in plenty of time to help with the evening meal."

"Do you want company?"

"I think Yahweh wants to keep me company on this one."

Natalia's understanding smile gave me great reassurance. *Thank you, Yahweh.*

I headed out the Horse Gate and walked through the valley to the hills just outside of town. I had no idea where I was headed, but Yahweh called.

The trees on the hill provided lovely shade, so I sat down to pray. This was the first time I'd ventured outside the walls of Jerusalem since Avraham brought me home but something about this place felt familiar.

The flowers growing at the base of the trees reminded me of the flowers Miriam and I had been picking for Natalia's . . .

And just like that, fear overwhelmed me. I rose and ran. In my panic, I lost my bearings and headed deeper into the grove. A man hid behind every tree, and with each apparition, my anxiety level rose. Soon tears robbed me of my sight, and I dropped to the ground, helpless to save myself.

With my face buried in my knees, every horror from the day of my capture rushed back. Each terrifying moment from those eight years wrapped itself around me. I couldn't move, I was a slave again, but this time, a slave of my own making. And even though the rational side of my brain confirmed this was all in my mind, the memories proved stronger—memories I'd pushed down and hadn't thought of since I'd come home. Every recollection controlled me. I might as well have been tied, gagged, and blindfolded again.

With the fear came guilt and shame. The questions that haunted me surfaced.

Why didn't you fight harder when those men took you?

Why did you let them separate you from Miriam?

Why didn't you tell anyone Dohd was governor?

"I just wasn't strong enough," I shouted into the silence. Tears flowed as I grieved my guilt. "I'm sorry I didn't fight for you, Miriam. Yahweh, I'm sorry I didn't find a way to escape."

"You couldn't have escaped, wee one."

Was that Ab's voice? I raised my head, but I was still alone. Even the images I'd seen running between the trees disappeared.

"You carry shame that's not yours to carry, sweet Adira."

"Yahweh?"

The voice didn't respond, but I knew.

"Yahweh, I didn't even know I carried that guilt. Miriam hadn't wanted to gather flowers. I talked her into coming with me. It's my fault she was taken."

Weeping caused my prayer to be broken. "And how many lashes did I bring on myself with my attitude? I always blamed the mistress and Amin, but what if it was me?"

"You are never responsible for the evil actions of others, my child."

And with that simple word from Yahweh, my tears of shame turned into tears of cleansing. They washed away the guilt of abandoning my family and ruining Natalia's wedding. My shame for not trying to escape melted. I remembered my nakedness in front of the stable boy, and my embarrassment faded as peace overwhelmed my being.

I could feel love and joy fill the tiny places that had held remorse and disgrace. Contentment replaced my restlessness. Belonging took the place of loneliness. Wholeness consumed my empty places.

By the time I stood, all that Yahweh had been trying to teach me since I lived in Susa made sense. I knew He had more for me to learn, but today I passed a milestone, and I celebrated my new freedom.

Freedom—my parents had talked about freedom all my life. In Susa, Jerusalem had been the synonym. But I finally understood what they meant.

The walk back into the city bolstered my confidence. I stopped at the river to splash cool water on my swollen eyes, and by the time I returned to the kitchen, I felt new.

As I fell into work alongside Natalia, she joined me in the

familiar hymn I hummed, a song of thanksgiving we'd learned from our parents in Susa.

"It's good to hear you sing again. I've missed that."

"Me, too."

One Hundred One

It took a few weeks for me to feel confident the new nudge I felt came from Yahweh. I didn't want to give up this freedom the Holy One had given me.

One afternoon I found Ab shaping something out of wood, "What are you making?"

"I'm carving ornaments for the doorways. I had a free afternoon, and I like to keep busy." He laid down his knife and patted the bench. "You look like something's on your mind, wee one."

"I think I might be ready to start thinking about my future."

"And what did you have in mind?"

"I want children, Ab. I want what you and Em had."

"Have you met a young man?"

"No, but I trust you and Yahweh to find the perfect match."

"You're sure."

"I trust you, Ab. I know you won't settle for anyone who isn't a dedicated man after God's heart. I want someone like you and Dohd, someone like King David."

Ab laughed, "I'm not sure you can compare Nehemiah and me to King David."

"You're comparing me to whom?" Dohd asked as he walked into the courtyard.

I ran and gave him a huge hug. "King David. You and Ab have hearts like the great king, hearts that follow Yahweh."

"That's a daunting expectation, Adira. But I accept the challenge."

"So, what do you say, Ab?"

"And you're sure?"

"How many times will you ask?"

"Sure of what?" Dohd was lost.

"Adira thinks she might be ready for a match."

"You will make some young man very happy, niece."

"Thank you, Dohd."

"Let's all pray about this." Ab's deep reassuring voice began, "Lord of Creation, thank you for protecting Adria. Thank you for bringing her home and setting her free. Yahweh, bring to us the man you've chosen to match her with. Bless our search for a man who shares your heart. Amen."

One Hundred Two

We didn't mention the conversation to Natalia or my brothers. And though I tried to be patient, now that I'd made the decision, I woke each day with expectation. After three weeks passed, I turned my prayers to praise as I looked for contentment in what I had.

The first meal of Shabbat brought a great deal of contentment each week. Jok, Jon, Avraham, and their families joined us for the evening meal.

As always, on this day, Avraham was the last to arrive. With men and posts to check, we found ourselves waiting on him every time.

"Good evening, family."

"Avraham, just once couldn't you leave post check to one of the other officers?" Anna scolded.

"Probably, but tonight I'm late because I invited one of my men to join us. He just arrived from Babylon. His mother is a Jew, and he hasn't enjoyed a proper Shabbat meal for more than a year. He's washing up in the trough outside."

"Let me get an extra plate," I went into the kitchen to get everything we needed for our guest.

Avraham was making the introductions when I returned, "And this is my sister, Adira."

I dropped everything.

Jok scurried to pick up my mess, "Are you al . . .?"

"Michael?"

"Admara? Avraham, this is your sister?"

"You two know each other?"

Everyone started talking at once, but I couldn't hear anything except my heart pounding. He hadn't changed a bit. His smile still made my legs weak.

Natalia's voice finally broke through, "Okay, let's eat while the lamb is still hot, and these two can fill us in. Dohd, will you give the blessing?"

Michael sat down across from me. My own prayer of thanksgiving drowned out Dohd. *Yahweh, I can't believe he's here. I feel so blessed that you would bring Michael to Jerusalem.* When Dohd said Amen, I forced my eyes toward the food.

Ab picked up the platter of lamb, "Alright, Adira, this seems like a part of the story you've left out."

"Adira?" Michael asked. "Not Mara."

"Your father bought me just after they'd changed my name on the papers. Your mother agreed a new name would keep me safe."

"You started to tell me your real name on the day we met, didn't you?" His smile would always have my heart. I could feel my face burning.

"Well fill the rest of us in." Jok broke into the private world Michael and I had temporarily created.

They all knew about Derora, so Michael and I filled in the holes beginning with him finding me milking, me stumbling over my name, and then him discovering I was his mother's personal maid. We managed to leave out the part where we'd fallen in love.

After we finished eating, Ab led us in a Psalm and shared the story of Joseph being reunited with his brother. He finished the evening with a prayer of thanksgiving.

"I have to get back for second watch," Michael rose to leave.

"We should be heading home, too," the twins ushered their wives to the door.

"Thank you for making me feel so welcome. Enjoy your days off, Commander."

Ab walked everyone out to the courtyard while Natalia and I moved plates, platters, and cups to the kitchen for cleaning after Shabbat.

"What did I see between you and Michael?"

"His father made sure there was nothing between us."

"That doesn't answer my question."

"I haven't seen him for five years, Natalia. His father had marriage plans for him when he sold me." I wanted to tell my sister that I knew he'd joined the army to avoid the arranged marriage, that he'd promised to marry me, but I couldn't be certain he hadn't found someone.

Natalia let it drop, but my thoughts wouldn't. Everything I'd felt for him in Calah flooded back. It was as if it was just yesterday he'd promised to find a way to marry me.

I didn't sleep. My mind bounced from excitement that we'd finally be together to fear he no longer cared. When I did drift off, my dreams replayed the day I'd mistaken him for a barn hand.

One Hundred Three

We enjoyed a quiet Shabbat. Dohd, Av, Natalia, and I walked to the temple and listened to Ezra read the scrolls. Then we sat in the courtyard and enjoyed the warm evening.

Exhausted from lack of sleep, when the sun dipped behind the hills, I excused myself.

"Will you walk with me before you rest, wee one?"

Ab and I strolled the streets in silence until the house was out of view.

"What do you know about Michael?"

"His mother saved my life twice."

"But what about Derora's son? Do you only respect him because of his mother?"

"Oh no, Ab. He's always been a gentleman. He never made me feel like a slave. And he treats his mother like Avraham treated Em."

"I thought I saw something between you."

"Natalia told me the same thing." I tried to brush off his suspicions.

"So, you wouldn't want him to call on you?" Ab's voice held a hint of teasing.

"Why do you ask?" My heart quickened.

"Answer my question first."

"No, Ab," I smiled up at him and tightened my hold on his elbow. "I would not object if Michael dropped by to see me."

"Good. I told him he could come to next Shabbat meal."

I stopped and looked at him, "You already invited him?"

"No, he invited himself when he asked if he could see you. He said something about a betrothal promise."

I was thankful the dark evening hid the warmth that crept into my face. "We did discuss it. That's why his father sold me. He didn't want Michael to marry a slave."

"Michael told me he thinks his father will object less to the niece of a government official." Ab winked. "We'd better get back. We have a big day tomorrow."

One Hundred Four

Exhaustion gave me a good night's sleep, but joy and excitement woke me before the rest of the house. I washed Shabbat dishes, then fixed a big meal to commemorate the day.

Though the outer wall had been completed in record time, the inner wall and the fill between the two had taken a lot longer. Most of the men who'd originally helped secure Jerusalem hadn't been able to stay to rebuild the inner wall. Fields needed tending, and other iron and brickwork took precedence, so the dedication of Jerusalem's fortress had been put off for twelve years—after the project was finished.

Levites from all over Judah had been invited to celebrate. Leaders from nearby towns crowded into the city to commemorate the occasion, and Jerusalem's musicians had prepared special songs of praise.

With so much extra food, I sent Natalia to invite our brothers' families to the morning meal. I never imagined Dohd would be so appreciative, "What a perfect way to start the day, Adira. Today we celebrate everything we've worked for since we arrived."

"And as long as we're celebrating, I have one more joyous

announcement."

"Ab, where have you been? The food is getting cold."

"We needed one more person to make the morning complete."

Just then Michael walked through the door.

Ab continued, "I've entered into a betrothal contract for Adira."

Yahweh, when you answer prayer, you really do it right.

Congratulations mixed with confused looks filled the small dining hall.

"Thank you, Hanani. From the moment I met Admara . . ."

Avraham interrupted, "Michael, if you plan to marry her, you should probably know her name is Adira."

My beloved smiled, "Commander, the girl I fell in love with I called Admara, so unless your sister objects, Admara she will always be."

Jok and Jon looked a bit concerned, "This is kind of fast, isn't it?" Jon spoke for the duo.

"I appreciate you worrying, brothers, but we wanted to make this announcement almost six years ago."

"My father wouldn't let me marry my mother's slave." Michael and Ab chuckled as my beloved squeezed my hand. "I believe hearing about her relationship to the governor should change his mind."

"Well then, let me ask a blessing on your betrothal as well as this food," Dohd said.

After we finished our meal, Michael had to return to his post, but not before he whispered, "I'll be back. There's still the matter of a kiss I've been waiting six years to collect."

I floated through the feast preparations. The entire market had been set up as a festival banquet.

About mid-day, Dohd began the dedication ceremony. Levites had spent the prior week purifying the wall as well as all the people. Merchants and traders had been turned away. No buying or selling would go on. The gates had been anointed before they'd been shut for Shabbat, and they would remain closed today.

The Judean leaders led the procession. They went up the stairs and divided at the top. Ezra led the procession to the left as far as the Water Gate, and Dohd followed the line that went right stopping at the Gate of the Guard. Each group boasted a huge choir, priests with trumpets, and temple musicians.

The musicians played, the choirs sang, and the entire city rejoiced. Dohd later said they heard the celebrating in Bethlehem.

I joined in the loud praise. As much as I wanted to focus on the joy of this massive wall that held hundreds of worshippers, the morning's announcement had me flying high. Thanksgiving for this new chapter in my life flowed like a fresh spring.

The processional descended and headed for the temple. Many brought sacrifices and danced in the streets. As Dohd came down the stairs his face revealed the joy in his heart. He'd dreamed of this day twelve years ago when he served Artaxerxes.

"Who would've ever imagined he'd go from cupbearer to governor?" I said to no one in particular.

"Who would've thought you'd go from slave to wife of Michael ben Rajif?" My beloved had snuck up behind me.

When I turned to greet him, the promised kiss waited for me. But before our lips could meet, I stopped him.

"Michael! What will people think?"

"Look around, my love. Everyone is busy celebrating. They don't know we exist. But if it makes you feel better . . ." He pulled me behind a tent. "May I finally give you that kiss I promised you on my father's garden bench six years ago?"

He didn't wait for an answer. Soon the sounds of celebration faded as six years of frustrated love found a bit of fulfillment in a kiss.

"I love you, Admara. I've loved you since I saw you on that milking stool. Your father gave me permission to set a date as soon as we like. He said we've already waited more than an appropriate amount of time, but if you want a full betrothal year, I won't rush you."

"I'd thought maybe tomorrow." His tight embrace felt so good. "Or maybe as soon as your mother can get here," I smiled.

"I was hoping you'd say that. I'll have your brother send word by royal carrier. We'll set the date for a week after she arrives."

"So, a Tishrei wedding?"

"I expect Em will travel at the speed of merchants. I'm sure she'll be here by then."

"We should probably rejoin the festivities."

"Yes, we probably should," he said as he pulled me close for one more long kiss.

One Hundred Five

Natalia took over for Em. She prepared a lovely wedding garment and helped me gather all the things we'd need to set up our own home. Derora and Rajif arrived before even two moons had passed.

"I miss Em today, Natalia."

"I knew you would," my sister replied as she handed me an ornate hairpiece. "This was hers. You should have it. She wore it the day she married Ab."

"But where did she get something so lovely in Susa?"

"When she gave it to me to wear on my wedding day, she said her great-grandmother attached it inside her robe when they carried her into exile."

A headband woven from the finest silk held twelve beautiful leaves of gold dangling from intricately woven leather cords. Brightly colored braided threads, each boasting three perfectly round polished beads, two jade and one lapis lazuli, were evenly dispersed between the intricately carved leaves.

"Natalia, this is lovely, but Em gave it to you."

"She meant for both of us to have it. Had you not been

collecting flowers, she'd have shared the story with you, and you would know all the details of this two-hundred-year-old hairpiece. You always loved those ancient tales."

A knock interrupted our embrace, and the door opened slightly.

"Derora! Come in!"

"Adira! I'm so glad this day has finally arrived. I brought something with me from Calah." She handed me a small package wrapped in linen and tied with silken thread. "I believe you left this in my room."

As I untied the small parcel, the linen separated to reveal a bone bracelet adorned with gold and silver. I gasped. "Michael gave this to me the day he suggested we marry. I couldn't bear to take it. I knew it would just taunt me. Thank you so much Derora."

I slipped the precious gift on my wrist, as Erith opened the door. "He's here."

My love had come to whisk me off to our wedding ceremony.

"Oh, Derora, today, I will truly be your daughter."

As we stood before this group of people I loved, I got lost in my thoughts. Every person represented a piece of my life.

My childhood stood on one side of the courtyard. Memories of Susa and the journey to Jerusalem bubbled up. I saw my father with a sword in one hand and a hammer in the other. Six of us had traveled to Jerusalem in my thirteenth summer. Our number had grown to sixteen, and today we'd add one more.

Abba looked so proud. I know his tears were a mixture of joy for me and sadness that Em missed the day. I praised Yahweh for a father who showed me how to live free even when he was a slave in the king's household.

On the other side of the garden stood Rajif and Derora—a part of my past I once thought should be forgotten and cast aside. I'd never have known them if not for those merchants who stole me that day. I felt a bit like Joseph. The journey to my best life had also started in the prison of a trader's wagon.

I'd learned a lot in my seven years of captivity. Who would have dreamed slavery would lead me to discover freedom in Yahweh and the secret to true joy?

Beside me stood all my tomorrows. Michael's eyes met mine as I realized my slavery had held the key to my future. I'd come to cherish the scars on my back because without them, I'd have never met this man. Though I resented Rajif when he sent me with Jurjis, I now know I wasn't ready to marry Michael six years ago. Rajif may have been wrong about my social status, but I agree, Michael deserved more than that girl who served Derora. It wasn't my position in Rajif's household that made me unworthy; fear, regret, shame, and guilt had kept me from being my best me. Yahweh had helped me release those chains in the grove, and now I was ready to join my free life with Michael's.

Adira bat Hanani . . ." hearing the priest say my name jarred me back to this moment. My face hurt from the joy that spilled out.

Our families would party all night, but after a wonderful feast, they ushered Michael and me into the largest guestroom in the governor's house. We wouldn't have our own home until Michael resigned his position. Eventually, we'd return to Calah where my husband would inherit his father's estate.

But on our wedding night, in a room lavishly prepared by my sisters-in-law, I was finally alone with my beloved. Free to love him, free to live where we chose, free to serve Yahweh together. And tonight, free to get lost in the first moments of our new future.

$\mathcal{A}$ Note from $\mathcal{L}$ynne

Thanks so much for reading Adira's story. I've considered writing fiction before, but in March 2020, the idea of Nehemiah's niece wouldn't leave me alone, so Hanani's middle child was born.

I loved researching the time of Nehemiah and discovering life in fifth-century B.C. The book of Nehemiah gives a detailed timeline, so the dates you find in Parts One through Three come straight from the Bible. Part Four is strictly fiction; however, the slave and bride markets were a real thing. Even though King Cyrus banned them, historians tell us the horrendous practice continued in some parts of the Persia-Median empire, and as you know, similar practices go on today.

In addition to an extensive timeline, Nehemiah shared many names in his account. Sanballat, Tobiah, and Geshem the Arab were true enemies of Israel. Meremoth and his grandfather Hakkoz were mentioned, and Baruch son of Zabbai helped on the wall. In fact, every person or group mentioned by name or by city when Hanani took Adira to check on the wall's progress can be found in the third chapter of Nehemiah. Each of the priests' names in Adira's story come straight from scripture also.

The other characters, Michael, Miriam, Chava, those who traveled with Nehemiah, and Adira's mistresses and masters are all figments of my imagination. Some I planned from the beginning.

Others, like Michael, surprised me when they appeared in the scene.

When I began to study the timeline and realized Queen Esther could have possibly still been alive, I had to include her in the story. After I'd already created Natalia's position, I discovered many historians speculate that Artaxerxes executed Hadassah when he came to power to honor his mother, the deposed Queen Vashti. I prefer to believe Queen Esther had the kind of personality that drew people to her, so Artaxerxes simply confined her to a suite with the harem.

I'm considering sharing Miriam's story as well as Michael's so you can find out what their lives were like before they met Adira and while they were apart. If you're interested in reading their stories, let me know. As of July 2022, they're just ideas rolling around in my brain.

If you've enjoyed *Adira: Journey to Freedom*, I'd appreciate your stars and comments on Goodreads and your favorite bookseller. And even more important, be sure to tell a friend!

God bless you as you journey toward freedom and find your way home,

Lynne

Thank You

Thank you to everyone who helped bring Adira to life. I have a very small launch team, but several of them went the extra mile to help me get the word out. Thanks to Julia, Sylvia, Nikki, Jackie, and Linda for reading, reviewing, and spreading the word.

I'm grateful to my mom for her support in everything I've written. When I sang, she came to every concert, and now she reads every book. I'm blessed to have her on my team.

My girls and their families have been behind me in every endeavor. Monica, Matt, Sylvia, Bobby, Julia, Travis, Josh, Corryn, Elizabeth, and Jaycee, I love you more than you can imagine. Sylvia, thanks so much for reading Adira more than once to help me get it proofed. Julia, thanks for leaving one of the first reviews and sharing with your friends. I am grateful for every word of encouragement.

Finally, there's one person who watched me fill notebooks with words and type it all in. He tolerated my countless edits and never said a word when I spent money on proof copies and swag. He's reserved the first copy for himself. Thank you, Steve, for letting me write, for encouraging me to write, and for loving me while I write. Loving you for the last forty-three years has been the best gift God has ever given me.

And while I'm at it—thank you for reading! I can't help but

write. The words leak out. But without someone to read it, a book is incomplete. So, thanks for doing your part in bringing Adira to completion. Because of you this story of freedom and finding a way home will touch hearts and change lives.

Resources

This is a list of some of the websites I used in my research
I apologize if any of the links become broken before you read this.
All worked in April 2022.

"Achaemenid Empire." Wikipedia. 2020.
   https://en.wikipedia.org/wiki/Achaemenid_Empire

"Ancient Civilizations/Persia." Wikibooks: WikiJunior. 2020.
   https://en.wikibooks.org/wiki/Wikijunior:Ancient_Civilizations/Persians

"Months of the Jewish Year." My Jewish Learning. 2020.
   https://www.myjewishlearning.com/article/months-of-the-jewish-year/

"The Palace of Darius in Susa." Wikipedia. 2020.
   https://en.wikipedia.org/wiki/Palace_of_Darius_in_Susa

"The Persian Empire: Culture and Society." TimeMaps. 2020.
   https://www.timemaps.com/encyclopedia/persian-empire-culture-
   society/

Mark, Joshua J. "Ancient Persian Culture." World History Encyclopedia. 2020.
   https://www.worldhistory.org/Ancient_Persian_Culture/

Parsons, John J. "Introduction to the Jewish Calendar." Hebrew for Christians.
   2020.
   https://www.hebrew4christians.com/Holidays/Calendar/calendar.html

Williams, Elizabeth. "Baths and Bathing Culture in the Middle East: The
   Hammam." Heilbrunn Timeline of Art History. New York: The
   Metropolitan Museum of Art, 2000-. October 2012.
   http://www.metmuseum.org/toah/hd/bath/hd_bath.htm

Did you enjoy
Adira: Journey to Freedom?

If so, be sure to tell a friend!

Plus, I'd appreciate your review!

Leave it on your favorite bookseller

or use this QR Code to leave a review on Goodreads!

In addition, if you visit my website,

LynneModranski.com

you'll find Book Club questions

and a Five-Session Bible Study

based on *Adira: Journey to Freedom*

and the book of Nehemiah.

And look for me on Social Media

@LynneModranski

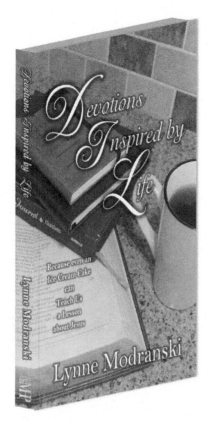

Devotions Inspired by Life

What do buzzards, blue jays, ice cream, and snowflakes have in common? Each teaches us something about Jesus! In the same way Jesus used illustrations from everyday life to teach His disciples, God blesses us daily with aha moments. In "Devotions Inspired by Life" you'll find more than seventy happenstance experiences that offer a new perspective on life and help deepen our relationship with our Savior. With scripture to lead the way, each of these short meditations invites you to search for Jesus in the midst of your mundane day-to-day.

Available at
LynneModranski.com
and from your favorite bookseller.

Lynne Modranski

Lynne Modranski grew up in the church learning how to follow all the rules of religion. When she started reading scripture for herself and began meeting with small groups who wanted to grow in Christ, she started to understand the concept of a relationship with Jesus.  Now, she loves helping others discover their true identity and reach their full potential in Christ.

Wife to Steve, a local church pastor, Lynne is mom to Monica, Sylvia, and Julia and "Hada" to Joshua, Corryn, Elizabeth, and Jaycee. Worship Leader and Small Groups Coordinator at Sycamore Tree Church, Lynne is first and foremost a follower of Jesus Christ. She has a passion to help others find a real relationship with the One who has given her true life as she shows them how they can become the very best they can be in Christ Jesus!

Made in the USA
Monee, IL
27 August 2022

11572011R00249